I0731382

In Due Season
(Gifts of the Heart)

by Lea Carter

Chapter 1

"I assure you that in due time you will receive all the blessings promised to the faithful." Grace paused Sister Allred's 2010 conference talk and turned off her truck.

"In due time," she repeated quietly. Still single at thirty-three, she was struggling to hang on until whenever that was. Offering up a prayer for patience, Grace hopped out of her Chevy and slammed the door. Hooked the heel of her rubber boot on the running board and leaned back against the truck a moment, appreciating the splendor of an Ozarkian sunset.

This was the one perk to daylight savings. Since most of her farm visits were scheduled in the afternoon, after her in-town clinic hours, she got to enjoy a lot more sunsets in the fall. Today, burnt orange and brilliant pinks ran across the western horizon as far north and south as she could see.

The Rockin' R Ranch, the client she was calling on, also stretched as far as she could see. In every direction. To her left stood a massive building that housed the best of the ranches' equine breeding stock plus an indoor arena that put the one from her alma mater to shame. Further out were the feed barns, bunkhouse, storage buildings for equipment, and so on.

Right next to the path that led to the manor house was the small menagerie that belonged to Mrs. Brooke, the ranch owner's wife. She was an amazing horsewoman but had very little sense otherwise when it came to animals. No, she was more the type to go on a buying spree—usually without consulting anyone—and poof, a small herd of pygmy goats would arrive. Kept Grace on her toes and that was the truth.

"Hey." Mike Williams, one of the younger ranch hands, approached her with a wide grin. "How you doin', Doc?" His eyes wandered down her five foot ten inch frame in a leisurely fashion.

Grace kept her eyes on his face. A fact which may've contributed to the slight flush in his cheeks when he got back around to looking her in the eyes. She didn't bother answering his question. Mike might've been the latest and greatest Hollywood had to offer and it wouldn't have made a difference. She lost her heart seventeen years ago and had never recovered it.

"Want to go to a movie sometime?" He grinned hopefully.

"No thanks." The ranch had a strict non-fraternizing policy and she wasn't about to break it for the summer help. Not that she worked for the ranch as such, but she was the on-call vet since Doc Baxter, um…left. Anyway, it made for a convenient excuse if it came down to that.

Mike came closer, stuffing his hands in his

pockets against the rapidly cooling evening air. "Dinner?"

She gave up and rolled her eyes. "No thanks."

"What'samatter, Doc?" He rocked back on his heels. "Too good for me?"

"Too different." She cocked her head at him. "What movie would you have taken me to?"

Coming another hopeful step forward, he leaned in her direction. "Whatever you wanted."

"Hmm. So it doesn't matter to you what they're rated or what kind of content is in them, that sort of thing?" Predictably, his smile dimmed a bit.

"Uh…no? Should it?" Confused, Mike stared at her. What did that have to do with the two of them having fun?

"It matters to me." She lifted one shoulder.

The crunch of a boot heel on gravel brought Mike's head around. "Okay. Um, see you around."

Grace watched, still lounging against her truck, as he scuttled into the deepening shadows between the buildings. Her heart gave a glad little flip at the sound of someone special calling her name.

"Gracie!" Alec Fitzsimmons strode toward her from his trailer, broad shoulders and narrow hips usurping her focus. He held out one of the twin travel mugs he was carrying, his wedding band catching the last of the fading sunlight. A widower of some eighteen years, the ring was more or less a part of him. "Fresh made."

"Thanks." Their fingers brushed when she accepted the mug, standing the hairs up on the back of her neck—but he didn't seem to notice the contact. As usual. If only she'd been older when they first met, maybe she would've known how to make him notice her. Now, with seventeen years of her silence between them, she wouldn't even know how to begin.

Taking a cautious sip of the hot chocolate, she smiled. "Hot chocolate is perfect on a day like this."

"Which must be another way of saying we should get inside before we freeze." He winked and lifted her carryall out of the back of her truck, his blue-black hair long enough to sway with his motion. Somehow, the silver hairs that were starting to show only served to make him look more attractive. "C'mon. You are not going to believe this."

She fell into step beside him. "Bart's message was so mysterious that he's got half my team convinced Mrs. Brooke's is opening a petting zoo." The woman had a varied enough collection of animals.

He chuckled. "Not exactly. The Rockin' R is still a horse ranch at heart." The pride in his voice was only natural coming from the ranch foreman. Draping an arm around her shoulder, careful of her red braid, he guided her inside the horse barn. "And there he is. Yashrab Alriyh, our newest acquisition." He used the word 'our' out of loyalty to his boss, who'd only informed him of the purchase after the fact.

Grace moved free of his 'just pals' touch and walked up to the fence that surrounded the indoor arena. Resting both arms on the chest-high bar, she leaned in. And stared. A dream in white pranced around the arena, his dainty hooves barely seeming to touch the ground or stir the soft dirt. Inquisitive ears swiveled in every direction while his nostrils flared, testing the unfamiliar scents coming from all around him.

Alec sipped his hot chocolate and watched Grace watch the stallion. She was a little taller than his wife, Melinda, had been. Beautiful, intelligent, and kind, he sometimes wondered that she was still single. Of course, Grace was just a kid. Or…wait, was she? Someone had let her age slip on her last birthday, but he found it difficult to believe she was really thirty-three. Why, he'd been widowed for nearly a year by that age.

He grimaced. Cheerful thought.

"Oh, Alec. He's exquisite."

"He is that," Alec agreed. It rankled that his boss, Mr. Brooke, bought the pure white stallion without consulting him first, but who could argue with perfection? Grace must've agreed, for there were stars in her maple-syrup brown eyes when she looked around at him.

"He's also…high-strung." Alec scratched his chin. That was an understatement. He'd waited as long as he was comfortable for the horse to settle on his own.

"Well sure." She turned back to staring at the magnificent animal. "How long has he been here?"

"Not quite forty-eight hours." Eddie Brooke shoved herself away from the wall where she'd been leaning.

"Eddie?" Alec blinked.

Edna Mae Brooke, a twenty-year-old beauty who insisted on being called 'Eddie.' Mostly to spite her parents if he read the signs correctly. As for what she was doing home basically in the middle of a college semester, well. Was it assuming the worst to suppose that it was for the same reason as the last three times? Eddie had a knack for causing trouble. And a weird sense of delight, it seemed, in taking the blame. Especially where it meant getting kicked out of expensive colleges.

"Alec. Hey, Grace." Eddie shoved her hands into her pockets and resumed watching the stallion.

"Eddie." Grace smiled and didn't ask questions. These days she hardly saw Eddie, though she used to follow Grace around when she was an inquisitive tweenager.

Alec cleared his throat. Privately, he thought Eddie wasn't half bad. Once she figured out that there was more to life than being entertained, she'd settle down. Until then…

"Anyway." Alec shook his head and turned back to the horse. "He had a personal escort all the way from Saudi Arabia. I can't pronounce the guy's name, but after we got through with all the paperwork and loading, he vanished. That's when things started going wrong."

Grace frowned and reassessed the stallion. She didn't see any injuries. "How do you mean?"

"He's not eating." Alec gestured toward the portable feed bin they'd attached to the arena fence. "We changed out the whole thing this morning. Still nothing."

"Drinking?"

"Not enough. He's got the whole place to himself." Alec's eyes flicked over the spacious accommodations. He'd hoped the animal would run off some energy in there, then accept a regular stall, but if anything he seemed more agitated. "And still he races up to the trough, takes a drink, then races off again like there's a mountain lion after him. Hasn't slept, either." He raised her bag. "How about it? Got something in here that can help?"

"Mmm, I don't think so. We'll have to use this instead." She tapped her head. "Let's start by turning about half of these lights off. And all the noise."

"Noise?" Alec grinned as he realized he'd tuned out the twenty-four-seven country western music the majority of the employees preferred.

"I'll get the radio." Eddie headed off at a brisk walk, eyes still fastened on the stallion.

"Anything else?" Alec quirked an eyebrow at her.

"I'm going to get some carrots. See what he thinks. Um…what's his name?" Unzipping her fleece vest, she started to hang it on the fence. Changed her mind. He was already spooked enough.

"Yashrab Alriyh." Alec stumbled over the pronunciation. "It means Drinker of Wind, a reference to his speed, I think. His escort called him something shorter, but I didn't catch it."

She nodded. "There is one other thing."

"Fire away." Alec took the fleece from her and hung it on one of the numerous wall hooks, then set her bag on the ground beneath it.

"Clear out the spectators."

His eyes flicked around the arena. Eight or nine people leaned against the fence in various spots, watching the stallion. He couldn't blame them—the horse's grace was mesmerizing. But Grace had a valid point.

"On it."

Nodding, Grace went over to where they kept the treats. Setting the insulated travel mug down so she'd have her hands free, she studied her choices. After two hours at a nearby dairy, she had to smell wrong. Saudi Arabia had cows, of course. She simply doubted that the stallion spent a lot of time in their company. Or that they smelled of the same medicines, feeds, and disinfectants that were used in the U.S.

Emptying her pockets, she tucked a carrot into each one. Started to turn away, then hesitated. Picking up her phone, she ran an internet search for Saudi Arabian music. Farfetched? Absolutely. Worth a try, though. She changed the volume to low and carried the phone with her to the fence.

A quick look around confirmed that the spectators were gone, but the stallion was still pretty agitated. One moment, he looked like an ice statue. The next, he screamed and raced halfway across the arena.

A steel guitar was cut off mid-wail. Snorting, he danced in place.

The lights dimmed suddenly and the horse froze again.

Biting her lip, Grace admitted to herself that she'd have given her eye teeth to know more about him. What his previous stable conditions were. Did he have a mascot back home, a companion animal that they kept around to help calm him? Surely they would've sent it along, though. A few minutes later, Alec hadn't returned and the horse hadn't calmed. Okay. Stage two.

"Marhaba," she called, exhausting her Arabic vocabulary. "Welcome to the U.S., Yash…um." She was never going to get his name right. It meant something about wind, didn't it? "Windy. Is it alright if I call you Windy?" Even in the dimmer light the whites of his eyes were starting to show. "Carrot? Want a carrot?"

Pulling one from her pocket, she held it out. Nothing. Hmm. Wait, maybe if she…

When the carrot snapped, so did the stallion. The soft dirt flew as he reared, kicked, and bucked, putting on a wonderful display of temper.

"What's going on here?" demanded a voice.

Grace jumped in surprise. "Mr. Brooke! You startled us."

"Us?" The tall man frowned down at her. "What're you talking about? What's wrong with my horse?"

"I called the vet to help sort that out," Alec responded cheerfully. "Mr. Brooke. Mrs. Brooke." He nodded at the couple, always glad to see them together.

"Fitzsimmons." Brooke greeted him gruffly. "What's this all about?"

"Yashrab Alriyh," Alec flattered himself that he was getting the pronunciation down, "is still getting used to his new home."

"He's on the far side of the world from his home, Mr. Brooke," Grace agreed. "The smells are different. The sounds. Even the food…" She stopped. Turned to Alec. "What do they feed horses in Saudi Arabia?"

"Umm." Alec scratched his head. "I'd have

to look that up, but now that you mention it, I noticed barley in his tub on the plane."

"Barley." Grace nodded. "And what's in his feeding tub over there?" She jerked her head in the direction of the makeshift feeding setup.

"The same grain everyone else gets," responded Eddie as she returned.

Both of her parents stiffened and nobody said anything for several seconds.

"If he doesn't like that..." Grace started to turn toward the arena and froze.

The stallion stood a few feet away from her. Neck arched, ears pricked forward. Eyeing the carrot pieces she still held.

Silently, she offered one to him.

He lowered his neck. Looked away. Looked back. Nodded his head emphatically.

Mrs. Brooke started to speak, but someone shushed her.

Grace held her breath as the stallion lifted a front hoof. The carrot wasn't coming to him, so... His hoof came down, bringing him nearer. Step by step he picked his way over to it.

She opened her hand, getting her fingers out of his way. His velvet muzzle daintily brushed her palm and the carrot disappeared in a few satisfied crunches.

Grace giggled as his inquisitive muzzle stretched toward her through the fence. "Silly fellow." Not liking the risk of his neck being extended through the bars, she offered him the other half of the carrot, pushing her shoulder forward as far as she could while her feet stayed rooted to the spot.

Once she was certain that his neck was out of danger, she took a tentative step closer. Bribing him with the extra carrots, she kept him near until it was her arm through the bars. Only then did she risk stroking his nose.

Someone cleared their throat and the stallion snorted—but stayed.

Grace looked over her shoulder to find Mrs. Brooke watching with hopefully arched eyebrows. In fact, her entire body language was that of an eager fourth grader pleading, 'Pick me!'

Grace debated briefly. On the one hand, this was the boss's wife. On the other hand, she had her patient to consider. Spooking him now might make things ten times harder in the future. On the third hand, Alec had apparently slipped off somewhere without bothering him.

In the end, the hopeful expression proved irresistible. Mouthing 'slowly,' Grace nodded.

Windy shifted and blew, but the lure of the final carrot held him fast as Mrs. Brooke inched nearer. When she was in position, Grace showed him the carrot. Broke it in half and put one in each of Mrs. Brooke's hands. Knowing that she was an ardent horsewoman, Grace let her take it from there.

Movement on the far side of the arena—near the stallion's feed and water—distracted Grace almost immediately. Sure enough, it was Alec. Stealthily, he removed the feed bin. Replaced it. Began pouring something into it.

Mrs. Brooke made a disappointed pout as the stallion's head swung around to look at the new sound.

Grace gave Mrs. Brooke a conspiratorial wink. This was an important moment and she needed the other woman to be patient.

Alec stood stock still as the stallion meandered in his direction. He read tension in the animal's muscles still, but this was nothing like before. The wild, harried look was gone.

Yashrab Alriyh snorted once. Paced to the right, then to the left in front of the feed bin. Finally, when Alec didn't morph into a leopard and attack, the stallion plodded up to the bin and stuck his nose in. The sound of crunching filled the otherwise quiet arena.

"You did it!" Mrs. Brooke stage-whispered. Squeezing Grace's arm she celebrated, "He's eating!"

"He'd better be." Mr. Brooke was wise enough to keep his voice down, but the scowl on his face shouted his displeasure. "That's a very expensive investment." His nod indicated Yashrab Alriyh. "I expect that stallion to produce the finest string of horses this ranch has ever seen."

"I understand." Grace really did. A good stud should sire good progeny. A matchless stud such as this one? Mr. Brooke would command the local field in terms of stud fees while simultaneously matching him with his own finest broodmares to ensure that the Rockin' R's next round of foals would be of impeccable quality. "We'll arrange to have food shipped in that's more to his liking. Once he's had a chance to adapt to this new environment, we can start adjusting his diet."

"Is that all that matters to you, Dad?" Eddie scuffed her toe in the dirt. "The bottom line?"

"Edna Mae." Mrs. Brooke's rebuke was sharp and instant. "Don't think that you can come home in disgrace and talk to your father like that!"

Eddie rolled her eyes and leaned on the fence as if she didn't care.

Grace cringed inwardly at the public scolding. One thing she'd learned over her years of working here was that vinegar sure didn't taste any better on a silver spoon.

Chapter 2

"Providing food that he's used to is an excellent idea, Grace." Alec was too much of a professional to acknowledge the family tiff; or to give his boss the earful he deserved. Anyway, he wanted more processing time before he diplomatically brought up the subject—again—of why it was important to consult the ranch foreman before bringing in new stock.

"And that will do it?" The concerned wrinkles in Mr. Brooke's face smoothed ever so faintly even as his hands came up to rest on his trim waist. "Something that simple?"

"Food is never simple when it comes to horses," Grace corrected. Hearing her own tone, and noticing his frown returning, Grace cleared her throat. This man was definitely not Neil, the newly graduated vet she'd just hired. "Especially for domesticated horses."

"Think of him as a competitive athlete," Mrs. Brooke interjected abruptly. Taking her husband's arm she continued, "Accustomed to a special diet. Particular foods."

"Exactly," Alec agreed, immediately clueing in to her tactic. Mr. Brooke was one of the few hardcore businessmen he knew of who didn't have a paunch to go with the paycheck. And that was mostly because he'd maintained his college basketball lifestyle. "He's hungry enough to eat what we have for now, but to keep him in peak condition, we'll have to go the extra mile."

That last was Mr. Brooke's motto. How had he led his college team to state four years in the row? Yep. By going the extra mile.

Grace, recognizing a bit of soft-soaping when she heard it, held her peace. Mr. Brooke's money would pay for the feed. The smart thing to do was make him comfortable with the idea. Needing something to keep herself occupied, she walked over to the treat bin, where she reclaimed her pocket junk and took a swig of hot chocolate—mmm, it was still warm!

"Yashrab Alriyh is important to the future of this ranch." Mr. Brooke's expression as he eyed the stallion did indeed give the impression that he was calculating the horse's net worth. "Get whatever he needs."

"Yes, sir." Offering Grace his arm, Alec headed for his office.

As she accompanied him, Grace couldn't help being impressed with the sincerity in Alec's tone. A lot of men would resent a boss who only saw the dollar signs.

"Those two," Alec's smile stayed firmly in place, "are going to be the death of me."

Grace kept her laughter contained until Alec's office door had shut behind them, then let it bubble quietly out. The office had wall-to-wall windows, which only provided so much sound-proofing. "They never learn, do they? Although

Mrs. Brooke at least orders whatever supplies that she thinks the ranch wouldn't already have." In bulk, of course. Cheaper that way, after all.

"Which I then have to implement or store," he pointed out. Shrugging, he seated her and circled his desk to where his own chair waited. "A horse is a horse to them both. Hopefully, though, we won't actually have to order from Saudi Arabia."

"Fingers crossed." She showed him her fingers, then took a long draw of hot chocolate. Shifted her multi-tool so it wasn't digging into her waist. "By the way, I bought some Stephen's dark hot chocolate mix. The kind you say you use? It doesn't taste like this." She raised her eyebrows as she took another drink.

"Hmm?" Alec pretended to be engrossed in his research. He would never admit that he added a smidgen of ground cayenne pepper to a pot of hot chocolate. Not even to Gracie, whom he'd known since his eleven-year-old son dragged her home one day, proudly announcing her as his first best friend in their new home.

"C'mon, Alec." She leaned forward and rested her forearms on the edge of his desk. "Confess. There's a secret ingredient, isn't there?"

"Rolled barley."

"What?" Grace wrinkled her nose and looked at the travel mug. "That can't be it."

"Sure it can." Alec swiveled his monitor to show her what he'd found. "Barley in his feeding tub on the plane. And as a major component of the feed from this store." He told himself he was imagining the flicker of disappointment in her eyes, but he couldn't misinterpret the way she leaned back and folded her arms. If the secret ingredient meant that much to her, he might have to reconsider sharing it.

His work cell began simultaneously to vibrate and play "Chisholm Law." Bart, his right hand man, preferred talking in person, so whatever he was calling about must be pretty important. Frowning, he answered.

"Yeah, Bart?"

Grace watched his frown deepen and leaned forward again. Taking advantage of his distraction, she allowed her eyes to drift over him. It was about as satisfying as smelling food, and yet she couldn't help it. Her heart had belonged to Alec from the first moment she'd seen him.

She was sixteen years old. Officially old enough to drive. Officially old enough to date. Still struggling to figure out if she liked things because everyone else did, but sufficiently self-confident to draw reasonable lines.

She'd gotten up one perfectly ordinary Sunday and gone to church with her parents. Both of her brothers were long gone to marriage and college, so it was only the three of them on their pew that morning. Innocently, she'd glanced around to see who'd come back from summer vacation. And made eye contact with

Alec Fitzsimmons, a broad-shouldered, gray-eyed stranger—whereupon her life was forever changed.

How her heart had sunk when she saw Danny huddled under his arm, as much as any eleven-year-old boy would do in public. The protective way he'd shepherded Danny to an empty pew convinced her that they were father and son.

"That's Danny Fitzsimmons," her mother had whispered, mistaking her interest for curiosity about the new boy. "Just lost his mother, poor darling."

Oh, she'd fought with herself forever about that. Finally came to terms with the idea that she wasn't *glad* about Melinda's death, only that Alec was free. Free to ignore *her*, as it turned out. Not that the average thirty-three-year-old man was interested in a sixteen-year-old girl.

"Be right there." Snapping his phone closed, present-day Alec got to his feet. "Something's wrong with one of the pygmy goat does. Do you have a minute to check her out?"

"Anything for Bart." Grace's lips quirked upward. Bart's complaints about the pygmy goats bordered on legendary, but she privately thought he had a soft spot for the little creatures.

On their way to the menagerie, they stopped to collect her fleece and carryall. Halfway there, she smacked her forehead with her palm.

"I left my phone in the main barn!"

"You did? Why?"

"Why?" She shook her head. "It wasn't on purpose, silly. I turned on some music for Windy and forgot about it." Lifting her bag off his muscular shoulder as she spoke, she slung it over her own. "Would you grab it before Windy gets too curious?"

"Windy?" Alec admired her graceful form as she walked backwards a few steps.

"Yashrab Alriyh." She rolled her eyes at her mangling of the stallion's name. "You said it meant wind drinker, right?"

"Drinker of wind."

"So, Windy." She shrugged.

"Right." Chuckling, Alec waved toward the menagerie. "Need me for this?"

"If we do, I'll have Bart call you." Her lips quirked up in a smile. "Go knock some things off your new to-do list."

"Thanks, Gracie." He enjoyed the grimace she made at his use of her nickname.

Returning to his office, he hunted through the available information until he found what he needed for Windy. Over an hour had passed by the time he hung up his office phone and returned to the menagerie.

"The feed's on its way." Alec recoiled slightly when Grace jumped. "Whoa! Sorry, didn't mean to startle you." He offered her a winning smile along with her phone. "Paid a small fortune to get the feed here by morning. And, Windy's in his very own stall." The more he said the name, the better he liked it. They simply had to hope Mr. Brooke didn't object, because it was definitely going to stick.

"Oh, good." Grace tapped her phone screen and blew out a breath. "I better check these messages."

Alec nodded and walked over to talk with Bart.

"Everything alright with Pat?" Looking into the odd, makeshift pen next to Bart, his jaw dropped. "She had twins?"

"Yep." Bart shoved his hat back on his head. "Didn't even know she was expecting."

"Me, neither." He scratched his chin. "Maybe from now on we should have someone check on the goats after Mrs. Brooke plays with them. Y'know. In case she doesn't get the bucks separated out."

Bart snorted his agreement and changed the subject. "Got in touch with the roofers. They'll be here at first light."

"Great." Alec nodded. It was the tail end of October and the weather was only going to get worse. "I'd like you to take care of that, if you would. I need to spend some time with Windy." Briefly he explained the horse's new handle.

"A little light work will probably be good for him." Grace commented as she rejoined them. "Help him feel at home. Careful not to overdo it, though."

"Right." Alec scrubbed a hand over his face.

Found himself inches away from Grace and took a discreet step back. "Grooming. Lunging. Pick up his hooves." She was nodding and he smiled. It was cute the way she bit her lip when she was thinking. "Routine stuff like that."

"Good." Grace tossed the last of the rubbish and washed her hands thoroughly. The kidding had gone well and Pat, the doe, was busy nursing her adorable new twins.

"Are we your last stop?" Alec kept his tone casual, as if he hadn't noticed her jaw-popping yawn.

"Yeah. I mean, I had a couple more stops, but with all of this…" She shrugged and zipped her fleece in preparation for leaving. "Neil made the deliveries for me." She never charged for deliveries, which would've made this the perfect opportunity to check on Wheelwright's small dairy, but that would have to wait for another day.

"I've got it." Alec shouldered her bag before she could. Looped his free arm around Grace's shoulder. "Going straight home?"

"More or less." Grace allowed herself a split second of crazy while she thought about how much she'd like to kiss him. Then smiled as if she didn't care about his proximity. His clean, warm cologne. The heat of his hand on her shoulder. "I've got a few patients in the barn right now, so I'll check on them first." They'd had a few milk cows when Grace was younger, but now that it was just her and her parents, she'd had their small barn renovated for the occasional larger patient. "Then it's movie night over at Noella's."

"Noella? Is that the cute French girl?" His concern about her fatigue faded into the background when she shot him a look that bordered on angry. "Now, don't take that the wrong way. We've barely met. Anyway, I'm old enough to be her father," he floundered. Grace shook off his arm and strode ahead of him to her truck. "I'm old enough to be *your* father!" he called desperately. What in the world was she so mad about?

Grace blinked back the tears stinging her eyes and unlocked her truck. Heard the sound of him putting her bag in the bed. Did he have to be so polite while she was upset with him?

Pausing, her foot on the running board, she mumbled, "I left the hot chocolate mug in the menagerie. Sorry."

"No problem." He watched her worriedly, but she refused to turn his way. She couldn't be that mad about his slip. They'd worked together for the last five years and he'd always treated her with respect, so she had to know he wasn't some stupid chauvinist. Even if he wasn't blind. "Drive safely!"

"Yep." Grace waved and climbed into her truck. Slamming the door, she let the engine warm up while she put on her seatbelt.

The sun was long gone, so she drove home by starlight and headlight, kicking herself all the way. Why shouldn't he notice that Noella was cute? Alec was a perfectly normal, healthy *single* adult male who had no idea how she felt about him.

Parking between the barn and her entrance to the house she shared with her parents, Grace climbed down and trudged into the barn. Mechanically, she checked on the animals and updated their charts. As she'd expected, they had plenty of feed. Her dad might've retired as the local vet, but he'd never stop being a farmer at heart.

Only when she set the last chart down did she allow herself to face the simple truth. Alec Fitzsimmons was never going to look at her and see a woman. As far as he was concerned, she was…well, frozen in time as the sixteen-year-old kid who used to hang out with his slightly younger son, Danny.

She laughed and wiped away a tear. It was such a cruel twist of fate—being almost the same age as the son of the man she'd never stop loving.

Chapter 3

Monday morning, someone knocked on Alec's office door. It was open, as usual, but Mike stood right outside, shifting his weight from side to side. Good. After hours of puzzling, Alec had finally settled on Mike's brief interaction with Grace as the probable source of her odd behavior on Friday.

"Mike." After acknowledging the man, Alec got up rather than inviting him into what he knew could feel like the principal's office. Closed the distance between them by carrying a stack of papers over to the filing cabinet by his door.

"Yeah, boss?"

Alec chuckled. "Mr. Brooke is the boss. I'm only the ramrod." He used the old—nearly archaic—term, thinking it might help the younger man relax. "I saw you talking with Doc Myers the other day." It felt weird to refer to Gracie so formally.

"Yeah." Mike scratched the back of his neck. "Asked her out."

Alec flicked a glance at him and saw consternation on the man's face, as if he couldn't believe he'd just blurted that out. "You're aware there's a strict non-fraternization policy on the Rockin' R."

Mike hesitated. "Yeah…but she don't work here." Or live there. Like most of the hands, he'd figured out that the boss' daughter was the underlying reason for that rule.

"That's true." Alec shut the filing cabinet with more force than necessary. "Where are you taking her?"

"Huh?" Startled by the abrupt sound, Mike had to stop and consider the question. He dropped his eyes. "Oh. She turned me down." He lifted a shoulder like he didn't care.

"I see." Alec hoped the relief he felt didn't show on his face. Sure, he wanted Gracie to grow up and get married someday, but he had personal—painful—experience with trying to raise a family when you didn't marry someone of the same faith. It was especially hard on the kids.

"So... We cool?" Mike raised his eyebrows. "I mean, I didn't know she was your girl."

Alec felt remarkably like he'd been kicked in the head. "My... Are you serious? She's the same age as my son!"

Mike retreated two steps. "Whoa, sorry." Rubbed the back of his neck nervously. "Didn't know that, either. I only saw how she...I mean...um..."

"How she what?" Again, Alec closed the distance without quite leaving his office.

"Y'know, man." There was a faint whine in Mike's voice now. "The way... How she looks at you."

Alec folded his arms across his chest. "You can go." Mike took off like a scared rabbit and

Alec smacked himself in the forehead. "That went well," he muttered as he returned to his desk.

The radio was still off in deference to Windy's nerves, so all he could hear as he tried to work was the clacking of keys and Mike's last words. *How she looks at you. How she looks at you. How she…*

Alec shoved his chair back from the desk. Was it true? Did Gracie, little Gracie, have a crush on him? Ridiculous. He was quite literally old enough to be her father! Which was precisely what he'd told her.

Oh no.

He drew his hand down over his face. Mike hadn't been the cause of her upset. No, that was his own smooth self. He was the culprit.

Providing, of course, that he could believe Mike. Alec leaned back in his chair and thought that over. What would Mike gain from lying? No. As convenient as it would be to believe that, it made no sense whatsoever.

Rising, he began to pace. Three strides to one wall. Three more to the other wall.

Leaving his office with a grunt, he got a grooming kit from the tack room. Let himself into Windy's stall.

"Hey there." Latching the gate behind him, he stood for a moment to let the horse look him over. "It's about time we got acquainted, big fella." Lifting out a soft brush, he slipped his hand through the strap. "Bet you know what this is." Holding his hand out, he waited for the horse's curiosity to bring him over.

He'd grown up around so-called cowboys who figured that if they shoved hard enough or kicked hard enough, and the horse moved, great. Mission accomplished. Because as long as they could force a horse to do what they wanted, it was just as good as willing obedience.

In his experience, that approach caused more problems than it solved.

"Here." He touched the brush lightly to the horse's neck. Stroked it toward his withers. Windy's neck stretched out, then he looked back at Alec as if to ask why he'd stopped. Chuckling, Alec resumed brushing, trying to get as much of the arena dirt out of the horse's white coat as he could. Instinctively remaining in tune with the animal's body language while he worked, he allowed his mind to resume puzzling over the potential ramifications of Mike's declaration.

If he was being honest with himself, *little* was not the right word for Gracie. He stood five foot ten in his socks and didn't have to look down very far to make eye contact with her. If he was being brutally honest with himself, she hadn't only gained a couple of vertical inches since he'd been introduced to teenage-her at church his first Sunday in Cadmia. She'd grown into an attractive woman. A bit thin, perhaps, but given the hours she worked and how many meals she probably missed...

He stopped and wiped his forehead on his sleeve. Right. He needed to get a grip.

Windy nudged him and he began brushing again.

They had a good professional relationship—or so he'd thought. However, even handled with the greatest care, this situation could turn into a nightmare. Yes, now that he was aware of her feelings, he was starting to agree with Mr. Brooke. The Rockin' R really should have its own, dedicated vet. One that was nothing like their last one, Doc Baxter.

He winced. Talk about nightmares. Whatever Baxter touched withered. Including the account balance Mr. Brooke had assigned to the ranch's vet needs.

Well, he'd simply have to be careful. Put out some feelers through friends in the area. Wait until he was sure he had an honorable, qualified applicant, then tell Mr. Brooke what he had in mind.

Sighing, he traded the brush for a hoof pick. Patted Windy's withers. Smoothed his hand down a front leg, then gingerly lifted it to inspect the soft tissue.

Getting a new vet would only solve half of the problem. Now that he'd started thinking about it, he couldn't ignore the question. Was he ready to date again? Not Gracie, obviously. No, she might be a little infatuated, but from his perspective sixteen years was too big an age gap.

But seriously. Was *he* ready to date again?

Between raising his son, Danny; working on the Rockin' R; and getting used to a new town, well—time had gotten away from him. He couldn't use Danny as an excuse anymore. Danny had his own life, his own business in a nearby town.

He frowned. When was the last time he'd seen his son? When had they last talked on the phone? He swallowed hard. When was the last time he'd missed Melinda? Had it really been over a decade and a half since he'd run his fingers through her bouncy black hair? Complained about her snoring? That such a petite woman should have a snore like a wood chipper had always boggled his mind.

As he finished checking Windy's hoofs, he was left with the uncomfortable conviction that there was no good reason for him not to be dating. He had a solid job and was in reasonably good health for his age. He grimaced, not liking how that sounded. Still, he wasn't the type to sugarcoat things. Forty-nine wasn't dead, but it wasn't just starting out, either.

"Well, Windy." He held out his hands, palms up. "Neither is the man without the woman, neither the woman without the man, in the Lord," he quoted 1st Corinthians 11:11. "I sure hope I don't make too big a fool of myself."

Shaking his head, he returned to his office and finished the day's paperwork. By the time

Bart called to give him an update on the roofers, he'd made up his mind. He was going to ask Julie Rogers to go out with him. They'd talked fairly often over the years at church. He tried not to reflect on how many years. It was bad enough to have to start dating all over again without worrying that he was too old.

"Good job, Bart. Listen. Something's come up that I need to take care of tomorrow evening. Is there anything you'll need me for? No? Okay." He coughed to clear the disappointment out of his voice. "Alright, thanks."

When he left the office for lunch, he automatically headed to his trailer. As he walked, his stomach tied itself into what his scout master would've called a hatchet knot. Either that or one of those ridiculous neckties—cravats?—from the movies Melinda used to like to watch. To delay the inevitable, he showered and shaved. Put on one of his nicer button-ups. Walking himself into the kitchen, he picked up his phone…and set it back down.

Kneeling, Alec prayed for help. "Forgive me for being so dense," he whispered. "I realize that's no excuse, but I'm going to do better. Except, I'm terrified of making this call. Please— help me." Ending in the name of his Savior, Alec remained on his knees for several heartbeats before reaching for his phone again.

"Hello?"

"Hi, Julie?" He swallowed, his throat suddenly

dry as the rolled barley they'd started feeding Windy. "This is Alec."

"Alec! Hi!" Some of the tension left his shoulders at her friendly greeting. "I was just thinking about you."

"You were?" Alec asked blankly.

"Yes," she laughed. "I'm currently serving in the young women's organization and we've been going over our plans for the first quarter of next year. Turns out that we have quite a few horse-crazy girls." She paused. "I volunteered to ask you to let us come out to the Rockin' R for a visit. Maybe even arrange for them to ride? If they want to, that is."

Alec mentally back-pedaled from his thoughts about asking her out. "That sounds like a great idea. I'll have to check with Mr. Brooke, of course," he continued smoothly. Reaching for the nearest pad of paper, he tore off his grocery list and prepared to take notes. "When were you wanting to come?"

Julie happily provided him with the basic details, but couldn't be more specific than January for the activity.

"We try to plan three months out, but the weather is chancy in the winter, y'know."

"Which makes it harder," he agreed. "That's alright, though. Let me run this past Mr. Brooke and see what he thinks. If he says yes, we can probably flex the date to accommodate you."

"That's wonderful!" she gushed. "Thank you

so much! Have a great day!"

"Thanks, you, too!" Alec set his phone down and got to his feet. Sank back onto the kitchen chair. "I'm an idiot."

If calling her the first time was hard, this was impossible. Wiping his face with his hand, he brought up the list of recent calls. Took a deep breath and hit her number.

"Hi, Julie. It's me again." He tried to laugh at her surprise. "Well, I forgot…I mean, I called *you*. That is, I called you to ask you…" The word stuck in his throat, nearly choking him. He coughed into his hand. "Would you go out to dinner with me tomorrow?" Tuesday wasn't a typical date night, but since she worked part-time in the mornings, he hoped she would agree. If he had to wait until Friday or Saturday, he'd be a basket case for sure.

"Oh!" He endured a painfully long pause before she said, "I'd love to."

"Great!" Oops, too enthusiastic. "I'll, um, I'll pick you up around six?" He tried for a casual tone.

"I'll be ready." Alec couldn't think of a single thing to say during the subsequent silence and was sincerely grateful when she finally ended the call with, "See you tomorrow!"

"See you," he echoed lamely. Setting his phone down once more, he sagged back against the chair. Yanked on his too-tight collar. "What have I done?"

The date loomed before him all the next day, sort of like a dodgeball that's on an intercept course with your face.

It got so bad that Bart gave up and asked, "You feeling alright?"

"Not really." Alec tugged at his collar. "Why do you ask?"

Bart snorted. "You keep repeating yourself for one thing. For another, you're an ugly shade of green around the gills." His eyes narrowed. "If I didn't know better, I'd say you turned into a lovesick teenager."

Alec folded his arms across his chest and glared at him. "I'm not a teenager."

"Does that mean you're lovesick?" Bart's eyebrows lifted. "Is it Grace?"

"Grace?" Alec exploded. "What're you talking about? She's a child!"

Bart snickered. "Well, if it ain't Marc Antony. How's de Nile these days?"

It took Alec a minute to recall the old, *old* play on words—denial and 'de Nile'—but when he did, he muttered something about juvenile jokes and stalked off.

Halfway through Windy's second grooming, it hit him that he couldn't arrive at Julie's house covered with horse hair and smelling like, er, a stable. Cursing himself for a fool, he did a quick check on Windy's feed and water, then bolted for his trailer.

Turned out that he was easier to clean up than

the cab of his work truck. Panic surged through him as he tossed dirty gloves, a tool box, and a spare pair of boots into the back of the cab, then slapped as much dust off the seat as he could. Which effectively ruined his third clean shirt of the day.

Driving over to Julie's with the windows partially open in an effort to air things out left him chilled and out of sorts, but he pasted on a smile anyway as he prepared to go knock on her door.

Except the door to her house opened before he could get out of his truck! His smile slipped as he saw that she was wearing what could only be an 'ugly sweater' contest winner, lightweight pants with a drawstring, and…well, he guessed those were shoes. They looked like exaggerated slippers to his untrained eye. Belatedly, it occurred to him that she was hustling around to the passenger side door while he stared rudely.

Hitting the release on his seatbelt, he just about strangled himself in an attempt to get out so he could at least open her door for her. But he was no match for this modern woman, who plunked herself on the bench seat and grinned at him.

"Punctual as always." In the back of her mind, Julie wondered how he'd managed to get so tangled up in his seat belt, but she kept that to herself. "I brought my church book," she patted the small bag she was carrying.

"Oh?" Alec was getting a headache. Maybe he *was* too old to start dating again. No, that wasn't it. Back in Nebraska, Brother Harrison remarried at seventy-something. He and his wife were an adorable couple, too.

Alec sighed. He definitely had no excuse for his ineptitude. Catching on to the fact that Julie was watching him curiously, he roused himself to say, "Great!"

"I thought it might help us plan." She wilted under his blank stare. "Am I missing something?"

Alec blinked. "I…don't think so?" He'd always appreciated Julie's straightforward approach, but right now, his bruised ego could've used a little coddling.

"Well. If you're sure." The longer they sat there, the more uneasy Julie became. His gray-and-blue plaid shirt, the polished boots… The startled drop of his jaw when she stepped out of her house. "It seems like you were expecting," she hesitated, wondering how off-base she was, "something different."

"No, it's fine." Alec gave himself a quick mental shake. He didn't have to act like a boor because the world had gotten more casual since his last turn on the dating merry-go-round. Not that he would *say* that, but he felt the need to say something more. "I don't mind mixing business with pleasure." He flashed her what he hoped was a winning smile. And watched in amazement as her hands flew to her mouth while her eyes got wide as dinner plates.

"Ith-thith-uh-day?" Her words were muffled by the hands she still had over her mouth

Confused, Alec leaned closer. "I beg your pardon?"

"Is this a date?" She lifted her hands fractionally away this time.

He felt his forehead crease and was too worn out to stop it. "Yes?" Truthfully, if she wasn't sure, neither was he.

"Oh no." Julie's face disappeared behind her hands, but enough of her neck was visible to show that she was blushing royally.

"Julie?" Alec tapped the steering wheel lightly with his fingers. "Is there…something you want to tell me?"

She peeped at him over her fingertips. "I'm dating someone."

"Ah." Unaccountably, Alec felt his whole mood take a turn for the better.

"It's Roger Wilkins. From over in Marshfield? I am *so* sorry for this misunderstanding." Nervously, she shoved her hair out of her eyes and gave Alec a once-over. "I thought you looked awfully spiffy for a conversation about a young women's activity."

His lips began curving upward. His shoulders started to shake. A laugh escaped and, thankfully, Julie smiled.

"It's okay," he told her at last. "I mean," his

manners kicked in, "it's…it's not prom night or anything."

Julie hooted. "Prom was many longs ago," she agreed, relieved that he was taking it so well.

"Yeah." That sobered him. "Quite a while." The pressure completely off now, he shrugged. "Well, friend. What do you say to us planning the young women's activity over scrambled eggs and waffles at Blinky's?" The local diner was a few vinyl seats short of swanky and breakfast for dinner wasn't what he'd originally planned, but under the new circumstances…

Julie's grin was back in full force. "Sounds great."

Chapter 4

Grace woke up to a light touch on her shoulder. Disoriented, she blinked at the blurry figure standing beside her. She wasn't at home. As she came more fully awake, her nose registered the distinctive odor of professional-grade disinfectants. And the sickly sweet scent of the hand soap they used at…

"What's wrong?" she croaked, starting to sit up. Whoever it was wouldn't have disturbed her rest unless it was important.

"What's wrong, young lady," her office manager, Mrs. Ivey, told her firmly, "is that it's five o'clock on a Tuesday afternoon and you're asleep on the Murphy bed at your office!" The older woman let Grace swing her feet to the floor, then sat down next to her. "When was the last time you went on a date?"

Grace, whose eyes felt like their lids had eighty-grit sandpaper on the insides, declined to respond. "Five o'clock? Already?" The last word turned into a yawn. "Wow, I better get back at it." 'It' being the mountain of paperwork that took second place during the day to every emergency or walk-in or stray cat that wandered through the clinic door.

"You better get home," insisted Mrs. Ivey, who'd only returned to the office because she'd happened to notice Grace's truck while she was driving past. Her boss didn't want to talk about dating? Fine. She had another string to her bow. "When was the last time you had supper with your parents?"

Grace shrugged guiltily. "Sunday?"

"You mean two days ago?" Mrs. Ivey frowned at her. "Was that before or after Luke Talbot's dog got hit by a car and you spent four hours patching it back together?" Like father, like daughter. She'd started as Eric Myers's receptionist some forty years ago and knew all the family tricks.

Oh yeah. She'd spent the night at the clinic to keep an eye on him, which always threw off her internal calendar. And obviously forgotten all about the whole incident. Just like she'd completely forgotten about seeing her best friend, Merry McKinney, introvert extraordinaire, arrive at church with the ward's most eligible bachelor. Yes, the hysterical call Grace received as she was getting ready to walk inside that Sunday had pushed everything else to the back of her mind... At least the dog made it.

Dredging up a light laugh from somewhere, she hedged, "I must've meant the week before last." Mrs. Ivey's eyes narrowed and Grace shook her head before she could be corrected again. "So it's been a while." Shoving herself to her feet, she tried to use the room's sink and got a face-full of loose hair when she bent forward. Groaning, she remembered that she'd taken her braid down so she would rest better.

"Let me." Mrs. Ivey gently took her. Smoothed it and twisted it up into a loose bun that she secured with the hair tie Grace took from around her wrist. "That ought to hold long enough to get you home. Maybe." She folded her arms across her chest. "If you leave right now."

Grace threw up her hands with a laugh. "I surrender! I'll just leave the piles and piles of paperwork on my desk and go home." Turning the tap on again, she bent down and drank.

"And how much of that paperwork should be done by Neil?" Mrs. Ivey raised her eyebrows.

"I…um…" Grace shut off the water and cleared her throat. "Don't you think he's got enough to do with all the clinic appointments, learning his way around town, plus pinch-hitting for me?" She pursed her lips. "I didn't hire him that long ago, Mrs. Ivey. And I don't want to kill him off before he really gets the hang of things."

"Better than killing you off. Or don't you remember your first two years here?"

That stopped her. "Dad did run me pretty hard, didn't he?" Grace had to squint in order to think back that far. Fresh out of college, the ink barely dry on her vet's license.

"Hard enough to keep you out of trouble," Mrs. Ivey concurred sagely.

"Trouble?" Grace blinked at her. "What do you mean?" One of the many things she'd liked about Neil was that he came highly recommended. "Sensible" was how one former employer described him.

"Oh, nothing." Mrs. Ivey shrugged. "I saw him at Blinky's with Eddie Brooke is all."

"Great," she groaned. Splashing some cold water on her face, she dried her hands on the towel and started toward the bed.

"I'll tidy up here." Mrs. Ivey blocked her way. "You get on home."

"Thanks, Mrs. Ivey." Grace hugged her. "I'll do that. Right after I tell Neil about his new schedule."

"New schedule?" Mrs. Ivey parroted hopefully.

"Yep." Grace slid into her fleece. "I'll need him to come in an hour before the clinic opens until we get the paperwork caught up."

"I suppose it'd be alright if he stayed late, too," suggested Mrs. Ivey, a twinkle in her eye as she followed Grace as far as the hall.

"Whatever it takes to keep us compliant," Grace agreed. Winking at Mrs. Ivey, she let herself out. Checked to make sure the door had locked behind her like it was supposed to, an old habit from her stay in college housing.

Frozen grass crunched under her feet as she walked over to her truck, chuckling slightly. The more she thought about it, the more she liked this idea. Neil was up on all the new rules and regulations, so it would actually be easier for him to do the paperwork. Sure, she stayed current with her continuing educations requirements. However, she also caught herself documenting things the way she'd originally been taught.

Blinky's was insanely packed for a Tuesday, so much so that she had to drive the parking lot twice before a spot opened up. She frowned at the dark blue truck she found herself next to. What was Alec doing in town? Not that it had to be Alec, even with the distinctive RR2 license plate. Bart might've borrowed it. Or Alec could've sent any of the boys into town for any reason and…

She shook her head. "No use worrying about your 'father,'" she told herself sarcastically. Shoving her hands into her pockets, she picked her way across the slippery parking lot.

Stepping into Blinky's was like stepping into her childhood. She used to jump along the black and white linoleum diamonds on the way to her dad's favorite booth. Used to spin on the counter stools until she was too dizzy to walk. Sighing, she admitted to herself that she missed it. Missed the carefree days when having to choose a shake flavor was her toughest decision of the week.

Spotting Neil's blond head, she headed in his direction. On her way, she passed the initials that some empty-headed teenager had carved into the side of a booth long before she was born. And then there was Susan—the diner's manager as well as the owner's daughter—waving to her from behind the serving counter.

"Gracie!"

She did her best not to wince at the babyish variation of her name and waved instead.

"Finally decided to come in for some of my pumpkin pie, did you?" Susan grinned.

"Can't tonight," Grace laughed. Her mom's pumpkin pie beat Susan's all to pieces, but she'd never admit it to the friendly woman. "I'll take a large hot chocolate to go, though." Blinky's hot chocolate was so dark it was a little grainy. Perfect way to stay warm on a cold drive home.

"You got it!" Susan immediately set about filling the order.

"Hey, boss." Neil greeted her from over his plate of fluffy scrambled eggs, waffles soaked in strawberry syrup, and what looked like a shared order of crisp bacon. "What brings you here?"

"Hey, Neil." She smiled at Eddie, privately impressed at how quickly the younger woman had found and arranged a date with the one new man in town. "Eddie."

"Doc." Eddie slouched and shoved her elbows onto the table in a slightly childish, slightly insolent move.

"How're the kids, um," she did *not* want to imply her best client's underage daughter had children when she didn't, "the baby goats doing?"

Eddie's face softened instantly. "They're so cute!"

Grace nodded sincerely, assuming that meant they were also in good health. "Have you named them yet?"

Eddie's lips curled, marring her good looks. "Mom calls them Hansel and Gretel. Says she's going to put it on their paperwork."

Grace flinched at her word choice, then watched in amazement as Eddie transformed from the petulant, twenty-year-old child back into a beautiful young woman when she noticed that Neil was studying her with a vaguely puzzled expression. Eddie might not have a clue what she wanted out of life, but she was a past master of amusement. Her own, of course.

"Speaking of paperwork." Grace felt her hair starting to slip out of its bun. "Neil, we're getting behind at the office. I'll need you to come in an hour early every day until we get caught up, alright?"

"Why should he do all the work?" Eddie pouted. She had plans for Neil, and none of them included him spending extra time at work.

"Unless I miss my guess," Neil's sharp eyes had already taken in Grace's loose bun and the light markings around her face, as if it had recently been pressed up against a pillow, "she's just finished putting in about six hours of overtime." She'd certainly been there when he left for the day. He shifted on the bench so that he was facing Grace more directly. "Don't worry, boss. I'll be there dark and early."

They both grinned at his terrible pun and Grace gave him an approving nod.

"Not on Sunday," she reminded him.

"Open for emergencies only," he nodded. That was half the reason he'd decided to come to Cadmia. He wasn't particularly religious, but having a boss who drew a clear line between work and life was a real selling point after years of non-stop school and work.

"See you tomorrow." She gave Eddie a polite smile, then drifted over to the counter. Froze at the sound of a familiar laugh.

"Here you go, honey." Susan waited expectantly for Grace to offer to pay, fully intending to wave it off. The Talbot's were cousins of hers and she knew for a fact that Grace wasn't charging them full price for the work she'd done to save Luke's no-account dog. Belatedly, she noticed Grace's white-knuckled grip on the edge of the counter. Followed the slant of her eyes to a booth near the kitchen door where Alec sat beside Julie.

Never one to pass up a bit of gossip, Susan leaned in closer. "Cozy, ain't they?"

Grace's mouth opened, but no words came out. Tears were threatening, though. At last, she forced out, "Thanks." Slid a five onto the counter, snagged her hot chocolate, and stumbled outside, where the frigid air delivered a stinging slap to her face.

It felt positively friendly compared to the

shock she'd gotten inside.

Hauling herself into her truck, Grace locked the door. Seventeen years. Five months. Three days. That was how long it had been since she looked up from her scriptures at church and watched Alec Fitzsimmons walk into the chapel. In all those years, he'd never looked at a woman. Well, maybe he had while she was off at college, but she hadn't heard about it.

And now…and now… Folding her arms across the steering wheel, she put her head down and took some deep breaths. Each one brought a fresh lungful of hot chocolate steam up to her face.

"Why, Heavenly Father?" she whispered. "Why did I have to see that?" Even as she asked the foolish question—'why' questions had never proven useful to her—she knew the answer. Finding out for herself was marginally less painful than having someone giddily share the 'latest,' assuming and embellishing with benign intent.

Groaning, she started her truck. Even worse would be if some well-meaning person decided to 'break it to her gently,' with tissues or gift bag in hand and promising that, 'You'll get through this.' That actually happened to her in college.

The drive home was a blur, but she knew exactly what to do when she got there. Dropping to her knees by the couch, she prayed for guidance and comfort. Then she got up and reached for her scriptures. It wouldn't matter where she read. As Paul said in 2nd Timothy 3:16, "All scripture is given by inspiration of God and is profitable…"

While Grace sought peace in the scriptures, Alec was trying to finish his supper at Blinky's—and struggling to ignore the amused lift to Julie's eyebrows.

He might have thought she was laughing at him except that things were going fine between them until he'd looked up to see Grace staring at him like he'd grown a second head. Grace had gone pale, then grabbed her order and bolted out the door before he got a chance to wave hello.

Ever since then, Julie's entire demeanor had changed. He was about to suggest they order dessert and get out of there—his headache was only getting worse as he tried to figure out not one but *two* women who were behaving strangely—when Julie's eyes narrowed.

Clearing her throat, she leaned closer. "You…weren't aware?" she asked.

"Of what?" Alec made a valiant attempt to feign ignorance. Under Julie's scrutiny, and the rising pressure of her arching left eyebrow, he grumbled, "Aware of what?"

"Uh-huh." Julie patted him lightly on the arm. "Shall I tell you when you're older?"

Alec rolled his eyes. "Let's go." She had to mean Grace. Did everyone know but him?

Laughing, Julie complied. Let the matter rest all the silent way to her home. Then she hesitated before getting out.

"What's holding you back?" Julie rested her shoulder against her seat while she waited for his answer.

Alec put his elbows on the crossbars of his steering wheel. Rubbed his eyes. "I'm old enough to be her father." He'd finally figured out what Julie was talking about, mostly thanks to what Bart had said earlier.

"That's never bothered her." Julie shrugged.

Alec straightened slightly. "What do you mean by that?"

"Men can be so dense." Julie shook her head. "Are you seriously trying to tell me that you never noticed she was in love with you? Never even had the faintest inkling?" From the way his hands were slowly shoving their way up through his hair, she decided that was exactly what he meant. "Wow."

Feeling suddenly exhausted, Alec closed his eyes. "Just say it." The subsequent silence was the loudest he'd ever heard.

"I know what it's like to lose the person you love. To not be able to think straight because you've shattered into a billion pieces." Julie stroked her bare ring finger. "I waited five years before I even considered taking my ring off."

Alec twiddled the ring he'd forgotten he wore, recognizing the voice of experience when he heard it. Opening his eyes, he swallowed hard.

"And dating?"

"Another three years." She smiled a little sadly. "I started letting my friends set me up before that, but I wasn't really ready. It was…pretty awful."

Alec nodded. He'd had a tiny taste of dating for the few hours today that he'd thought he was going out with Julie. The idea of a blind date was enough to make him want to jump in a hole and pull it in after him.

"But I didn't have a Grace waiting for me."

His brows knit together in confusion. "Why do you say her name like it's a title or something?"

Julie inhaled slowly. Let it out. "Because the way she loves you? It's right out of a love song." Concluding that she'd given him enough to think about, she unfastened her seat belt.

"Thanks for tonight." She smiled. "I had fun."

"Thanks." He scrounged up an answering smile. "So did I." And he had. Right up until he'd noticed Grace exiting the diner looking like death warmed over.

"Night." Julie was out of the truck and halfway up the walk in what felt like half a heartbeat.

"Night," he mumbled. Once she was safely inside, he navigated her circle drive and started headed for the Rockin' R. As soon as he reached the first property gate, he swung in. Parking, he got out and stepped into the insulated coveralls he always carried. Swapped his newer boots for the work ones he was suddenly glad he'd dumped behind the seats instead of tossing into his trailer.

Shoving his hands into a pair of worn work gloves, he exhaled slowly, watching his breath crystallize in the moonlight. Driving carefully over the uneven ground, he followed the fence to the section Bart reported as needing repair.

Spools of wire and new fence posts lay waiting for tomorrow, but he needed to work now. Setting an alarm on his phone, Alec took another deep breath of cold, clean air. Then picked up a post-hole digger.

Slamming the digger into the ground rattled him down to his boots. It felt good. He lifted out the dirt he'd captured and set it aside. He repeated the process again and again until he'd dug out the old hole enough for a new post.

For the next four hours, except for a short breather, Alec dug holes, planted fence posts, and strung wire under a full moon. His shoulder muscles were burning and his back aching when his cell phone sang out that it was almost midnight.

Returning the tools to where he'd found them, Alec crawled into his truck and wearily drove to his trailer. It was worth it, though. A much needed sense of peace had settled over him as he worked. There was still plenty that he didn't know about his future. What he'd remembered, though, was that with faith, it would all work out.

"Gettin' soft, old man," he told his reflection while he gingerly stripped off his shirt. Silently blessing Mr. Brooke for splurging on the deluxe trailer—complete with a bathtub—he ran a hot bath and let himself soak until at least some of his muscles had stopped screaming.

Chapter 5

"Oh, Eric, stop." Sarah laughed at her husband, who was surreptitiously trying to wipe the makeup off his cheeks. "All you're going to do is smudge it and ruin the effect." It was Wednesday night and they were getting ready for the ward trunk-or-treat.

Eric shook his head and asked Grace, "Where were you when your mother talked me into this?" His hands came down from his face, fingers stroking outward to indicate that 'this' was meant to include the bowtie, blue overalls, and the red and white striped socks that his wife had gleefully provided for him. Not to mention the *blush*.

"You are an adorable Raggedy Andy," Grace laughed. It felt good to laugh. She'd spent every available moment studying or listening to the scriptures since spotting Alec with Julie, and the peace she felt was amazing. She didn't understand it, given that her feelings for Alec were as strong as ever, but she was grateful.

"How do I look?" Sarah lifted her blue skirt and flowery, white apron together. Naturally, her socks matched Eric's, though she had agreed that it would be sensible for them to wear their own, comfortable shoes.

"I think you look perfect." Grace bent closer and kissed her mother's cheek, careful to avoid the concentrated blush. "You, too, grumpy."

Wrinkling her nose at her dad, she stretched enough to give him a peck on the cheek as well.

"Grumpy? Me?" Eric feigned a pout. "Just because I had my heart set on going as the circus strongman?" He flexed his arms in an impressive display of seventy-year-old muscles.

Grace felt herself starting to blush as she considered her outfit. "Do you think it's too much?" She'd taken a silks class as an undergraduate elective and fallen in love with the discipline. She had a small setup of her own in the barn, which she didn't use nearly enough.

Still, unless she was actually performing, the catsuit often felt sort of…snug. The tops of her powder-blue, lace-up calf boots overlapped the bottoms of the suit legs by a few inches. The lined bodice was a black base with blue piping around the waistband and shoulder seams. Silver sequins on the bodice and collar glimmered in the faintest suggestion of light, in direct contrast to the costume's inky black sleeves and legs.

"You look gorgeous." Her father's assessment came easily.

Grace smiled. It was her own fault, really. If she'd been paying the least bit of attention, she could've gone as Raggedy Ann Jr. or something. Or she might take a page out of Merry's book and wear the same outfit every year.

But last year she'd gone straight from work. Still wearing her lab coat. She'd gotten plenty of friendly laughs and teasing. None of which she'd minded in the moment. She simply couldn't take it again this year. Not after… Not after seeing Alec with Julie. She couldn't stand being the boring vet anymore.

So, even if she wasn't completely sure about it, tonight she was going to smash some preconceived notions. Which, she told herself upon arrival, meant she needed to get out of her truck and go into the church.

Laughing shakily, Grace opened her truck door. Swinging her long legs around, she slid out. She'd chosen to wear black pumps to protect the soles of her barely there boots. Shifting her cape so that it hung straight, she strode inside.

Luckily, the first person she saw was Noella. Petite, vivacious Noella.

"Wow!" Noella grabbed Grace's hands and held her arms out from her body. Spun her. Too overcome to express herself in English, she announced in French, "I love your outfit! It's spectacular!!"

"Thank you!" Grace couldn't have asked for a more enthusiastic reception, though a slightly quieter one wouldn't have bothered her. She hadn't had this many eyes on her all at once since the last time she'd treated a pet tarantula.

"Are you a dancer?"

"An…" Grace paused. She'd never had to translate 'aerialist' into French before. "An acrobat of the air?"

"Trapéziste?" Noella's jaw dropped. "Amazing!"

"And you." Grace smiled, puzzled. "Are you…dressed as Anne Shirley?"

"Oui, yes." Noella leaned closer and dropped her voice slightly. "I tell someone I am from Prince Edward Island and it is assumed I must love this character. So, after a while I read the books," she laughed. "And tonight," she touched her wide-brim straw hat, "I become her."

"Soooo…now you actually do like her?" Grace clarified.

"Anne?" Noella shrugged. "I like her better after she has grown into her love for Gilbert."

Grace had to agree with that.

"Oh, not really. Not enough, I mean," Grace cautioned, suddenly remembering that her favorite Acadian-transplant was enthusiastically engaged in the local community theater. "C'mon." Linking arms with Noella, she steered her into the cultural hall where the costumed kiddos would hopefully provide a distraction. Heaved an inward sigh of relief when Noella dashed off to take a picture of an adorable nine-year-old Mrs. Claus.

"Grace? Is that you?" Sister Cutler had a slight deer in the headlights look about her as she approached that made Grace tug her cape closer to her. "What a stunning outfit!"

"Thank you. And you look adorable. Are you some kind of candy?" Grace guessed. It was a pretty good bet, given the stuffed, green trash bag Sister Cutler was wearing. At least, she thought it was stuffed. Sister Cutler was a darling woman who hadn't worried about her figure for thirty years.

"Oh yes." Sister Cutler laughed. "We look ridiculous, but it's the only couples' costume I could get Gary to agree to." She glanced around the room for her husband. Spying him cheerfully helping to set up the chili table, she turned her attention back to Grace. "I wish I'd known you dance," she assumed glibly. "We might have been able to use you in our spring production."

Grace scrambled mentally for some idea of what the woman was talking about and finally dredged up a hazy memory that Sister Cutler's daughter had a studio in the next town. It only took a few tries to convince her that Grace didn't know a tap shoe from a tutu, then the conversation moved on to more normal topics.

Sister Cutler stayed and chatted a little longer, then excused herself to take pictures of her grandchildren.

"Mmm, I think," Noella appeared at Grace's elbow, "that our Merry has a boyfriend."

Grace looked around and frowned. Tyrel Scott again. Dressed like…um. Like someone from one of Merry's favorite TV shows. And acting like he was glued to Merry's side. Merry, who shrank away whenever someone noticed her. Who was known to hide out in empty foyers during church events until something semi-organized happened.

Grace took a step forward, intending to rescue her introverted friend.

"Wait." Noella gripped her arm. A sensitive person, she all but felt Merry's pain and discomfort in the noisy, chaotic environment. However… "See? He's taking care of her."

Grace relaxed as Tyrel led Merry to a less congested area.

"Everyone!" Brother Murdock clapped massive hands and silence rippled out from him as if in shock waves. "May I have your attention, please? We're about ready to start the chili cook-off, so if you'll fold your arms, I've asked Sister Hixson to bless the food."

After the prayer, Noella squeezed Grace's arm. "I brought a pot. My mother's famous eight-bean chili!"

"Mmm." Grace returned the hug. Whispered, "Does it have cinnamon?" She almost hated to ask.

"Of course!"

"Naturally," Grace agreed promptly. She allowed Noella to hustle her into the line. Having never visited Prince Edward Island, she wouldn't claim to be an expert on Acadian cooking, but cinnamon certainly featured heavily in all of Noella's mother's recipes. Even in chili, though?

"This, it is Merry's mother's?" Noella asked, indicating Elaine McKinney's distinctive, chipped crock pot.

Grace smiled and nodded, fondly remembering the afternoon when she'd dropped the heavy spoon responsible for that chip. Somewhere back up the family tree, her parents were related to Merry's. Ever since they figured that out, the two families had spent so much time together that, in some ways, Grace was closer to Merry than she was to her own, much older brothers.

Snagging a second bowl, she filled it with the apparently plain beef chili—spiced with a drop or two of Monastario's Jalapeno Juice—while Noella put some eight-bean in her first bowl.

"We're holding up the line," Grace urged when it looked like Noella was going to give her a second heaping ladle of Acadian chili.

"Ah, yes." Noella chuckled. "Must leave some for the others." She winked conspiratorially.

Grace returned the wink and led her off in search of a table. She could've used Merry's company right then, but didn't want to intrude since she looked so taken with Tyrel. Instead, she found seats at tables in the primary room. Cautiously took a bite of Noella's chili. Hmm.

"This is great!" she grinned at Noella. That was all the invitation it took for Noella to launch into a monologue on the subject of chili, which was fine with Grace. It was super easy to listen and chew at the same time.

She'd almost forgotten her outfit until she noticed that the group of young men sitting at the next table were staring at her. She was debating what to do about it—exiting casually was at the top of her list—when Alec appeared. As always, her pulse went haywire when their eyes met, but he only smiled and turned his attention to the boys.

"Gentlemen." Alec Fitzsimmons put broad hands on his narrow hips. "Your mothers were right. Staring is rude." Pulling a chair over, he asked, "Who here has been to the circus?" Using a drawing app on his phone, he sketched the rough image of a trapeze swinging under a big top. Held it up. "Seen an aerial performance?"

Calling the boys' attention to the mechanics of the discipline, he helped them see that extra material *could* be life-threatening. Got them talking about skill. Timing. Force. Even the law of gravity. Anything but the skin-tight outfits aerialists were known for wearing.

And looked up to find Grace gone. Nodding awkwardly at Noella, the 'cute French girl,' he left the boys talking excitedly about going on a zip line, the closest thing they had to a trapeze in the area. Wandered aimlessly until he was confident Grace was no longer in the building. In the process, he got buttonholed by Brother Murdock and did his best to concentrate while he droned on about how well his plumbing business was doing lately.

Finally, he followed his restless feet out of the building. "I don't know exactly what this feeling is," he looked up at the night sky and spoke reverently to his Heavenly Father. "But it seems to be pulling me toward her." Running his fingers through his hair, he stared down at a loose gray hair that clung to his fingers. "She's…what? Thirty? Something like that. Not much older than my son, that's for sure. Meanwhile I'm…" His breath left him in a whoosh. "I'm going to be fifty next year." He hadn't stopped to think about his age for a long while. Not numerically, anyhow. He hated to admit it, but this particular number probably explained why he was having to use an ice pack after work most nights.

"Hitting the halfway mark, eh?" Eric Myers, who'd been afraid Alec was his wife coming to haul him back into the sweltering-hot building, stepped out of a shadow. "Must be nice to be young." Cocked his head to the side, assessing Alec's standard button-up, jeans, and cowboy boots. "Came as yourself tonight, eh? Have to suggest that to Sarah for next year."

Alec managed a weak laugh, but didn't say a word. He couldn't. Just gaped at the last person he'd expected to find there.

"Something troubling you, Alec?" Eric asked kindly.

Alec almost laughed. Of all the impossible situations. While he'd love to counsel with someone about his situation, he might have to draw the line at Grace's dad.

"There's…something I think I need to do."

He brushed his hands briskly together, knocking the gray hair off.

"Something you *think* you need to do. Hmm." Eric scratched his chin. "Don't you know?"

Alec slid his hands into his pockets. Shrugged with feigned casualness. "It's complicated."

"Ah. Like most things." Eric grinned knowingly. "Well, for what it's worth, my experience is that it helps to look around now and again. Take your bearings. Make sure that where you're headed is where you want to end up."

Alec tried vainly to swallow the lump in his throat. *End up?* He wasn't ready for retirement, let alone dying. And yet…the mental image of himself, still alone, in his trailer on the Rockin' R at Eric's age had less than no appeal.

"Gotta be careful, though." Eric scratched his chin. "Take my house, for example. Always wanted to build my own. Kept reading magazines. Telling my wife I was going to do it. Never happened." He chuckled. "Then we decided that we needed a barn. Something sturdy so we could raise milk cows, give the kids responsibility, that sort of thing."

Alec nodded, even though he had no idea where Eric was going with this.

"I drew up the plans myself. Three contractors tried to talk me out of it." Eric's shoulders started to shake. "I plum ignored everyone's advice

because it felt right. Know what I wound up with?
A barn big enough to handle a whole herd of
cows." He was openly laughing at himself now.
"A barn roof that peaks at nearly thirty feet.
I…the crew that built it for me still gives me funny
looks when I run into them in town."

Alec felt a tug at the corners of his mouth.
He couldn't help it. Eric's humor was contagious.
Giving in to it, he laughed with him, chasing away
some of the shadows he hadn't been able to shake
since his disastrous 'date' with Julie.

"And you know," Eric wiped his eyes, "it all
worked out in the long run?"

"Oh?" Alec was genuinely surprised. He'd
sort of expected a 'sometimes we make mistakes,
but we have to keep going' ending.

"Yes, it's been a real blessing. If I'd done it
the way the experts wanted, we'd have had a nice,
ordinary little barn. Cows would've been safe and
dry. But when Grace took over the clinic and
needed a place for some of her bigger patients to
recuperate, what would she have done?" He
shook his head. "She'd have wound up renting
some space elsewhere. More hours on the road,
more money out of pocket."

Grace. Alec noted that even her father didn't
call her 'Gracie.' Ooops.

"And that roof. It's perfect for her ropes
equipment."

"Ropes?" Alec wasn't positive, but he
thought… "You mean like you told me she did

in college?"

"Yep." Eric grinned. "She stuck with it. Says it keeps her limber. Keeps her…toned or something like that." He heard a door open behind him. "Uh-oh."

Alec smothered a grin as he watched Sarah Myers exit the building.

"What're you doing out here?" she half-scolded her husband. "You don't even have your coat on."

"Now, I've only been out a few minutes," Eric consoled her.

"I've been looking for you for the last fifteen," Sarah huffed, going up on her toes to wrap her own scarf around his neck.

"Have you?" Eric slipped his arm about his wife's waist, pulling her up against his side. He'd spent years out in the bitter cold tending animals and secretly loved her fussing. "Might be I lost track of time. Alec here has a problem we were talking about."

Don't pull me into it! Alec groaned inwardly. Getting caught in the middle was the worst thing about working for Mr. and Mrs. Brooke. Not that he'd ever heard the Myers exchange a cross word, but he didn't want to start tonight.

"Oh?" Sarah sent him a sympathetic look. "Have you asked Grace about it?"

"There's an idea." Eric winked at him. "She's got a good head on her shoulders."

Alec didn't know what else to do, so he started

nodding. "Yeah." His voice squeaked and he cleared his throat. "Yeah, thanks." He started retreating. "Night!"

Halfway down the parking lot, he realized he'd passed his truck. Groaned. Was there some law about dating neutralizing brain cells? 'Cause that was where the evidence was pointing. And he wasn't even dating yet! So if it turned out that there was a law to that effect, he was toast.

Pulling onto the highway, he tried without success to recapture the peace he'd felt while working on the fence posts. Instead, his truck drove him to the Myers'. Grace's truck was already in the drive. Blowing out a breath, Alec pulled up by the barn. Shut his truck off.

Wait a second. He thought he heard music. Didn't he? It got louder when he opened his door. Sounded sort of like rock, except with…bagpipes? He eased the door shut behind him rather than slamming it. Reached up to smooth his hair. Tugged on his collar. Did they offer refresher courses in dating somewhere? Online, maybe?

Unbidden, an expression of his father's sprang into his mind—'Putting it off won't make it any easier, son.'

Alec suddenly felt about sixteen again. "Miss you, Dad," he whispered hoarsely.

The music coming from the barn changed, became much slower. Lilting. Fanciful. It lifted him off the ground and drew him into the barn like he was some cartoon character. He half expected to be able to look at his back trail and see a string of hearts. But at least it got him inside.

Where he stood, dumbstruck, staring up at a dream. His heart shuddered, permanently shattering his carved-in-stone notion of her as an adolescent girl. Had she always been this beautiful?

Grace hung, perfectly still, suspended in mid-air by streams of cream-colored silk. One of the hardest things for her to learn had been the art of a timely pause. A subtle hesitation. Kicking one foot free of the silk she'd hooked it in, she dangled from one arm while pointing her toe and languidly drawing one leg up even as her other leg darted out to capture the silk in a different way.

Rolling. Twisting. Wrapping the silk around her body in rhythm with the music. Trying to reach the proper setup for a drop while looking graceful. Relaxed. Holding a stretch like her muscles weren't trembling. Never, ever letting the effort show.

There. Perfect. She let go.

"Grace!" Alec shot forward faster than he'd thought possible, desperate to catch her before she hit the floor. Pulled up short just in time to keep from knocking heads with her.

"Alec!" Stunned, Grace hung there, upside down, frantically pushing the silks out of her face. Why? That was a brilliant question, given that she'd actually rather like to disappear. "What're you doing here?!"

"I… That is…" He withdrew a step to reassess her situation. "You weren't in any danger, were you?" So much for his dramatic rescue attempt. Sheesh, his ego was taking a beating this week!

Grace hesitated. Bending in the middle, she caught hold of the silks. Unwound herself the rest of the way.

Alec stared in amazement as she touched down as softly as a butterfly landing on a flower, one streamer draped over the front of her right shoulder.

"You thought you were saving me?" she asked, dropping her eyes demurely.

"Yes, well." He stepped closer. "I've never seen anyone successfully fall ten feet before." He touched the flimsy-looking streamer where it hung loose over her head. "Let alone do it elegantly."

She had to tilt her head back to meet his gaze. It felt good to be seen. Good like…like the sun on her face after a backbreaking night of pulling calves.

Chapter 6

"Grace." Alec's hand strayed to her hair, smoothing it away from her face. "Will you go out with me Friday?" The invitation came straight from his heart, because his head was still warning him it was a dumb, *dumb* idea to date someone so much younger.

Grace tore her focus away from the scent of his cologne. "What about Julie?" Ummmm, maybe she should've taken a breath before she blurted that out. Or maybe he liked women that were clingy and possessive. *As if.*

"You saw us at Blinky's the other night?" He watched her stiff nod, confirming that they were thinking along the same lines. "She wanted to talk to me about having a young women's activity night at the Rockin' R." The lips he'd never noticed before were so close that he could smell her strawberry lip gloss. It had been so long, though. Did he even remember how to kiss? His right hand settled on her waist. Was it his imagination or were her eyes starting to close?

Grace pulled away with a jerk. Moved so that she was on the other side of her silks, which had never seemed so thin and paused to try to catch her breath. Good grief. All he'd done was look at her and she nearly swooned. If he actually ever got around to kissing her, she was in serious trouble.

Bewildered, Alec let his hands fall to his sides. Had he… No, had *everyone* read her signals wrong?

"Would Saturday be alright?" Grace held her breath. It was Merry's turn to host movie night on Friday and Grace realized how important they were to her friend.

"That works for me." Was she playing hard to get? But no, her counter-offer had come at once.

"Then yes." She closed her eyes and tilted her head forward, laughing silently at herself. No artistic pause there.

He bounced lightly on his toes. Put his hands in his pockets because he didn't know what else to do with them. "Pick you up at six?" He did some rapid mental calculation. "I mean, five?"

"That's fine." She couldn't see more than a blurry figure through the streamers, but he sounded uncertain. As he turned to leave she hastily asked, "What should I wear?" She caught a glimpse of his face through the gap between the silks and her cheeks warmed when his eyes flicked over her form. Not that he could really see her, either.

He hesitated, trying to figure out the answer. He hadn't paid attention to women's clothing for a good twenty years. "Your blue dress?" he suggested.

She parted the silks to get a good look at his face. "My *blue* dress?"

"Um. Yes?" Maybe she had more than one blue dress? While he only recalled the one that was no guarantee he was right. He snapped his fingers. "Turquoise. With the gold…" Unable to come up with the word, he began moving his hands along his own belt line. "Gold…thing around the waist." It wasn't a belt, exactly. It didn't have a buckle or anything like that for one thing. What was that word?

"Sash," she supplied, ducking behind the silks again.

"Sash," he repeated. He'd seen enough of the smile she was unsuccessfully trying to hide to be worried. Had he just made a fool of himself? "Great." Nodding, he began backing toward the door. "See you Saturday. At five."

Grace waited for the sound of his truck to fade, then released an excited shriek. The clinic's residents registered their shock at her jubilation with bleats, oinks, and other sounds. But for once, she didn't care.

"Can you believe it, Oscar?" she asked the pot-bellied pig she'd disturbed. "He remembered a specific dress!"

Securing her silks, she double-checked everyone and raced inside the house. Which was dark. Empty.

What?! Her parents weren't home yet! But…she had to tell someone. Celebrate with someone! Preferably someone who would do more than 'moo' in response.

Realizing she'd left her phone—still playing her exercise soundtrack—in the barn, Grace buried her face in her hands. Took a couple of deep breaths. Swapped her catsuit for a pair of boys' basketball shorts and a loose tee, then jogged out to get her phone.

Unable to wait any longer, she dialed Merry.

"Grace? Are you alright?" Merry's voice asked anxiously.

"Merry, I…" Grace hugged herself. "I have a date for Saturday!"

"Oh, really?" Her tone shifted to amused, though not surprised. "How many?" Grace rolled her eyes, but didn't respond fast enough to prevent her from adding, "I think every man in the room noticed you tonight."

"Yeah, yeah. One man is all I need, thank you." She held her breath while she waited for Merry to think that over. Merry was the only person she'd shared her secret with.

"Are you trying to tell me that Alec Fitzsimmons has asked you out?" Merry squeaked.

"Yes!!!!" Again, the animals protested her exuberance.

"Wait, what? Grace, I can hardly hear you over that racket. Are you in the barn?"

"Yes," Grace said again as she stepped outside and closed the door behind her. "Is that better?" Her breath hung in the air above her, visible in the weak rays from the security light.

"Much." Merry blew out a breath. "Now. Start at the beginning."

Grace laughed. "You don't really want me to do that, do you?"

"Well." There was a short pause, then a guilty sounding, "Noooo. But you probably want to tell me. Why else would you call?"

Grace shook her head, glad Merry couldn't see her. Merry had never quite found a balance between honesty and tact. Still, she made an excellent point. Grace *had* called so she could tell someone she trusted her exciting news. Of course, the fact that she had a date with him was the most important part, so...mission accomplished.

"There's not that much to share." Grace meandered across the lawn, leaving dark footprints where she'd scuffed the frost off the grass. "I saw him at the trunk-or-treat, but we didn't talk or anything."

"I saw him, too." The amusement in Merry's voice was impossible to miss.

"What?" Grace demanded when she stopped there.

"He couldn't take his eyes off you."

The chill air did nothing to assuage the heat creeping up her cheeks.

"Grace? Are you there? You're blushing, aren't you?" Silence. "Honey, it's not a bad thing for the man you're interested in to want to look at you."

Grace clapped a hand over her mouth to stifle her laughter. Merry, whom she loved dearly, had a bad habit of imparting 'wisdom' gleaned from the books and movies she studied as if it was from her own life experience.

"Grace? Don't make me come over there, young lady."

That did it. Grace wrapped her free arm around her waist and gave in to the laughter. "Don't you 'young lady' me, you goofball. You're only four years older than I am."

"Four years is one thousand…"

"Four hundred and sixty days. Yeah, yeah." Grace cut in. How many times had she heard this?

"Well. Learn something new every day, right? That means I know one thousand four hundred and sixty things that you don't," Merry said loftily.

"And what did you learn today?" Grace looked at her phone when the silence dragged on. They were still connected. "Merry? I know you're there." Suddenly remembering seeing Merry with Tyrel, Grace paused. "Hey. Are you alright? Do you need me to come over?"

Merry laughed. "I guess that threat works both ways, doesn't it?" she asked softly.

"Call it what you like," Grace teased back, relieved to hear Merry joking about it.

"I'm… I'm seeing someone, too."

Grace's phone started beeping urgently. She

groaned and headed for the house at a jog. "Shoot. Hang on, I've got to plug my phone in." No way was she going to let her phone die in the middle of Merry's big announcement! Careening into her room, she made a mad dash for her charger. "Okay, your turn."

Haltingly, Merry shared what Grace instinctively knew was the short version of the story.

Grace contributed as needed. Remarked that she hadn't been able to loan her truck for the move-in that prompted Tyrel's first call. Was suitably impressed at his innovative gift of a food delivery from Fresh, the most popular frozen food delivery service in the area.

"Anyway, I got home from Noella's meeting yesterday and started to eat one of the pizzas."

"You what?" Grace gasped in dismay. "Oh, honey, he probably planned for the two of you to eat it together. I mean, it's a pretty bold move, practically inviting himself over like that, but..." Her voice trailed off as she realized Merry had gone quiet again. *Ouch.* Merry often struggled to pick up on the subtleties of social interaction. Grace opened her mouth to reassure her.

"I hadn't thought of it that way." Merry half-laughed. "I was so focused on apologizing for making a mistake that I just...didn't even realize he was being cheeky."

"Oh?" Grace began mentally gearing up for a very direct conversation with Tyrel about the consequences for hurting Merry. "You've already apologized?"

"Yeah. When he picked me up tonight, it sort of came out. Y'know?" Merry laughed again.

"How'd he handle it?" Grace coaxed, though it didn't sound like it had gone badly.

"He hugged me."

"Hugged you?" Grace's eyebrows rose. Merry had very clearly defined spatial restrictions. It was one thing for Grace or someone she'd accepted to hug her, but a relative stranger? A *male* stranger?

"Swept me right off my feet."

"Did he now?" The corner of Grace's mouth quirked up at the faintly dreamy note in Merry's voice. How about that? "I'm glad."

"Thanks."

There was a comfortable moment of quiet as they each followed their own thoughts. Grace blinked away happy tears. If anybody deserved a happily-ever-after, Merry did. Being single truly represented failure to her. Failure and a bleak, empty future. All things Grace had learned while wiping away tears few others were allowed to see.

"Are you going to see him again?"

"Yes, we're going to watch some *Pool of Stars* tomorrow."

"Perfect!" Grace laughed in delight as it clicked in her mind. *That* was where their matching outfits came from! "By the way, did you two plan your costumes?"

"No, it took me completely by surprise." Merry giggled, something she never did. Abruptly, she sobered. "Hey. Do you still have open vaccinations on Thursdays?"

"Hmm?" Grace made a face. "Ugh, why'd you remind me?" They deliberately scheduled Thursdays lightly to accommodate harried run-ins.

"Because it's almost nine and you need your sleep."

"My sister, my keeper?" Grace teased, projecting a smile into her tone. She didn't doubt for a second that Merry's concern was genuine, but she'd known her far too long not to recognize the 'I'm tired, too' in her voice. "It's been a big night for us both."

"Historic," Merry's voice quietly corrected.

Surprised, Grace considered the statement. "You're right."

"Congratulations, Gracie." Merry's voice held a barely stifled yawn.

"Congratulations, Merry. Night."

"Night."

Grace set her phone on the desk and lay down to think. She'd gone on a few group dates in high school, mostly to be polite. Halfheartedly accepted dates in college for the same reason. No, not even halfheartedly. Whole-headedly, maybe, once she'd talked herself into it. Much to her dates' exasperation, she'd been invulnerable to their charms.

Her date with Alec promised to be a completely different experience.

She pressed cool fingers to warming cheeks as she replayed his answer to her simple question. It was always good to have a clue what kind of clothes to wear on a date, but that was usually all she dared hope for—a single clue. Something 'comfy.' Or 'dressy.' And there was the old favorite: 'jeans.' Tonight was the first time she'd ever gotten a request for her to wear a specific outfit. He'd completely taken her off guard.

At some point in her pondering, she yawned. Blinked. Dozed. Woke to her alarm going off the next morning.

The day passed as a hectic blur of "the usual" mixed with vaccination walk-ins, which was pretty good for a Thursday.

Friday went much more smoothly. In fact, things wound down enough that she seized the opportunity to visit the Wheelwright dairy that afternoon.

"Are you sure you don't want me to make the delivery?" Neil frowned at her. "You've been a little…distracted today."

"Don't be so dramatic," she laughed, hoping he was joking. She prided herself on being able to focus while at work. She couldn't help a few nerves, but that was normal. Right? "Besides, you've got paperwork to do."

Shrugging, he picked up the box to load into the bed of her truck. "Have fun."

"Fun?" Mrs. Ivey hooted. She'd shown the last patient out, so she knew there was only the staff left to hear her. "Wheelwright was the last and the loudest of the I-don't-wanna-woman-vet protestors."

"Because why?" Neil rested the box on his hip and gave Mrs. Ivey his full attention.

"Because that's how he was raised," interjected Grace before Mrs. Ivey got started. "Several of my father's clients were wary of a female vet at first. Of course, everything changes. Once I had a chance to show them what I was capable of, they capitulated." She rolled her eyes, realizing she'd practically quoted the state motto. "This is Missouri, after all. As for Wheelwright, this last year we worked extensively on his herd management."

Mrs. Ivey harrumphed, but didn't say anything. She didn't have to. They both knew what Grace meant was that she'd practically camped at Wheelwright's in June. That he'd only agreed to pay for half of the supplies until after the spring calving, when he'd consider paying the rest. Still, if his next batch of calves turned out to be all-star heifers, she'd figure it was worth the effort. Why? Because, honestly, she was just as bull-headed as he was. And…because a small part of her wanted him to come out of the dark ages. To see ability, not stereotypes.

As she drove, she offered yet another prayer for things to go smoothly. For both their sakes. Her prayer was answered in the form of Wheelwright's eleven-year-old grandson, Willie. He spent over an hour with her, helping her record results while he peppered her with questions. With his help, she was able to ultrasound nearly the entire bunch of serviced cows, all of whom were confirmed pregnant.

It was all brought to an abrupt halt by Wheelwright's bellow from the near end of his milk barn.

"Willie! You done played enough. Get back in here."

"I gotta go, Doc." Willie handed over her clipboard. "Soon!"

"You bet!" She chuckled as she watched him jog away. "That's one apple that rolled quite a piece from his family tree!"

Chapter 7

"Grace?" Sarah smiled at her daughter as she came into the front room. "You're home early, darling. Especially for a Friday." Sliding a picture into a plastic sleeve, she asked, "Will you be joining us for supper?"

Grace endured a small pang of guilt as she shook her head. "Thanks, but I bumped into Danny Fitzsimmons at Stock's and we ate at Blinky's." Where she'd spilled the beans about—oh, everything. Her date tomorrow night with Alec. That she loved him. Yeah, she'd told him that she loved his *dad*. "Plus, tonight is movie night at Merry's."

"Danny Fitzsimmons?" Sarah brightened. "I haven't seen him in forever. How's he doing?"

Grace laughed. "I'll tell you while I help with those photos." Her mom had been the unofficial family photographer for years, but lately she'd started branching out.

"Oh, thank you, sweetheart." Sarah gestured at the stack of photos in front of her. "I'll label them if you'll put them in the sleeves?"

"Deal." Taking the chair beside her, Grace began gingerly adding photos to the half-finished page.

"I've always loved the Sorensons," Sarah sighed, flexing tired fingers, "but if I'd known how many of these albums they wanted for their

~ 80 ~

extended family, I think I would have asked for more money!"

Grace cracked up. "I can't believe they're not sending a digital album, to be honest."

"They talked about it." Flipping over a photo, Sarah neatly recorded the name of each person, their age, and the year the photo was taken. "But I guess Brother Sorenson has had too many unpleasant experiences with computers to trust them much. And, Sister Sorenson is of the opinion that a Christmas gift you can't actually wrap—and therefore open—isn't much of a gift."

Grace head-shrugged. "Fair enough!"

For the next half an hour they chatted while they worked, until…

"You left him with Noella?" Sarah was aghast.

"That's right." Grace cocked an eyebrow at her mother. "You sound disappointed?"

"Oh." Collecting herself, Sarah waved the idea away. "Not disappointed."

"Sad?" Grace made eye contact with her. "Mom?"

Sarah sighed. "Are there so many eligible young men around that you can give them away?"

Grace practically dropped the stack of pages she was trying to add to the binder. "Mom!" Shocked, she struggled to find words to express herself. "Mom, I promise, Danny and I… We were never interested in each other. Not like *that*."

"You wrote to him the entire two years that he was gone on his mission," Sarah pointed out, confused.

"Because we were friends." Well. That wasn't the whole truth. She bit her lip. And it wasn't like she was going to be able to keep things a secret after they started dating—which was what she was praying was happening.

Sarah started to turn away, to get another binder, but something in Grace's face held her there.

"I love Alec Fitzsimmons, Mom. I always have." Under other circumstances, watching her mother's jaw hit the floor might've been funny.

"Grace." Sarah took her daughter's face in her hands. Studied her eyes. "You never told me."

"I never told anyone but Merry." She *tried* to tell her mom about Alec once, but she'd gotten a verbal pat on the head and a canned answer about how crushes on 'older men' were normal. It was no surprise that her mom didn't even remember.

"Grace." Taking a deep breath, Sarah folded her daughter into a hug. "I don't know a thing against the man, as such. On the other hand." She drew away and looked at Grace with troubled eyes. "Honey, I'm afraid the man's still mourning his wife."

Grace's heart shuddered. "He...might be." She hesitated, thinking back to his invitation.

"But I have to give this a chance."

"You don't mean…" Sarah narrowly avoided wringing her hands. "When?!"

"We're going out for dinner tomorrow."

Sarah picked up her pen. Uncapped it and recapped it. "That's a bit sudden." Grace's face fell and Sarah mentally kicked herself. How would either of them know if Alec's decision was sudden? Were they mind readers now? "First I find out you're in love." Dropping the pen, she took Grace's hands in her own. "Then I find out you've already got a date lined up!"

"A date?" Eric stepped in from where he'd been unabashedly listening for the last couple of minutes. "When and with whom?"

An hour later, Grace parked in front of the huge, renovated barn where Merry worked and lived. Harmony's hatchback was already there, right next to Noella's car. *Hmm. Noella and Danny…* The more she thought about it, the more she liked the sound of that.

Exhausted from her parents' persistent banter, Grace bypassed the front door and went to Merry's hydraulic lift box instead. One of probably three people in the world who had a spare key to the double doors on Merry's second story verandah, she knocked lightly, then let herself in.

"There she is!" Harmony waved her over to the kitchen island where they were all working. "Thought we were going to have to watch *Mr.*

Scoutmaster without you."

"Oooh, that's a new title." Grace stepped out of her shoes and hung up her coat. "Who's in it?"

"Clifton Webb." Noella held out the movie case she'd been studying while she waited for a turn with the spatula.

"Nice!" Grace grinned at Merry. "A new title *and* rice krispie treats!" Giving the case a quick once-over, she nodded. "I remember this guy. He played the dad in the original *Cheaper by the Dozen.*"

"And Souza in *Stars and Stripes Forever*," Merry supplied. While she hated making rice krispie treats, it was worth it to see everyone's smiles. "I haven't liked him in all his movies, but this one sounds pretty good."

"So you've never seen it, either?" Harmony was openly shocked.

"Not this one, no." Merry scooped up her paper plate of treats and a napkin. "Same rules, ladies. If it turns out to have questionable content, we shut it off and watch a session of general conference instead."

"Good deal." Harmony spoke around half of a sticky treat, making the others laugh.

They all fit on Merry's massive couch, which made giggling at the movie a lot more fun. The main character turned out to be a television writer who didn't understand his considerably younger audience. He joined a local scout troop in dignified desperation and the quips commenced.

"Awwww." Harmony snuggled a little closer to Grace as the final credits rolled. "What a cute ending."

Hearing a hint of longing in her voice, Grace wrapped an arm around her and wondered again about Harmony's story. She never talked about her family.

"Yes," Noella agreed. "The boy, he is much better with this new family."

"Absolutely." Merry rose and began collecting trash. "Now, who's going to take rice krispies home with them?"

"Not it!" Grace ducked behind Harmony, who laughed. Substituting junk food for three square meals wouldn't be a smart move.

"I'll take some." Harmony patted Grace's hand. "Whatever I don't eat, I can drop off at the airport breakroom."

"Sold!" Merry transferred the rest of the leftovers to a nine-inch paper plate and wrapped it within an inch of its life in plastic wrap. "For the lucky winner." She winked as she nudged it in Harmony's direction.

Harmony hauled herself up off the couch and yawned her way over to the island.

"You better get some sleep," Merry admonished her. "If I know you, you'll spend all day at the track tomorrow."

"What else is there to do around here on a Saturday?" It didn't bother Harmony in the least that none of them knew the track was closed for the season.

Grace frowned at Harmony's humorless laugh. "If you're volunteering," she started, "there's the ward wood cutting project tomorrow at eight."

"In the morning?" Harmony whistled. Of course, she'd known about the project all along. She just hadn't planned on attending. "Are you going?"

"I am," Merry announced. She preferred to do her wood working in the quiet confines of her own workshop downstairs, but for a service project she'd make an exception. A lot of families in the ward boundaries wouldn't make it through the winter without their wood stoves.

"I signed up to bring hot soup." Noella also had plans with Danny for the next evening. Something about helping him be "out of the way"? While that made no sense to her, she didn't have any trouble understanding that she wanted to spend time with the muscular young man Grace'd introduced her to.

"And I'll be there in thermal coveralls and thick gloves." Grace rose and stretched, reaching up toward the ceiling, then down to touch her toes. "Though I'll only stay until my feet are frozen." Her feet were always the first to succumb to the frigid temperatures.

Harmony chuckled. "I give. I can spare a couple of hours."

"Awesome." Merry surprised her with a bear hug, the kind that Harmony usually initiated. "Tomlinson's at eight tomorrow."

"Got it." Harmony gave Merry a grateful smile. Usually the weekly movie nights were a great break from her pell-mell life. Once in a while, though, the happy endings acted like a magnifying glass, emphasizing her bare ring finger and empty social calendar. Not to mention the empty house she was heading 'home' to.

"I can ride with you tomorrow?" Noella asked, handing Harmony her coat.

"Are you sure? I don't know how long I'll be there."

"It is alright." Noella nodded. "The Petersons will be there." She often rode to church events with the Petersons. She loved children in general and their triplets in particular.

Harmony chuckled. "The Petersons. If we somehow managed to harness the energy and teamwork of their triplets, we'd get enough wood chopped for the whole town in less than an hour."

Grace joined in the laughter, but made no move to collect her things. "Be careful out there," she waved as Harmony and Noella headed out the door.

Merry waved, too, then continued cleaning up. "Set a spell," she invited Grace, gesturing toward the stools surrounding the island.

"Thanks." Grace slid onto one of the hand-made stools and rested her arms on the walnut island top. "I told my parents about Alec tonight."

Merry was putting a glass into the dishwasher and missed the slot she was aiming for. Leaving the rest of cleaning up for later, she pulled out some hot chocolate and started microwaving water.

Grace chuckled at that. Chocolate was Merry's favorite flavor and, over the years, most of their important conversations had taken place over steaming mugs of cocoa. She sobered slightly when Merry set a tiny bottle of strawberry flavoring in front of her.

"Wow," she said around the lump in her throat. "That's the good stuff." The kind that only took a few drops to turn an entire mug of ordinary hot chocolate into strawberry-hot chocolate. And Merry kept it around especially for her.

"C'mon." Merry slid a mug to her and carried her own over to the couch where she settled herself comfortably.

Grace followed her, sinking happily into the couch. Some couches swallowed her whole like an unwelcome hug, while others were as stiff and uncomfortable as a wary dog on its first visit to her office. This one was perfect. When she joined Merry, their feet reached roughly to the other's knees, letting them lean back while they faced each other.

Merry let her enjoy her drink, then coaxed quietly, "How'd they take it?"

Grace licked the hot chocolate foam off her upper lip and sighed. "Enthusiastically." With a small hand shrug, she corrected herself, "Mom warned me that he's probably still mourning."

Merry hoped her wince didn't make it to her face. She'd known Sarah Myers since she could remember. She wouldn't have warned Grace if she hadn't believed what she was saying.

"Is he still wearing his ring?"

Grace blinked. Nodded slowly.

"How do you feel about that?"

Grace bit her lip. "Like maybe Mom's right." Slowly she raised a shoulder. "Like maybe he's not really ready to date and…" Her throat seized up and hot tears rushed to sting her eyes. "And he picked me because then he'll have an excuse if it fails." She accepted a box of tissues from Merry, who thankfully let her sniffle in peace for a minute.

"What you said just now?" Merry cocked her head to one side. "You don't actually believe that."

Grace crumpled the tissue and considered before shaking her head. "It's simply a fear." Blown out of proportion by the fact that she was standing on the threshold of getting everything she'd ever wanted.

"And we know there's never only one fear, right?" Merry's disgusted scowl was genuine.

"Sort of like chiggers."

"Gross!" Grace groaned at the mention of the tiny red parasites. "Only you could bring up chiggers in a conversation about love."

"Am I wrong?" Merry knew she wasn't. "Fear's parasitical, right?"

"I…" Grace blew out a breath. Even thinking about the ugly things was making her itchy. "Yeah, okay, I guess so." She wrinkled her nose at Merry. "I hope that's as far as your analogy goes."

"Sort of." Merry hesitated. There weren't many people in the world she could be herself with, and while Grace was one of them, they still had to work at communication sometimes. "Remember that time your cousins came to visit?"

Grace rolled her eyes. "I assume you mean the summer we spent a perfectly good Saturday at the ER because they were all covered in chigger bites." And Merry, her best friend, came along to keep her company.

"Yep. Your mom must've warned them a hundred times: stay out of the long grass. A simple rule, but none of them could bring themselves to obey it."

Grace narrowed her eyes at Merry. "And what simple rule should I follow here?"

"Don't put the cart before the horse."

Grace stared at her. "Don't put the cart before the horse?"

Merry had to take a gulp of her dark chocolate mint to keep from answering the question, even though she knew it was rhetorical.

Meanwhile, Grace covered her eyes with one hand, trying not to feel too silly. "You mean I shouldn't worry about breaking up with him until after the first date?" She was rewarded with a warm smile. "Thanks, Merry. I needed that."

Sighing, Grace leaned her head against the couch's wing. "Must be something about coming face to face with a dream that flusters me."

"I know what you mean." Merry nodded, thinking about her own slowly developing relationship with Tyrel.

"How's that coming?" Grace asked, almost as if she could read Merry's mind.

Merry ducked her head. "It's coming."

"Is he nice?" she coaxed. To her surprise, Merry bobbed her head from left to right, a sort of yes-no answer.

"We got off to a rough start," Merry admitted awkwardly. Tugged on her dark ginger braid, making her natural highlights flash in the light. "We've swapped apologies, though, and since then we've mostly been having fun, so…" She drew her knees up protectively. "So he's pretty nice, yeah."

Grace had to think about the rapid-fire words twice before she felt she really grasped what Merry was telling her. "You've…been having fun since then," she repeated haltingly, needing the reassurance. Worrying about Merry was second-nature by now. All their lives she'd run interference for Merry where possible, but she knew this was an experience Merry had to have for herself.

"Yeah." Merry nodded. "It helps that we both really like *Pool of Stars*."

"True." Grace chuckled in relief. Asked gently, "Scared?"

"Every second." Their eyes met and their friendship tree grew a new ring or two.

"Not much choice, is there?" Grace twisted her lips wryly. "I mean, I suppose we could throw away the chance of a lifetime. Move in together and get a dozen cats apiece."

Merry kicked her lightly with her stockinged foot.

"No?" Grace winked. "Then I guess we'll just have to give love a try."

"I hope you get to live all the plans you've made." Merry met her gaze seriously. "You'll be the best thing that ever happened to him if he gives you half a chance."

Grace tried hiding her flaming cheeks behind her mug. The horrible thing about road trips and girls' camp and some twenty-eight years of friendship was that eventually a best friend could get to know you better than you knew yourself.

"I don't want anything so terribly special," she hedged at last. "A temple wedding. Children."

"To live in a trailer?" Merry teased.

Grace wrinkled her nose. "Maybe not." Which probably meant Alec would have to give up being foreman at the Rockin' R? He had to live on site for his job… That was a lot to ask. "Well. Maybe. I don't know."

"Mr. Brooke might spring for a bigger one," Merry suggested. "As a wedding present."

"Anything's possible." Grace finished her hot chocolate.

"Hey." Merry nudged her. "Need to stay over?"

A smile tugged at Grace's lips, but she shook her head. "Thanks, I better get going. Dad plans to get up early tomorrow so he can practice for grilling Alec when he comes to pick me up."

Merry burst into laughter. "Oh, you are so lucky I wasn't swallowing when you said that!" Hot chocolate out the nose *hurt*. "Please tell me you aren't serious." Rising, she took Grace's empty mug and set it in the sink.

"Serious as taxes." Grace reluctantly got up, too. "Claims he never got to do it for my prom, so now Alec gets the full treatment by default."

"The full treatment?" Merry was appropriately awestruck. "Can I come watch? Ow!" She yelped as Grace punched her playfully in the arm.

"Thanks." She wrapped Merry in a warm hug that comforted them both. Inhaled the scents of wood, butter, and sugar that clung to her best friend. "Love you."

"Love you," Merry whispered at the same moment.

They laughed, but they were both a little teary-eyed as they drew apart.

"We better get some sleep." Merry nudged her toward the verandah. "Early day tomorrow."

Stepping out of Merry's lift box when it reached the ground, Grace waved goodbye and hurried to her truck. The sound of her teeth chattering was barely drowned out by the engine, prompting her to reach into the back seat for the fleece blanket she carried year-round. It was as cold as she was, but at least it captured the heat she was losing, instead of letting it vanish into the frigid air.

Eyes peeled for deer, dogs, and pedestrians, she carefully made her way home, where she slept like a log. A log that couldn't seem to get wherever it was going, no matter how hard it rolled and bumped along—until her alarm went off at six the next morning. Dutifully, she got up and stumbled into her clothes.

"Grace?" Her mother's voice penetrated a thick, sleepy fog. "Honey, wake… Eric, look at this. I'm not sure she should go today."

"What's wrong?" Grace forced her eyes to open and found both of her parents frowning at her. Glanced down to see if she'd missed a button or something. No, her long-sleeved flannel shirt was buttoned correctly and tucked neatly into the bottom half of her coveralls. Thermal undershirt? Check. Wriggling her toes, she confirmed that she was wearing woolen socks. Knit cap? Yep, in hand. Not that she remembered changing out of her pajamas, but that was nothing new. "Oh." Stooping, she re-tied her right boot so that it was double-knotted.

"C'mon, sweetheart." Eric pulled her into the kitchen. "You can sleep while we finish getting breakfast ready." Seating her at the table, he chuckled at her perplexed expression and returned to his station at the waffle irons.

Sarah tsked, but resumed running her spatula through the scrambled eggs. "I hate to say anything against your movie nights." She really did; they were almost the only fun Grace had outside of work. "But when you're tired enough to fall asleep standing up, young lady, I think you might need to reassess matters."

Grace opened her mouth to respond and wound up yawning so hard she popped her jaw. "Ow." Massaging the offended muscle, she sighed. "I was in bed by nine-thirty, Mom." Her stomach growled menacingly. The food smelled great; that wasn't the problem. The problem was that, even after talking things over with Merry last night, she was so filled with dread that she doubted she'd be able to swallow a bite of breakfast.

"You've had a rough couple of weeks. Probably didn't realize how tired you were," Eric observed, squeezing her shoulder as he set a plate of waffles on the table. "Better nap before your date tonight."

"That's a good idea," Sarah agreed. She smiled at her husband as he picked up two plates mounded with golden eggs to carry over to the table for her. "Take a hot bath, too," she suggested, picking up her own plate. "Otherwise you'll be sore from the service project."

Grace buried her face in her hands. Somehow, she'd never expected her parents' dating advice to include recommending a *nap*. How old was she again? She peeked through her fingers when her dad cleared his throat, then meekly took her parents' hands for prayer.

"Are we ready for Sunday School tomorrow?" her dad asked after the amen. "Everyone keeping up with the reading schedule?"

"I am!" Sarah volunteered perkily. "I struggle a bit with Paul's writing style, but I finished Titus yesterday and plan to read Philemon right after I do the dishes." Forking a waffle onto her plate, she reached for the honey butter. "So far, I think my favorite verse is from 2nd Timothy."

Knowing that her mother tried to memorize a verse a week, Grace kept an ear open for it as she halfheartedly spread homemade grape jelly over her waffle. One of her pet peeves was wasting food. Especially her favorite foods, like waffles.

Nor was she looking forward to the inevitable lecture on her health from one or both of her parents when they noticed she couldn't eat.

Should she call Alec? Postpone the date? She couldn't believe she was even considering it. She had to be insane. In fact, there was probably a clinical term for someone who spent a lifetime yearning for something only to get cold feet at the last minute.

"God hath not given us the spirit of fear; but of power, and of love, and of a sound mind," Sarah quoted 2nd Timothy 1:7.

Energy shot through Grace, making her arms break out in goose bumps and almost forcing a shocked gasp from her. The Spirit sent the words pulsing through her—*God hath not given us the spirit of fear.*

Chapter 8

Grace was still thinking about that verse two hours later when Alec's truck pulled up at the Tomlinson's. It didn't stop her from blushing lightly, but it did help her resist the urge to duck behind Merry. Which wouldn't have been a good idea anyhow, given that Merry was currently wielding a sixteen-inch chainsaw. She waved at Alec and Danny as they got out of their truck and wasn't sure if she was relieved or disappointed when they were immediately drafted them to help one of the other groups.

Harmony, who'd been keeping close to them, brightened when Merry turned off her chainsaw and took out her earplugs. "Out of gas?"

"Out of oomph." Carefully setting the chainsaw down, Merry shook out her arms, twisted right and left, then touched her toes. "I might help stack for a while, but then I'm done."

Harmony grinned. "Awesome. I'm going to check in with Noella before I head out."

"Good luck at the track!" Grace waved as Harmony dashed off, racing her own shadow as usual. Shifting cold feet in her boots, she sighed. "I better get going, too."

"That's right, you have a date." Merry hip-bumped her lightly. "In a dress."

"Big help you are." Grace returned the friendly bump. "Are you going to stay and have some of Noella's soup?"

Merry shook her head. "I'm bushed. I'll probably take a hot bath and fall asleep on the couch watching *Zorro* episodes when I get home."

"Mmm, Guy Williams." Grace wasn't kidding. Nine times out of ten she hated facial hair with a passion. Somehow, though, Guy Williams really made the pencil mustache work for him. Of course, the fact that he had a fabulous black horse named Tornado didn't hurt.

Looking around, she spotted her dad leaning against a Jeep and smiled. She'd been worried about leaving him, but apparently he had already downshifted into his 'loafing gear,' as he called it.

"Always good to see him come out." Merry pointed with her chin at the man Brother Myers was talking to.

Surprised, Grace took another look. "Oh, yeah. I didn't realize who it was."

"Well." Merry took a slightly awkward sideways stance, like she wanted a hug without being certain she'd get one if she asked. "Where are you going for your date?"

"No idea." Grace glanced around for Alec and was disappointed when she didn't see him.

"Seriously?" Merry's tone held a wealth of disbelief. "Wow, I couldn't do that." Picking up her chainsaw, she began walking slowly toward her truck and was happy to have Grace fall in beside her.

"Mmm, I think you could. It's a matter of

trust. I've known Alec for years. Even if he picks something awful like—like trying to take me roller skating after asking me to wear a dress." She gestured dismissively. "It'll all work out."

"Yeah, that's…" Merry stopped to clear her throat. "That's a *lot* of trust."

Grace mulled that over for a while. Merry had holes of all shapes and sizes in her self-confidence, which Grace had never been able to understand. She knew it made Merry's life a hundred times harder than average, though.

"He made the effort of asking me out," she explained slowly. "I believe he'll follow through by doing his best to make tonight an enjoyable experience for us both."

Merry put her chainsaw in her truck and stuffed cold hands into her pockets. "Must be nice," she said wistfully.

"What?" Grace held her gaze so Merry would know she really wanted to hear the answer.

"Having the courage to be optimistic like that."

Grace waited, but Merry refused to expound. "Hey." She touched Merry's arm. "Is everything okay?" She didn't dare ask directly about Tyrel. Once Merry associated something negative with a person or thing it could be difficult for her to change her own mind.

"I guess." Merry rubbed her eyes. "I'm tired. Cold." She offered Grace a wry twist of her lips and a shrug. "Must be making me gloomy."

"Must be." Grace wrapped her arms around her friend and could tell that Merry needed it. Worried about her Grace invited, "Want to come with? Run interference for me with my mom while I get ready?"

Merry chuckled. "You're more tired than I am!" She pointed at the sun, which was still vaguely on the eastern side of the sky. "It's not even noon."

"Good grief, you're right!" Laughing, Grace massaged her stiff neck.

"Go home. Take a shower." Merry gently shoved her toward her truck. "Take a nap. Then call me. We can talk while you get dressed."

"Deal." The word morphed into a yawn and Grace pointed at Merry. "Text me when you get home, alright?"

"I will." Merry's smile warmed her eyes, reassuring Grace considerably.

Waving, Grace sauntered over to where her dad was still leaning against a Jeep, talking with Jerry Fulton. The best friend of her oldest brother, he'd been a fixture at her house when she was a kid. They'd all celebrated when he joined the military. And welcomed him home with open arms when he received a medical discharge after his deployment to Iraq. She didn't quite catch what they were saying as she walked up, but eavesdropping wasn't her goal, so no loss there.

"Hey, Dad." She kissed his cheek out of habit. Nodding at Jerry, she remarked to her dad,

"You look comfortable."

"Doin' alright," he agreed with a chuckle. "Giving these whippersnappers a turn."

"And jawin' with an old friend," Jerry inserted, giving her a gap-tooth grin. His pre-enlistment clothes hung off his now-gaunt frame like yesterday's washing.

"It's good to see you, Jerry." She smiled sincerely at him. "Sorry to interrupt. Dad, would you mind getting a ride home? I'm bushed, but," winking broadly so Jerry would see it, she teased, "I know how you older fellas like to work until the cows come home."

"I can't even tell you," Eric responded promptly, "how many times I've done exactly that."

Jerry cracked up, enormously amused at her dad's old joke.

"Alright, alright." She hugged her dad. "You tell Jerry all about it while I go home and warm up." As usual, her toes were blocks of ice by now.

"When is he picking you up tonight?" Eric squinted at her. "I want to be home early so I can properly prepare for the pre-date interview."

"Grace has a date?" Jerry gave her a look that was all question marks.

Grace was abruptly warm all over. Alec just *had* to come into earshot in time for that, didn't he? Dropping her gaze, she mumbled something under her breath and took off in the direction of her truck.

Alec frowned as he watched Grace hustling off. Didn't she want to talk to him? And…what exactly had he overheard? He sort of recognized the younger man talking with her father. Had seen him around town occasionally. He also had a hazy recollection of seeing the man at other church events—usually with the Myers. Which added up to his being some sort of family friend, but did that really make it his business that Grace had a date?

Clearing his throat, he stepped around the Jeep the men were leaning against and took the bull by the horns. "Morning, Eric." He looked at the other man expectantly.

"Alec, hello!" Curious as to how much Alec'd heard, Eric ignored his not-so-patiently waiting to be introduced to Jerry and nonchalantly remarked, "Come to get it over with?" Alec's reaction was all he'd hoped for. His eyes widened and his shoulders tensed.

Startled, Alec turned his attention back to him. "Get…what over with?" The hairs on his arms rose at the way the younger man began sizing him up.

"This is him, huh?" Jerry took Alec in at a glance, then reviewed his outward appearance more carefully. Noted the worn spots on his boots. The neatly done patch on his left sleeve. And, of course, there was the Rockin' R truck he'd driven up in. At his best guess, this Alec person made a comfortable living.

"That's right." Eric answered Jerry while grinning at the clearly discombobulated Alec. "What do you think, Jerry?"

Jerry scratched his chin instead of answering right away. "You asking me as an available bachelor, Eric? Or as Grace's substitute big brother?" It was his backward way of letting Alec know he wasn't competition. Because, truthfully, Jerry liked what he saw. Mud on the boots and determination in his eyes.

"Either one." Eric already knew his own mind on the matter. However, he did get a kick out of teasing Alec.

"Tough job, filling Will and Adam's shoes," Jerry joked. "Hey. I'm Jerry Delaney." The hand that was thrust into his own had a plenty good grip without squeezing. And plenty of callouses. "Don't mind me," he added. "Just keepin' an eye out for my kid sister."

"Alec Fitzsimmons." Alec relaxed, grateful that he hadn't given into the adolescent urge to try a hand-crushing contest. "And I can respect that."

Eric kept a straight face even as he chuckled inside. It had been a while, but he remembered his own courting days. He couldn't imagine his much-younger self having the self-possession to look Sarah's brother in the eye and say something like that. Must be a whole different animal coming at it as a middle-aged man…let alone the second time around.

"Pull up a stump," Jerry invited, grinning boyishly. "Tell me about yourself."

Alec ran his hand through his hair. Grimacing, he straightened the knit cap he'd knocked askew. "Usually when people say that, I tell them I'm the foreman at the Rockin' R. Start talking about how many acres it is or how many employees, that sort of thing. I'm not sure how to answer it in this context anymore." Well, that was awkward. He might as well have said he needed to get out more. Which he did.

Jerry shot a glance at Eric, then straightened away from the Jeep. "I reckon I ought to take a turn with that maul." With no more explanation than that, he sauntered off.

Finding himself alone with Eric, so to speak, Alec shoved his hands in his pockets to keep from fidgeting. "I can't imagine that there's much you don't know about me."

"S'pose not," Eric agreed. "I've heard you bear your testimony. Ridden with you to the temple. Seen you work." He indicated Danny, who had shifted over to help feed the log splitter. "And I know your son."

Alec felt his heart swell as he looked over at Danny. "He's the best thing that ever happened to me." Slowly, he went over and leaned against the Jeep beside Eric. "A week ago, dating was about as much on my mind as," he cast about for something ludicrous, "as becoming a first-time astronaut."

Eric chuckled. He hadn't been much older than Alec when he semi-retired from veterinary work. Honestly, the thought of remarrying at that age would've terrified him. Almost as much as the thought of losing his better half.

Alec relaxed a little, grateful for the understanding he saw in Eric's eyes. "Then, out of the blue, three different people…" He hesitated, debating whether he wanted to reveal that tidbit of information yet. Not that he wasn't grateful to Mike, Julie, and Bart for dropping the proverbial ton of bricks on him. "Well, three different people told me things that got me to wondering why I hadn't. I thought it over and realized I didn't have a single good reason."

"That's what was bothering you at the trunk-or-treat," Eric surmised. No wonder the poor man had seemed rattled.

"That." Alec nodded. Took a deep breath. "And…Grace. I…I fooled myself for years into thinking that she was still just a kid."

"Must've been something of a surprise, seeing her in that getup." Eric was openly amused. He was proud of his daughter for maintaining a healthy lifestyle and pleased to hear Alec acknowledging that he found her attractive.

"Yeah." Alec coughed into his elbow, then tugged his sleeve down straight again. He'd had plenty of awkward conversations over the years, but this one took the prize. "Brother Myers, don't you think she deserves to marry a man her own age?"

Faced with the blunt question, Eric squinted at him. "I think she deserves to decide who she wants to marry."

Caught by the blunt answer, Alec's shoulders slumped. That was it. His last, and arguably best, excuse for calling off tonight's date lay in metaphoric ashes at his feet. Rubbing the back of his neck, he searched his heart. Did he have any reason for not wanting this besides being terrified he'd make a fool of himself?

"In that case." Wiping suddenly damp palms on his jeans, he quietly told Eric, "There's something you ought to know. Something I would want to know about the person who intended to date my child."

Eric listened intently as Alec related the pertinent facts of his first marriage. Nodded now and again. Waited until he was positive Alec had finished.

"Have you told Grace?"

"No." Alec blew out a breath. "Danny knows, of course. And now you." It wasn't a deep, dark secret. In fact, it was common knowledge in Nebraska. Amongst those who cared. He simply hadn't felt the need to publicize it after his move.

Eric folded his arms across his chest. "You need to tell her."

"You're right." Alec held out his hands, palms

up. "It's hardly a typical first date conversation, though." First dates, those were for talking about favorite foods and colors and…

"Maybe not." Eric paused to consider. "But this isn't a typical first date, is it?" He waited for Alec to meet his eyes.

"No." Alec swallowed hard. "Not by a long shot." His mind leapt across the years to his first date with Melinda. He'd gotten his driver's license over the summer, which helped give him confidence to ask the prettiest girl he knew if she'd go to a movie with him. A girl he'd known since kindergarten. A girl who'd gone to church occasionally growing up, but had no particular interest in religion.

"Alec." Eric put his hand on Alec's shoulder. "You've known Grace quite a spell. You've gone to church with her. Worked beside her. Yes, dating her will change things. It's bound to be difficult at times." Eric shrugged philosophically. "Trust that she's woman enough to meet you halfway."

"That's…good advice." Alec looked away. Accidentally made eye contact with Danny, who was watching them with interest.

"Have you told him you're going to start dating again?" Eric wasn't trying to be nosy. He hadn't given Danny much thought before but now he realized that the young man had the power to influence the future of this venture. Possibly even more power than either Alec or

Grace, under the circumstances.

"I tried."   Alec lifted one hand helplessly. "Turned out he has a date of his own that he wanted to tell *me* about."   He thought that was great, especially once he'd figured out the woman in question was Noella.   Made him feel sort of preempted, though.

"Does he now?   Wellll, what do you know?" Eric slapped him lightly on the shoulder.   "Maybe we'll have a double wedding come spring."

Alec's heart seized in his chest, spun like an off-balance washing machine, then kicked into overdrive.   Somehow he forced a laugh. Nodding, he walked away, heading in Danny's general direction.

Danny assumed the neutral facial expression he usually saved for exasperating clients and sauntered over to meet his dad.   Whatever Brother Myers said, his dad looked like a stiff breeze would knock him over.

"C'mon, Dad."   Danny grabbed his arm. "Let's stack for a while."   Hopefully the rote actions would give his dad some space to think.

Alec allowed Danny to lead him into the barn where the three walls blocked most of the wind, which was picking up as the day wore on. Together they slipped into line, allowing a couple of other volunteers to step out.   Alec found solace in the methodical efforts, especially while his mind was struggling to process the idea that he couldn't possibly remarry without going through a wedding.

Stupid, really, that he hadn't put it all together from the beginning. Or perhaps it was a sort of self-preservation. He'd died the proverbial coward's death before managing to ask Julie out. The shock of considering a wedding at that point might have done permanent damage. Well. Probably not.

Strange how different it felt when he asked Grace out. Once he'd gotten over the shock of her controlled fall, the invitation came as naturally as wearing a white shirt to church. He hadn't even thought twice about where to take her.

Somehow, the whole thing started him chuckling. So much so that he was still randomly giving vent to it as he and Danny climbed into his truck to leave.

"Okay, Dad." Danny squinted at him. "Give. What's so funny?"

Alec shook his head as he started the engine. "Oh, something Brother Myers said about us having a double wedding this spring." He was so busy navigating around the haphazardly parked vehicles and over the rutted ground that he completely missed Danny's abrupt color change.

"Let's not jump the gun." The words came out tight, clipped. "It's only a first date!" Danny tugged on the seat belt, which suddenly felt like it was strangling him. He'd completely forgotten about his dad's date with Grace and was focused with laser-like intensity on his plans for an evening with Noella, such as they were. It wasn't easy finding something to do in a tiny little town like Cadmia. Especially for something this important.

Alec took his foot off the gas as he approached the ungraded road-access point. Turned the wheel to one side and took the opportunity to give Danny a careful look.

"As my grandmother would say," Alec let the truck bump onto the road, then hit the accelerator, "you marry who you date."

They rode along in silence for a while, fence posts and telephone poles whizzing by their windows with an occasional house to break up the monotony.

"Do you believe that, Dad?" Danny asked at last.

"I recommend it." Alec tapped the wheel with his thumb. "Dating's more than being with people you enjoy, son. It's getting to know them and yourself." Had they ever had this exact discussion before? Perhaps, but this couldn't have been more timely. "Dating with marriage in mind can keep you from wasting a lot of time that you'll wish you had back when you find the right one." At least a decade in his own case.

"I haven't really given getting married much thought, I guess."

Alec frowned. "That's half my fault, I'm afraid. I won't say you'd be a better person if you'd grown up with a stepmom, but I would've been setting a better example for you."

"Now hold on." Danny shifted to face him. "You're a great example! You taught me everything I know. How to study the scriptures. How to drive. To keep myself worthy of the priesthood." He paused, fighting the tears that so often plagued him when he ventured into deep waters. "How to make a grilled cheese sandwich."

Alec appreciated his son's words and understood his predicament. However… "You're a fine young man, Danny. You've built up a good business for yourself. You've kept your covenants. You have to know, though, that there are blessings you're missing out on."

"That's a tough one, Dad. I mean, it's true and all…" He ran his fingers through his hair, sliding his knit hat off in the process. "I guess I never stopped to figure out how it applied to me." Nor was he sure he should start trying right before a first date. Did he really need the added pressure?

"It's an easy mistake to make. I ought to know, because I've been living that mistake for years." Alec signaled and turned onto the Rockin' R. "But, let's see what the scriptures say. Open up to 1st Corinthians 11:11 and read it, please."

Obediently, Danny opened the scripture app on his phone and read, "Nevertheless neither is the man without the woman, neither the woman without the man, in the Lord."

"That one seems pretty straight forward." Alec winked at him. "Now read Psalm 127:3."

Danny cleared his throat and obliged. "Lo, children are an heritage of the Lord: and the fruit of the womb is his reward." *Children?* Children were for old people! He…he…um…

Alec eased off the gas, letting the truck slow to almost coasting on the clean, white gravel. "I lost your mother twice, Danny. I mourned her twice. Then, I got caught up in being both mom and dad." He winked so Danny would know not to take it the wrong way. "Finally, I lost myself in the grind of making it from sunup to sundown. Checking off those never-ending boxes."

Alec pulled up beside his trailer and parked. Gave Danny a final, meaningful look. "I wasn't living, Danny. I was going through the motions. And something happened recently that woke me up." A muscle in Danny's jaw twitched and Alec hesitated.

"Last night, I sort of announced my intentions. I should've asked if it would bother you for me to start dating."

"I think it's a great idea!" Danny throttled down his excitement when his dad's eyes narrowed suspiciously.

"Grace was your best friend growing up," Alec pointed out. "And I'm not planning to date so I don't have to be alone on Friday nights. There's a very real possibility that I will remarry."

"Dad, if you're worried about my having

feelings for Grace, don't." Danny was adamant. "Friends, yes. But it never went beyond that." Running his fingers through his hair, he continued, "In fact, when she told me you'd asked her out, I was thrilled. For you both." He clamped his mouth shut, worried what else he might say if he continued.

Alec couldn't decide if he felt relieved or painfully curious. Wait… He could be both, couldn't he? "What did she tell you?" His curiosity intensified when a grin crept across Danny's face.

"No soap, Dad." Danny hit the seat belt release and opened his door simultaneously. "You'll have to figure her out for yourself. Last one in gets a cold shower!" Whooping like a teenager, Danny slid to the ground, slamming the door behind him. Scampering across the ground, he bounded up the stairs and into the trailer.

Alec sat back with a frustrated groan. Shook his head and laughed.

Chapter 9

Grace left her boots outside to dry while she took Merry's advice—except she chose a long, hot bath followed by a cold rinse to wake herself up again.

"Grace, is that you?" Her mother, who must've been waiting for the water to shut off, knocked on the door between their living spaces. "I've got lunch if you're hungry."

Grace's stomach took her by the nose and she followed the scent of hamburger toward the sound of her mother's voice.

"Ah, there you are." Sarah looked up from the pot she was checking and nodded at the sideboard. "How about paper plates today?"

Grace's mouth watered as she set the table, glad for her mother's habit of letting her make at least a small contribution at times like this.

"Here we are." Sarah set a pot on the semi-permanent hot pad holder on the table. "Steamed stuffed peppers," she announced, lifting the lid to let Grace see.

They both took their seats and joined hands for prayer.

"Did your father say when he would be home?" Sarah asked, reaching for the milk.

"No." Grace shook her head and carefully lifted a pepper out for her mother's plate before setting one on her own. "He was talking with

Jerry, though, so he might be a while."

"Hmm." Sarah filled Grace's glass, then picked up her knife and fork. "As long as he wasn't trying to keep up with the teenagers?"

"No, of course not." Grace laughed as she cut a bite. Blowing on it, she watched the steam curl away from her while the cheese strings grew thinner and thinner. Lifted the forkful of hamburger and pepper and cheese to her mouth. "Mmmm. Mom," her eyes drifted closed, "you are the best."

"Oh, now." Sarah's eyes twinkled. "You say that no matter what I make."

"And I mean it." Helping herself to one of the hot, buttered rolls, Grace sighed. "I'm a terrible daughter."

"Well, that's news to me." Sarah slid the honey over in case Grace wanted some. "What have you done that I don't know about?"

Grace pulled her roll apart and drizzled honey on one half. "Besides always being the one to eat your food instead of the other way around?" That didn't stop her from enjoying the melt-in-your-mouth bread.

"Hmm, I suppose it has been a while since you've hosted," Sarah teased.

Grace sat up straight. "Mom, that's brilliant."

"I... What?" Sarah blinked.

"I'll host! It won't be fancy, but I think it's a great idea." Seeing the slightly puzzled tilt to her mother's brows, Grace phrased it more formally.

"Will you come to my house for supper tomorrow?"

"Tomorrow?" Sarah mentally reviewed their schedule. "Oh, dear. I think we've got an appointment to help the Halverson's with their family home evening tomorrow."

"Oh?" Grace was mildly surprised since family home evening, a church-recommended program for families, was traditionally held on Monday nights. She nearly rolled her eyes at herself. Tradition wasn't the point of the program, of course. The best day of the week to get together for family building was when it worked out.

"In fact, I think we're booked for the next few nights," Sarah mused.

"I look forward to that." Grace repressed a sigh as she reached for her glass. "To actually knowing what I'm going to be doing from one minute to the next."

Sarah patted her hand sympathetically. "That reminds me of how relieved your father was when you came home to work with him."

Puzzled, Grace waited for her mother to finish verbally connecting the dots between the thoughts.

"There used to be half a dozen big animal vets in this county, or near enough to call on in an emergency." Sarah shook her head and smeared homemade blackberry jam on her roll. "As the years passed, more of them closed or switched to pets-only until it was just your dad and a vet way to the east."

"Rollins," Grace supplied. "Two of his sons had their licenses, but one of them got stomped pretty badly by a bull last year. Though I haven't heard anything official," her appetite suddenly diminished, "I doubt he'll be practicing again." Her mom patted her hand again.

"Sooo." Grace gulped down the last of her milk and began gathering her dishes. "When do you think you can pencil me in?"

Winking, Sarah answered, "Let's plan for the week after this coming one. I'll keep our calendar clear, so we can do any night that works for you."

"Are you sure?" Grace lifted the milk jug and her eyebrows. At her mother's nod, she turned to put the milk away in the fridge. "Won't that make it hard for you to plan supper the other nights?"

"No, not with a little advance warning. I'll make a couple of double-batch suppers this week and we can do leftovers or throw-togethers." Sarah shrugged it off with the serenity of a woman who'd cooked for ravenous teenagers and now faced all meal-related situations confidently.

"Thanks, Mom." Bending, Grace kissed her mother's cheek.

"Leave the dishes." Sarah shooed her away from the dishwasher. "I need all the exercise I can get!" She patted her friendly figure and they both laughed. "You've got a few hours yet, so I'd think about that nap if you're going to."

"Yes'm!" Waving cheerfully, Grace closed the door behind her. She didn't expect to be able to nap under the circumstances, but she found it impossible to resist the siren song of her pillow on a full stomach.

It was probably for the best. The nap gave her less time to be nervous. Or so she told herself later as she arranged and rearranged her seldom-used makeup kit.

"Tell me."

In response to Merry's quiet admonishment, Grace stopped her fidgeting. Exhaled slowly as she set her strawberry-scented lip gloss down and picked up her purse.

"I love him." The lips of her reflection sparkled slightly as it spoke the words with her. A dusting of gold eyeshadow brought out her light brown eyes while jet black mascara emphasized each long eyelash.

"Then just be yourself."

Rising, Grace smoothed her dress. "That's great on paper." She did her best to laugh. "But right now, I'm wishing I'd specialized in lepidopterology. Then I could at least classify the butterfly collection I've got in my stomach."

Merry's laugh was classic I-didn't-see-that-coming, full-bodied and long-lived. "Nice!"

Grace touched the smooth, cool edge of the painted ceramic pot that was delivered that morning. A short, green stem poked out of the center of the dirt inside, teasing her to guess what kind of flower it would become.

The card contained a simple poem.

"We drop a seed into the ground,
A tiny, shapeless thing, shrivelled and dry,
And, in the fulness of its time, is seen
A form of peerless beauty, robed and
crowned
Beyond the pride of any earthly queen,
Instinct with loveliness, and sweet and rare,
The perfect emblem of its Maker's care.

This from a shrivelled seed?—
—Then may man hope indeed!"

~ "Seeds," by John Oxenham

As she reread the card, she stroked the stem, her heart fluttering. Thinking of Alec and poetry in the same heartbeat was a new experience for her. She liked it. A lot.

She looked up at the sound of someone knock. Wait… That was the wrong door.

"Merry? I have to go."

"Okey dokey. Have fun!"

Unplugging her phone, Grace slipped it into her purse. Went to the door that divided her half of the house from her parents' and opened it.

"Someone's here for you, honey." Eric stepped aside, giving them their first look at each other.

Grace caught her breath. She'd imagined this moment so many times. Pictured Alec in cowboy boots and the ridiculously fancy embroidered shirts that were so common at rodeos. Or the crisp white shirts and suits she'd seen him wear to church so many times.

Tonight he stood there, in her parents' living room, feet planted in his usual open stance. The peacock blue cable-knit sweater he was wearing made his gray eyes stand out in his tanned face. The corners of his mouth rose as she entered the room, as if he liked what he saw.

Alec watched her walk into the room, the ankle-length skirt of her turquoise dress swishing around her as she moved. Her flame-red hair rested in loose curls on her shoulders, free from its braid for once. It framed her face, which wore a dusting of makeup that only made her lovelier.

Speechless, Alec took a step forward and offered her his arm.

Grace swayed as if the sheer force of his presence pushed her back. Then her hand was reaching for his arm. The wool of his sweater was soft, the muscles underneath firm to her touch. It was so delightfully real that she found she could barely breathe.

She was so close that he could smell the faint, pleasant scent of her perfume, and he waited for her to look up at him. When she finally did, it was only for an instant, through a screen of insanely long lashes. Was she…nervous, too?

Taking her hand from where it perched lightly on his forearm, Alec tucked it securely into the crook of his arm. That drew her eyes to his again and his world shifted.

"Have fun, you two." Sarah leaned against Eric as they watched the young couple drift in the general direction of the door.

Alec came to himself in time to keep them from running into the wall. Stood aside to let her exit first.

In a matter of moments, Grace found herself tucked safely into the cab of his truck. Stretching her legs out, she smiled to herself as he closed her door. As often as not, she had to rearrange car seats to accommodate her taller frame. "I hope Dad wasn't too hard on you," she ventured as he turned onto the road.

"Eric?" He shot her a tight smile. For a moment he'd forgotten that he needed to figure out how to broach the subject of his first marriage…on a first date. "No. Not too bad."

Puzzled by the tension her question had caused, Grace studied him.

Sensing her scrutiny, Alec stroked his freshly shaved jaw.

"You look—fine." Grace was grateful for the dim lighting as her cheeks pinked. The subtle hesitation in her speech had added another meaning to the word 'fine.'

"You look exquisite." Signaling, he turned

east onto the highway.

Grace relaxed, cherishing the warmth stirring inside her. "Thank you." Remembering her manners, she added, "Thank you for the plant, too."

He chuckled. "That's it?" He let the question ride for a moment, then continued, "You're not going to ask me what kind of plant it is?"

Grace relaxed, relieved that he hadn't been hinting that he expected…more of a thank you. "I'll find out the old-fashioned way," she shrugged.

When he didn't turn toward Cadmia as she'd expected, she slanted a curious look in his direction. Her mind skipped ahead, confirming that there was basically nothing east of Cadmia. Not for miles, anyway.

"Where are we going tonight?"

Alec smiled. "You'll see." Hoping to distract her, he indicated his glove box. "There are some CDs in there, if you'd like to pick one. We do have a kind of long drive."

Grace touched her purse, thinking of the endless playlists on her phone. Squinted at the dash, but out here, where there were no streetlights, she couldn't really tell if there was a way to hook her phone into the older truck's speakers. So, biting her lip to keep from giggling, she got out the CDs. Held them up to the window to read them in the dying sunlight.

"Are these all mixes?" she asked at last. She recognized Alec's cramped handwriting on the burned discs. She'd seen it often enough over the years.

"Are they?" Alec glanced over, but kept both hands on the wheel. "I'm sorry, I didn't realize."

"That's okay." Selecting one at random, she popped it into the CD player. "Let's see what this one is." Light jazz bubbled around them and she smiled. "I like it."

They made it clear through that CD and partway through a second before they passed the Springfield city limit sign.

"Almost there," he promised. A block later, he pulled into a hotel parking lot. "I'll get your door," he told her, stopping at a sign that indicated valet parking.

Grace leaned on him a little more than she really needed to as he helped her down. Enjoyed the feel of his hand on her back as he guided her into the lobby and turned them toward the hotel's restaurant.

"I'm glad you liked the jazz." Alec tried to shake off the prickle of nerves that hit him as he reached out to open the restaurant door, where curving, swirling letters proclaimed 'Little Persia.' "They have live music here."

Grace stepped inside and paused to take it in. She smelled pepper. Curry. Cloves. Naan bread. And a dozen other aromas she recognized but had no name for.

Lamps that might've once housed genies were spaced around the room, short electric 'flames' emanating from their spouts, while the dew-drop shaped mosaic lamps that hung from the ceiling provided the bulk of the lighting. The dark wood of the walls sported carvings of what looked like the skyline of a fairytale Persian village. The booths that lined the walls were also ornately carved, each divider featuring a different parade of jungle animals.

"Welcome to Little Persia." A young woman smiled at them from just inside the restaurant door. "May I have your name, please?"

"Fitzsimmons."

Grace shivered slightly as his breath stirred her hair. When had he come so close?

"We have your table ready, sir." The woman led them to a table for two near the presently empty stage. Smiling brightly, she offered them menus. "We have several wines to choose from this evening…" She trailed off when Alec shook his head.

"We don't drink, thank you," he said simply.

"Very good, sir." She bobbed her head. "Your waiter will be with you momentarily."

Grace touched the thick tablecloth. Traced a finger down the heavy cutlery lined up on either side of her plate. Her suspicions were confirmed when she examined the menu and found that it had no prices.

Alec leaned over to ask if she had any questions

about the menu and noticed her shift in her chair as though she were uncomfortable. Suddenly, he couldn't swallow. Had he guessed wrong?

"Grace? What's wrong?"

How was she supposed to answer that? Grace shifted again. Realizing what she was doing, she willed herself to hold still.

"Good evening." Their waiter appeared, genie-like, beside the table. "And welcome to Little Persia. Have you dined here before?"

"We're not ready to order," Alec informed him, smiling to take the sting from his skipping to the point. "Could we have a few more minutes?"

"Absolutely." The waiter set a card with his name—Peter—on the table. "If you have any questions about the menu, I'll be delighted to answer them." He bowed, then left to tend to his other tables.

"Wow." Grace clenched her hands in her lap, where Alec couldn't see them. The waiter and maitre'd were both college age, but conducted themselves with all the suave assurance of veterans, almost as if this particular restaurant gave its employees more than an apron when it hired them. Like training or something. "This isn't what I was expecting."

"Would you like to go somewhere else?"

Grace jumped at a sound from her right, but it was only the band setting up.

"No, not especially." Biting her lip, Grace

hesitated. She didn't want to insult him. "This place is amazing." Striking suddenly upon a discreet way to find out what she needed to know, she asked, "Do you come here often?"

Confused, Alec shrugged. "Not as often as I'd like." Gesturing at the band he added wryly, "I keep trying to persuade them to open a place in Cadmia, but they have some obsession with money."

Startled, Grace looked over at the band. Watched the lead singer wave to Alec, who responded with a smile. Wow. Maybe she didn't need to worry about prices after all. It certainly raised a question she'd never bothered with before—exactly how much did ranch foremen make?

"They own the restaurant," Alec told her, misinterpreting her slightly raised eyebrows. "I honestly think they opened it so they'd have a place to play." A small smile played across her lovely features.

"What do you recommend?" she asked, tilting the menu toward him.

He hesitated, studying her eyes to be sure she wasn't trying to dodge his question about leaving. "Well, I usually order the baghaly polow." He pointed it out on his own menu. "Lamb shank with seasoned rice."

She nodded and studied the description. The dish names were all Romanized versions of the original Arabic, with a helpful description.

"This, um…polo ba morgue?" She had no idea how to pronounce 'morgh.' "It sounds good." According to the menu, that translated into some kind of chicken dish, which she felt fairly safe about ordering.

"It's delicious," Alec agreed, raising his hand. Peter materialized beside him. "We're ready to order now."

As the meal progressed and the music started, Grace noticed and appreciated a dozen little things about Alec. How he treated the waiter. That he offered his hand so she could join him as they bowed their heads in individual prayers over the food. That he knew how to handle a cloth napkin and having more than one fork to choose from.

Their conversation wandered from topic to topic, never getting too serious as they got to know each other on a different level.

"So." Alec eyed her drink. She'd opted for the same thing he ordered, a pomegranate mocktail. "Are you going to try it?"

She hesitated a moment longer, then gingerly picked up the glass. Sniffed it as discreetly as possible. Something…something reminiscent of cherry juice. A hint of orange. Lifting it to her lips, she took the tiniest sip.

"That's incredible!" Suddenly realizing how intently he was watching her, Grace blushed. "You're staring."

He shook his head. "Not staring. Admiring."

"There's a difference?" She made herself meet his eyes when she would've rather looked away.

"Certainly." Setting his utensils down, Alec focused on her even more as he explained, "I always knew you were pretty, Grace. However, tonight is the first time I've really allowed myself to enjoy it." Lifting her near hand, he brought it to his lips.

Astonished, she…she stared at him. Resisted the temptation to pinch herself. If she was dreaming, she had absolutely no desire to end it.

"Alec, I think that's the loveliest compliment anyone has ever paid me."

"Does that mean I can keep staring?" He winked roguishly, feeling half his age. The answering duck of her head was so charmingly demure that it nearly pushed him over the edge. She was so close. All he would have to do…

"How is your food this evening?" The maître d', having approached from the side, didn't realize until too late that she was interrupting.

"Excellent." Alec straightened. Grace's plate was pretty well empty, so he cocked an eyebrow at her. "Would you like something else?"

"Oh, no. I mean." Understandably flustered, Grace stumbled over her words. Had he been about to kiss her? "Everything was wonderful. But I'm, um, full."

Alec handed the maître d' his card. Which she handed off to Peter, who had once again apparently appeared out of thin air, mobile terminal in hand.

"Not too full, I hope." Alec gave Grace his attention again. "We haven't had dessert yet."

Maybe he was crazy to take her out for frozen custard in November, but if so he wasn't the only one. The line at the drive through was impressively long. At length, desserts in hand, they got back on the road.

"Mmm, this is the perfect ending to a perfect first date," Grace murmured as she dug into her strawberry concrete.

"It isn't quite over." Alec took them out of town, signaled, and pulled off on a patch of gravel. Reaching behind the seats, he brought two blankets forward. "Come over here." He patted the bench seat beside him.

Grace hesitated. Tentatively slid closer. She *knew* they were right on the edge of the highway, but she felt terribly isolated because of the sheer lack of light. Any concerns that he was planning a make-out session faded when he draped a blanket over his legs.

"Let me hold your concrete," he traded her for the other blanket, "while you put this on." With his free hand, he flipped the visors up so they'd have a clear field of vision.

"Thanks." Grace reclaimed her concrete. Watched curiously as he took a bite of his own dessert and looked out the windshield.

"There." He pointed. "That's the Big Dipper."

Dipper." She leaned closer to get a better site along his arm. "Got it?" Her hair brushed his shoulder when she nodded and he swallowed. "And the Little Dipper. And there's Cassiopeia."

Grace soon settled her head on his shoulder and watched his finger trace the constellations, her concrete forgotten.

"They go on forever, don't they?"

Alec paused. Was this the opening he needed? "As far as I know, yes." He felt her laugh and had to smile. "You know what I mean."

"Yeah." This was definitely, absolutely *nothing* like any date she'd ever been on before. She definitely enjoyed learning about the constellations—but she was also finding new things to love about him.

"Grace? I… When I talked with your dad earlier, I told him something that I need to tell you." He instantly missed her warmth as she sat up so she could see him. Or try to, anyway. "It's about Melinda."

Not sure what to say, Grace just nodded.

Where to begin? "I think we met in kindergarten, but I don't really remember." She didn't laugh, so he cleared his throat and tried again. "She was my first crush. My first date." He paused. "My first kiss. And, after my mission," he decided to skip to the important part, "I invited her to church."

He peered at Grace, but couldn't see much

more than a basic outline. "Thinking back, it should've been obvious to me that she wasn't really interested. At the time, though, I was dead-set on marrying her, so I ignored everything except what I wanted to see. Then, when I couldn't wait any longer, I asked the bishop to perform a civil ceremony for us."

Grace set her concrete in the cup holder, but that wasn't the source of the cold she was feeling.

"What I'm saying is, I was never sealed to her. In fact," he gripped the front edge of the seat, "she filed for divorce about six months before she was killed in a car accident." She gasped and he stopped. The ensuing silence was as thick as the dust at a rodeo, until he finally caved.

"The reason she gave the courts was irreconcilable differences. To me, in very plain English, she said she'd had it with me and my…" He started to choke up. With herculean effort, he forced the words out. "My stupid religion." It was several seconds before he collected himself enough to continue. "Apparently while I'd been waiting for her to soak in what I was teaching Danny, to take an interest in being part of a forever family, she was not-so-patiently waiting for me to get over it."

"Oh, Alec." The words were torn from her. "I'm so sorry."

"Yeah." He coughed. Reached up to wipe away an errant tear.

Impulsively, Grace closed the distance between them. Wrapped her arms around his waist and held on tight.

Slowly, Alec reciprocated, gathering her even closer. Her hair was silk against his cheek as he bowed his head.

Chapter 10

"Do you think that we could sit here?" Grace asked her parents as she gestured toward the longer, middle pews at church the next day.

"The date went that well, eh?" Eric winked, then let Sarah precede him. He liked having his girls on either side of him and felt a tiny pang at the thought that soon—he hoped—Grace would have Alec to lean on. It was a confusing enough mix of emotions that he sat down without another word.

Meanwhile, the twisting in Grace's stomach had little to nothing to do with the fact that it was the first Sunday of the month and she was fasting. No, this was all about Alec. He might sit next to her. Or not. If he did, there would be talk, to put it mildly. In some singles' wards, couples that sat together at church were considered practically engaged.

Of course, this wasn't the time to be worrying about things like that. Closing her eyes, she took a deep breath and let her mind review the events of her week. Paused to ponder things she wanted to repent of. Smiled as she remembered times when the Holy Ghost had helped her make better choices than she could've on her own.

The prelude music started, prompting her to think of the words from the prelude music the organist was playing. He'd chosen to start with a children's hymn, "All Things Bright and Beautiful."

The pew moved as someone sat down, but Grace didn't open her eyes. She didn't have to. Alec's crisp, clean cologne was unique in a town almost entirely composed of the 'how much is too much?' or 'soap and water's good enough for me.' camps.

Her heart swelled with love for him when he respected her meditation. How many times had she arrived at church early in her singles' ward, hoping for peace and quiet to ponder in, only to be interrupted by well-meaning members? She didn't want to be rude, but surely things like 'You look nice today!' and 'Study group has changed from Wednesday to Thursday.' were trivial compared with preparing for the sacrament?

The pew shifted again and now she did peek. *Danny and Noella? Sitting together already?*

The bishop rose and started the meeting, rescuing her from further speculation about them. Sharing a hymnal with Alec, Grace sang "High on the Mountain Top," then bowed her head for the opening prayer.

After the announcements and the passing of the sacrament, the bishop stood again to bear a simple testimony of the atonement, then invited the congregation to come to the pulpit and share their testimonies of gospel principles.

Her heart lurched within her when Alec got up. She hated that her biggest concern was whether or not he was going to mention their date and prayed hard in the few seconds that it took him to reach the podium that she could focus on remembering the Savior instead.

"After yesterday's woodcutting project, I am happier than usual to be inside and warm." Alec smiled and a few people chuckled. "I'm also more aware that no matter how imperfect or unqualified we think we are, if we will listen to and obey the Holy Ghost, the Lord can use us to build the kingdom of God on the earth." He closed in the name of the Savior and returned to his seat beside Grace.

A sweet peace settled over Grace as she considered his words, and the words of the other humble men and women who offered their testimonies over the course of the remainder of the meeting. One particularly precious primary child shared how she'd been learning about the pioneers, which helped her stay cheerful while her family helped at the woodcutting project. Grace was sorry when the bishop rose again to thank those who'd spoken and announce the closing hymn.

After the closing prayer, she looked shyly over at him.

"Hi." Her heart skipped a beat as his hand came to rest lightly on hers.

"Hey."

It wasn't until he laced his fingers through hers that she noticed. With a gasp, she lifted her eyes to meet his.

"What?" His eyes narrowed in concern. Looking down at their clasped hands, his gaze was drawn to the white line around his ring finger. The empty spot where his wedding ring usually rested.

"Alright, everyone." At the front of the room, Sister Phillips adjusted a wearable microphone. There were still some children and youth in the room who would be heading to primary, as well as a few adults-teachers. Long story short, it could be like herding cats to get folks re-settled for Sunday school, so she liked to start things in that direction as soon as she could. "If we can take our seats, please."

Alec smiled and returned his attention to Grace. He hadn't given much thought to how she'd react when she noticed he'd taken off his ring. Maybe he should've.

"It was time."

Grace tilted her head to one side as she considered the direct statement. Alec's clear gray eyes met hers without wavering.

He shifted to face the front when Sister Phillips asked for volunteers to help with reading certain scriptures, and his arm came to rest quite naturally around Grace's shoulders.

It was easy to tell that everyone had done their scripture study at home this week, because the discussion flowed freely. They didn't make it all the way through Paul's epistles to Timothy, Titus, and Philemon, but there were some wonderful moments as questions were asked about being 'an example of the believers.' Sister Phillips' didn't try to force things along, either, but rather let the members help teach each other.

"It's hard," Brother Burt conceded with a nod. "For myself, I've learned that the best thing I can do is just be myself. My friends at the factory where I work, they know I don't listen to or tell dirty jokes. I don't cuss. I don't drink. They also know they're welcome at my home. Had three barbecues this last summer that I invited them to. Did we talk religion?" He shook his head. "We talked about sports, cars, even barbecue grills. They sat at my table and let me offer a prayer over the food. They saw the pictures on the walls of my home. Saw," he paused to wipe at his eyes, "how I treat my wife and kids. They know as imperfect as I am, I'm trying to be a disciple of Christ."

"Thank you, Brother Burt." Sister Phillips looked suspiciously as though she was going to cry, too, but managed to announce the closing prayer and sit down.

Grace made a note on her phone to invite her staff to the family supper she was planning. As an afterthought, she leaned over to ask her parents if that was alright.

"Oh, that'll be fun, dear!" Sarah assured her brightly.

Relieved, Grace sat back. Looking up as Alec

looked down, her breath lodged in her throat. Somewhere in the back of her mind, she knew he wasn't actually going to kiss her right there in the chapel—but he was certainly close enough to.

Danny, oblivious to their moment, bumped his dad with his elbow. "Hey, Noella and I will be at the Peterson's, okay?"

Alec had some difficulty in switching gears, but nodded. "Let me know if you need a ride ho…um, to the ranch." It seemed strange to remember that the Rockin' R wasn't Danny's home anymore.

"Will do."

Judging by the grin on Danny's face, he wasn't expecting to need a ride anytime soon. Still, Alec wasn't worried. They'd had another short talk about marriage on the way into church this morning. Noella might be nothing more than a new friend in the long run, but Alec was confident he'd gotten Danny thinking.

"We'll see you later, dear." Sarah smiled at her daughter, then at Alec. "You're welcome to join us for supper if you like."

"Thank you." Seeing that she was already standing, Alec got to his feet quickly. This must be one of those awkward moments Eric had warned him about. As long as he'd known Sarah Myers, he'd never, ever, not even *once* considered the possibility of calling her 'Mom.' Now, suddenly, as they stood there facing each other, he couldn't *not* think about it.

Then Eric rose and stood between them, bringing Alec up short.

"She put a roast on before we left this morning," Eric said mildly. "So be sure you come hungry."

Taken completely by surprise, Alec's laugh was breathier than usual. "I can do that."

Grace got up as they left and shook her head. "I realize he didn't invent the so-called dad joke, but that was worse than usual." After fasting two meals, they would all be hungry.

"Hey." Alec tried to sound miffed. "Don't be knocking the dad jokes." Winking at her, he took her hand in his and followed her out into the hall. He let her lead him past the groups of chatting, watching people—had a foyer ever had so many eyes?—and into the parking lot.

"What're your plans for the rest of the day?"

Grace swung their joined hands a little as she considered her answer. Technically, she should take a nap. She'd gotten to bed before eleven last night, she just hadn't gotten much sleep.

"What did you have in mind?"

Grinning, Alec turned toward his truck. Spotting her truck, he hesitated. "Follow me and find out," he compromised.

Laughing, she raced to her truck as he quick-walked to his. He went straight out of the church parking lot, and again her mind ran ahead along the road, searching for his destination. Much to her surprise, he drove a good twenty miles before turning down a…no, it wasn't a road. It was barely a set of tire tracks in the dirt and weeds that ran up a hill and disappeared among the trees.

Eyeing the prominently placed purple 'no trespassing!' indicators on the property line, she bit her lip and kept going. Alec obviously knew where he was going. Right?

Three miles later, she pulled up beside his truck—in front of a small, snug-looking cabin! The two windows she could see sported curtains, making it look as if the cabin had blue eyes. The roof sloped down over a porch area that had two rockers and a long bench waiting for company.

"I never knew this was here!" she told him as she joined him beside his truck.

"It wasn't until recently. I mean, I bought the property quite a while ago. But I didn't do anything about it until a couple of years ago."

"Wait, this place is yours?" Grace looked more closely at the cabin. It wouldn't make sense for daily living, not so long as Alec was, for all intents and purposes, the man in charge at the Rockin' R. But the cabin was adorable on the outside.

Chuckling, he took her hand. "C'mon, I'll give you the grand tour."

"Alright." Grace enjoyed every minute of the tour, easily imagining supper on the back porch or looking out the window while she did dishes. The kitchen itself was sparsely furnished, with only a mini fridge and a card table. He laughed as he showed her the "laundry room," where the washer and dryer would go when he started living there full-time. Down the hall were two bedrooms and an office, which looked comfortable, if a bit barren. The master bedroom had a picture of the Savior and one of their local temple. The other walls were bare. "Alec, this is amazing!"

"You like it?" Returning with her to the living room where they'd started, he took a seat on the couch.

"Yes, of course." Smiling, Grace sat as well, careful to leave a reasonable amount of space between them. "I don't know how you can stand to live at the Rockin' R with this here waiting for you."

"Oh, I'll move here soon enough." He looked down at their intertwined fingers. "I've only got a few more years before I can retire."

"Isn't that a good thing?" She was puzzled at his tone, particularly on the word 'retire.'

"I guess so." He did his best to smile. "Are you looking forward to retirement?"

Grace considered. "Golly, I don't know." Tucking her stockinged feet up under herself, she admitted, "I haven't thought about it much."

He smirked. "Really?"

"Yes." She tilted her head to the side and squinted at him. "What's so funny?"

"Nothing." He cleared his throat. "I mean, I...I guess I thought I was the only one who didn't have a bucket list as long as a country driveway."

"I guess there's traveling." She wiggled her fingers vaguely. "If you can afford it."

"That won't be a problem."

"Great." His prompt answer surprised her. She didn't pry into folks' financial affairs, but plenty of local business owners were quick to complain that they couldn't afford to retire. Whereas most of the farmers she knew stuck with it until they couldn't drive the tractor anymore.

"It's not that I'm some kind of financial guru," he explained, not sure what to make of her thoughtful expression. "One of Mr. Brooke's quirks is that he likes to gives bonuses in the form of stocks."

"Wow." She'd never stopped to consider Alec's 'fortunes,' so to speak. Now that they were talking about money, though, she couldn't help remembering the divorce statistics she'd heard quoted a while ago. It seemed like financial problems headed the list of contributing factors.

"I did sell a few to help put Danny through school." He wished she'd say something else, give him a clue what was going on in her head. "The rest have been, well, um, accumulating."

"That's amazing." Settling deeper into the couch, she inhaled shakily. "Money's funny stuff, you know? I have to watch things at my practice carefully. Think about everything from paychecks to supplies to insurance." Her voice trailed off. She didn't know where she was going with this. Except that combining the lives of two people would almost certainly involve combining their incomes. Or at least, talking about it.

"Grace."   He squeezed her hand gently. "Your father built up a fine practice. You've even expanded it, taken on a junior partner. You're being careful and prayerful as you make decisions. And that makes all the difference."

The truth of his words resonated within her, bringing an unexpected rush of tears to her eyes.

He smiled and reached up to gently brush a tear away with his thumb. "I'd offer you a tissue, but I don't have any here." He looked past her at the kitchen door. "I might have some napkins in my truck."

The room tilted when he felt the pressure of her cheek against his palm and realized how close they were. All the air left the room and he could feel beads of perspiration starting to form. Thankfully, his palms remained dry as his brain screamed that he'd forgotten everything he ever knew about kissing.

Grace nearly fell over when he abruptly jumped to his feet and strode into the kitchen. Then he came back, empty-handed.   And returned to the kitchen.

Standing up, she intercepted him on his next pass. "Ohhhkay." She spoke soothingly as she rested her hands flat on his chest. His heart was pounding twice as hard as hers. "It's okay."

"No, it's not." Embarrassed and angry with

himself, Alec withdrew a step and shoved his hands through his hair, ripping a few strands out by the roots. "I don't have a clue what I'm doing."

Grace frowned. "You're doing fine." Not that she wasn't disappointed at not being kissed by the man of her dreams in this romantic setting. "Alec," she started to move closer, then stopped when he looked away from her. "Alec, this is only our second date. Give us a chance."

He made a move toward the door and her gears shifted. "Don't you dare walk away from me, Alec Fitzsimmons."

He froze.

"Look at me," she commanded. For some reason, he obeyed. "I am just as scared as you are, believe me. I have *just* as much to lose." Her voice started to shake and no matter how hard she swallowed, she couldn't seem to regain control of it. "But I'm here. And I'm trying. So don't you give up the first time something doesn't go perfectly."

"You're so beautiful." Lifting one hand cautiously, he tucked a curl behind her ear. How bizarre was it that she'd finally shown a temper to match her hair and it actually made him more comfortable with the idea of kissing her?

"Especially when I'm angry, right?" She made a face at the cliché.

Caught off guard, he burst into laughter. The romantic mood was shattered, but so was the insecurity that gripped him.

"You're not wrong." He dodged when she threw a feint at his shoulder. "I mean it," he insisted. "You are beautiful when your color's up and you get that intense expression on your face like… Like you're going to fix something if you have to turn the world upside down and shake it." He hesitated, wary of saying the wrong thing. "And I'll never forget three springs ago when I caught you asleep standing up. You remember, one of our mares had colic and you worked with her all night? You hadn't any right to look so adorable, but you did."

"I remember." Shoving her hands in her pockets to hide their trembling, Grace managed a smile. "I remember you had hay in your hair and the collar on your gray and green plaid shirt was crooked and I wished you would let me straighten it for you."

"Anytime." He brushed his lips across her forehead. "You can fix my collar anytime."

Smiling, she reached up to straighten his tie, which was the closest she could come right then.

Reluctantly, he eyed the compact travel clock that perched on one windowsill. "We better get going. Don't want to be late for supper."

She groaned and slapped his chest lightly. "What terrible timing for a dad joke."

They held hands all the way back to where they'd parked, then made the short run out to her parents', where a hearty meal followed by three hands of UNO left Grace trying vainly to stifle her yawns.

Taking pity on her, Sarah glanced at the clock. "Oh my, look how late it's gotten! Time certainly flies when you're having fun."

"Big day tomorrow, dear?" Eric asked blandly, though he knew full well that they didn't have a thing planned the next morning.

"Thank you for supper, Sister Myers." Taking the hint, Alec rose, his hands still deftly controlling the deck he was shuffling. "That was the best roast I've had in many months."

"Flatterer," Sarah teased, rising as well. "And many's the time you've called me Sarah, so don't be getting all formal on me now." They all chuckled at that.

"Thank you," he repeated. Shaking hands with Eric and giving Sarah a half-hug, he followed Grace outside. "Hey." He caught her arm as she headed for his truck. "This might be a little old-fashioned, but I'd kind of like to walk you to your door."

"I like old-fashioned." Smiling, she let him take her by the elbow. "But I do have to stop by the barn first."

"I think I can find my way around a barn." He winked and turned in that direction.

She moved away from him as they entered the barn, her heart fluttering anxiously. What if he tried to kiss her? Ugh. What if he *didn't*?

"Anybody on special feed?" Alec asked,

wondering if he could help.

"Pixy the pony is." She patted the mare. "Pixy got into the grain bin at home, didn't you, girl?" She shared a smile with Alec as the pony nodded vigorously. "She's staying with us for a few days while her own makes another try at pony-proofing his place."

"And she's behaving?" Alec didn't try to hide his surprise. A mischievous horse was literally trouble on the hoof.

"So far." Grace checked Pixy's water. "It helps that we have a double-bolt system on the outside where she can't reach it."

After she finished checking her last patient, she looked up to find Alec watching her, a light in his eyes that made her stomach flip. But she did her best to act nonchalant as she tucked her hand into the crook of his proffered elbow. Fluffy snowflakes spun and sparkled in the dim yellow of the security light as they crossed the patch of lawn to her porch.

He stopped at the steps, which meant she was a hair taller than he was when she turned to see why. For a terrible moment, they just stood there, looking at each other. Then, in a flash, she slipped inside and locked the door behind her.

It was either that or kiss him. And she didn't think he was ready for that.

Chapter 11

"Okay, what's going on?" Mrs. Ivey set her lunch on the table in the breakroom and fixed her most intimidating glare on Grace.

Grace blinked. "What?"

"You've been checking your phone every chance you get." Mrs. Ivey folded her arms across her chest. "That might be normal behavior for Amy, but when you do it, you make me nervous."

"There's nothing wrong, Mrs. Ivey." Laughing, Grace tucked her phone into her pocket. "In fact, I think something might be about to go right." Dropping a wink, she smoothed her white coat and went out to greet her next client.

At the end of the day, she corralled them all in the back room and cleared her throat. "Ladies and gentleman," she began. "I would like to invite you to…"

"You're getting married!" Amy clapped her hands and squealed.

Grace blushed. "I…not at the moment."

"Really?" Oblivious to Neil's attempts at waving her off, Amy blurted, "But my friend saw you at Little Persia on Saturday with some hot guy and…ow!" She broke off suddenly when Mrs. Ivey accidentally stepped on her foot while reaching for her jacket.

"Oh, are you all right, dear?"

From the corner of her eye, Grace saw Neil hide a smile behind his fist while Mrs. Ivey simultaneously comforted Amy and chastised her with her eyes. She abruptly slapped her front pocket as her phone vibrated. Perhaps with the long-awaited text from Alec? Great, one more thing to be nervous about.

She started to pull her phone out, then remembered why they were all looking expectantly at her. "I, um, I'd like you all to come by for supper on Thursday."

"What can I bring?" Mrs. Ivey asked, winding her scarf around her neck. "Is your dad grilling?"

"Just bring yourselves. And, I was actually planning homemade pizza." She grinned.

"I'll be there!" Amy's embarrassment from earlier had already evaporated.

"Awesome. And…" Grace's phone buzzed again, completely derailing her train of thought.

"I'll bring soda," Neil volunteered. They all looked at him in surprise and he shook his head. "I can't come empty-handed, sorry. It's not in my DNA."

Grace laughed with the others and nodded, conceding the point. Honestly, Mrs. Ivey and Amy would also probably bring something small; she simply didn't want them thinking they needed to. She slipped her phone out of her pocket, but before she could check it, Mrs. Ivey came over to walk beside her.

"A hot guy, hmm?" Mrs. Ivey certainly hadn't forgotten Amy's remark.

Grace fought it, but the heat in her cheeks let her know her face was a vivid pink.

"Do we get to meet him on Thursday?" Mrs. Ivey wheedled.

Grace hit the unlock button on her fob. "What makes you think you don't already know him?" With a cat-that-ate-the-canary grin, she hopped into her truck and drove off.

Two blocks away from the clinic, she pulled into a parking lot and checked her phone. The first text was from her mom and made no sense. Something about a bunch of balloons being delivered?

The second text was from Alec and read simply: [Call me when you get home.]

Every time she passed a speed limit sign on her way home, Grace deliberately eased off the gas pedal and let the truck coast until she'd slowed down to the legal limit.

"Mom?" she called, knocking on the door as she let herself in.

"Come in, honey, come in!" Sarah came bustling out of her sewing room, where she'd started some mending to get herself out of the kitchen where the balloons waited. "I'm dying of curiosity."

Grace covered her mouth with both hands as they entered the kitchen, where some dozen balloons hovered above the table.

"There's a card." Sarah held it out urgently.

"What in the world?" Grace accepted the card, but kept staring at the balloons. Pink, blue, green, purple, gold, silver, white, black with silver stars, red, brown… She snapped out of her reverie when her mother tugged on her sleeve. "Huh?"

"The *card*, honey."

"Oh. Oh!" Grace ripped it open, the envelope fluttering to the floor as she eased the card open and peeked at the message inside.

Sarah discreetly averted her gaze, but it wasn't easy. She almost pulled a muscle in her haste to respond to Grace's invitation.

"Mom, listen to this." Tilting the card so her mom could see it, which she was obviously aching to do, Grace read aloud, "I thoroughly enjoyed our date on Saturday and hope you'll go out with me again. Pick a balloon to see what we're doing next. Alec."

"How cute!" Sarah clapped her hands in delight. "Sort of like a 'choose your own adventure novel,'" she quipped, eyeing the balloons anxiously. She hated popping balloons.

"Yeah." Propping a fist on her hip, Grace studied the balloons. The instructions couldn't have been simpler. And, as she squinted at the lighter-colored balloons, she could see vague shapes inside them.

Reaching out, Grace fingered the lines of ribbon that tied the balloons to the small gift bag at the bottom. Unsurprisingly, the green balloon had a green ribbon, the blue balloon had a blue ribbon, and so on. All had ribbons except the black one, which was tied down with black cotton twine.

Though not exactly subtle, she had to give him points for creativity. Biting her lip, she considered her options. The black balloon was the only one that stood out. Closer examination of the gift bag at the bottom revealed that she'd have to untie all the balloons before she could get a look inside it.

"Aren't you going to pick one?" Sarah asked in dismay when Grace pulled out her phone.

"In a minute," Grace promised. Having just remembered Alec's text, she called him.

"Hey, beautiful." His deep voice held a caress that quite definitely weakened her knees. "How was your day?"

"F-fine." She pinched the bridge of her nose in an effort to get a grip. Shouldn't they have to be in the same room for him to affect her like this? "How was yours?" Somehow she got the mundane reply out without stumbling over the words.

"Staying busy, but not busy enough to keep my mind off of you."

Oh shoot. Grace leaned against the back of a nearby chair as casually as she could.

"Do you like the balloons?"

"Yes. Of course. I like…" She mentally dragged herself to a stop. "I like them a lot."

"I thought about getting you flowers, but I remember you telling me once that you don't like watching cut flowers die."

"Yeah, that's right." Folding an arm across her chest, she leaned more easily on the chair. "I didn't know you were listening."

Sarah, uncomfortable with eavesdropping, ducked around the corner into her sewing room.

"I probably missed a lot," he admitted. "Wouldn't be surprised if it takes me the rest of my life to get to know you."

Something about the simple frankness of the statement took her breath away. Perhaps it struck him the same way, as an almost-proposal, for several seconds passed in silence.

"Starting with our next date, I hope," he coaxed.

"I…I hate popping balloons," she confessed.

Chuckling, he suggested, "Tell me which one you picked, then."

"Um…" Scanning the bouquet again, her eyes returned to the distinctive black balloon with its stars. "How about the one with the twine."

"Excellent choice!" There was a hint of satisfaction in his voice as he cautioned, "We'll have to get an early start, though."

"How early?"

"Let's see, it's an hour drive, so four o'clock should do it."

"Four? *In the morning?*" She shook her phone as if that would improve a crystal-clear connection.

"I'm sorry, could you repeat that?"

"If you're free next Saturday, we could go then."

"You want me to get up…" Hearing a noise, she looked over and found herself face to face with her dad, who was eyeing the balloon bouquet. Turning away hastily, she lowered her voice. "At 4 AM on a Saturday?"

"No, don't be silly." The restrained laughter in his voice did nothing to reassure her. "I want you to be ready to leave at four."

"To do what, exactly?"

"You'll have to pop the balloon to find that out."

"Oh really." She wanted to be annoyed, but he sounded so doggoned pleased with himself that she found herself struggling against laughter instead.

"I'm afraid so. You'll want to wear jeans, shoes you don't mind getting muddy…and I recommend layering up in case it's really cold."

"Alec, you've got to give me more than that," she protested.

"I'll buy you a big breakfast afterward."

"*After*ward?"

"Is it a date?"

She rolled her eyes. "Fine. But I'm warning you." She cut him off as he started to speak. "If it turns out that you've dragged me out of a nice warm house at oh-dark-thirty for a less-than-phenomenal reason," she paused for emphasis, "I will get even."

In the profound silence that followed, she wondered if she'd gone too far. Then, she wondered if he'd already hung up. A quick glance at her screen showed that they were still connected.

"I look forward to seeing you try."

Aaaand she was blushing again. "Bye," she mumbled.

"Eric, there you are." Sarah, who'd emerged from her sewing room once again, hugged her husband. "Hungry?"

"Depends." Eyes twinkling, he jerked a thumb toward the bouquet. "If that's what we're having for supper, I'll pass."

"You big silly. Those are a gift from Alec to Grace. They each have a date activity inside and she has to pick one."

"Oh, I see. Like a fortune cookie."

Grace groaned.

Sarah cocked an eyebrow at her. "Have you picked one yet, dear?"

"I reckon she must've," Eric observed. "I heard her agree to go out with him next Saturday." He discreetly omitted the time, since he knew it would only make Sarah worry about them traveling in the dark.

"That's wonderful!" Privately, Sarah was relieved that no balloons had to be popped to get that arranged. "Where are you going, dear?"

"Crazy." Grace threw up her hands. "I just

agreed, again, to a date with no idea of where we're going or what we're going to do. Well, he did mention that I should wear shoes that can get muddy and layers against the cold."

"Sounds like it's an outdoor activity," Eric surmised.

"It certainly does." Sarah frowned. "An uncomfortable one."

Grace poked the black balloon thoughtfully. Sighing, she picked up the gift bag and headed for her door.

"Aren't you joining us for supper?" Sarah asked, surprised. "We're having pork chops."

"And that sounds fantastic." Grace kissed her mother lightly on the cheek. "Thank you for inviting me. I…I have some thinking to do right now."

The kind of thinking that she did best ten feet above ground, her arms and legs akimbo in various positions as she practiced a silks' routine. Twisting, reaching, holding the poses, in order and in rhythm with the music.

With most of her attention on the routine, that left only a tiny part of her mind free to review the situation with Alec.

As a teenager, her imaginings were the epitome of ignorant bliss. Dating would be fun and uncomplicated. They'd get married for time and all eternity in a Latter-day Saint temple…didn't matter which one, she wasn't overly attached to any of them. Merry would be maid of honor at the reception, which they'd have in Cadmia, of course.

Shaking her head, she waited for the music to change. The faster, more hectic song matched her current feelings. And would, until she had more answers than questions.

Arms shaking, she carefully lowered herself to the ground before another song could start. Her breathing slowly returned to normal as she meticulously secured her gear.

Barney, an aging gray tom who kept the mice population in line, leapt up onto the half wall beside her and butted her with his head.

"Hey, old-timer." She scratched under his chin and stroked his back. "You managed to miss my performance." Barney ignored the statement and shoved his head under her hand. "Well, don't take on so," she laughed, massaging behind his ears. "If you come by tomorrow evening after supper, I'll give another one. Just for you."

Rolling her neck to loosen her shoulders, she added, "Followed by a hot bath and hopefully some sleep." Giving Barney a final cuddle, she teased, "Appearing here the next two weeks only." Sighing, she headed for the door. "Or, I could pop that doggone balloon."

Chapter 12

No matter what she did or how busy she kept herself, Grace's mind kept straying to the mystery date.

Even on Thursday, while she laughed at Neil's biology lab stories so hard she'd cried. Even on Friday at Harmony's, where she sang along with the others to a classic musical

Especially on Sunday, when Alec sat next to her at church and held her hand.

Now here it was, her turn to host movie night, and she couldn't stop thinking about it. Less than twelve hours to go.

Merry, always the first to arrive, cracked up when she saw the stack of DVDs on top of Grace's TV. "This is awesome!"

Grace grinned and shook a bag of tortilla chips into a serving bowl. "I wasn't sure you'd approve."

"When have I ever objected to cartoons?" Merry moved the bowls of chips to one end of the counter. Transferred some jalapenos from a jar to a small bowl nestled inside a larger container of pebble ice while Grace finished browning the ground beef. Dishes of diced tomatoes and sour cream already waited for the rest of the guests.

"I think I hear someone." Grace wiped her hands on the mid-sized towel she'd been using as an apron, then tossed it into the laundry basket around the corner from the kitchen.

"Got it." Merry opened the door and ushered them in.

"Welcome!" Switching off the stove, Grace greeted them with hugs.

"Mmm, that smells good!" Noella hugged her back and, predictably, made a beeline for the kitchen.

"A nacho bar?" Harmony hung up her jacket. "This is definitely the right house."

"I was hoping you'd say that," Grace admitted. "It's my aunt's recipe and I always forget to only make half of it, so I've got enough to feed an army."

"Good food, good entertainment. Doesn't get better than that!" Merry stood at one end of the counter, ready to hand out paper plates.

"Oh, what're we watching?" Harmony did her best to sound cheerful instead of hopeful. More often than not, Grace chose movies about animals. Always wholesome and usually cute, but... Harmony could really use a laugh right now.

"You'll never guess." Merry's tone made it plain that she hoped Harmony would give guessing a try.

Rather than spoiling Merry's fun, Grace got the drinks out of the fridge and generally fussed over everyone until they were comfortably seated. Harmony startled all of them with a whoop of joy when the cartoon theme music began.

Despite her best efforts, Grace couldn't seem to concentrate on what they were watching. Every goofy gag sent her mind spinning around and around like a game wheel, inevitably landing on the mystery date. She'd ruled out bungee jumping, but without more information she was stuck. Alec had already proven he was willing to drive for over an hour just to eat at a favorite restaurant, and that meant there were a lot more options than if they stuck around little old Cadmia. Which, she had to admit, they might easily do. *Oh no. What if he wants to go fishing?* She'd never enjoyed fishing. She didn't even like eating them.

"I am lost," announced Noella. Television was a rare treat in her life as a child, which was a huge part of why she enjoyed the movie nights so much. The other part was that she got to spend time with her friends.

Grace scrambled for the remote and pressed the pause button, grateful that Merry and Harmony were already starting to try to explain the cartoon's peculiar humor. They paused a few more times for the same reason, but overall the evening was a success, which they topped off with strawberry shortcake.

"Mmm." Harmony sank into the couch, savoring the tangy fruit. "This is exactly what I needed."

"Rough week?" Grace leaned lightly on the other woman's shoulder.

"Something like that." Harmony dug out another bite.

"Business troubles?" Merry guessed. They were all self-employed, and more often than not their stresses stemmed from that.

"Actually, that's going pretty well." Harmony provided allergen-free ingredients and other items for a co-op she'd built since moving to Cadmia. "One of my customers brought in two more families this week."

"That's great." Grace pushed her dessert around in her bowl. Seven more hours. Ugh. She needed to get a grip. Of course, she'd already been waiting for what felt like forever. What were a few hours compared to years? "I guess you'll have to take on a partner soon."

Harmony almost choked on her dessert. "Not quite." Why had the word 'partner' brought *Grant* to mind?

"You okay?" Grace touched her arm. Noticed the tension in her muscles.

"Fine." Harmony cleared her throat in an effort to distract the often too-perceptive Grace. "Wrong pipe." That was basically the truth.

They both turned to look at Noella as she exclaimed, "Regardez l'heure!" She hastily scooped her last of her dessert into her mouth. "I didn't realize it was so late!"

"It's barely nine," Merry responded in French.

"Oui, me..." Remembering that they didn't

all speak French, Noella took a calming breath and forced herself to think in English. "In the morning, I have an appointment."

"Oh, that's right." Harmony shot Grace an apologetic look. How could she have forgotten so quickly? Noella had muttered to herself about the job for nearly the entire drive over. In Dutch, which meant Harmony only mostly understood her. The job was obviously important, though. "Hate to eat and run."

"Don't worry about it. I actually have plans tomorrow, too."

Merry came to her feet like someone had hit an eject button. "Now you tell us!"

Grace didn't protest as Merry shifted into a slightly myopic 'time to go' mode. She wouldn't have cared if the dishes got left around for her to pick up, but she knew it gave Merry something constructive to do, which would make her feel better.

"Thank you for the evening!" Noella sighed when she came up for a goodbye hug.

"Have fun tomorrow," Grace suggested hopefully. If she read Noella's answering body language correctly, her appointment had nothing to do with fun.

Harmony grinned. "See you Sunday."

Grace surprised them both by holding on a little longer than maybe she usually would've. "Take care," she murmured.

"Yeah." Harmony coughed in lieu of clearing

her throat. "You, too." And she scurried out the door with Noella.

"What's up with Harmony?"

Turning to answer Merry, Grace's jaw dropped. "Wait, hold it right there." Crossing to where Merry was starting to load the dishwasher, Grace wrapped an arm around her shoulders. "You don't have to clean my kitchen, goofball."

"I was just…" Merry snapped another lid into place.

"C'mon." Grace gave her a half-hug and started walking her in the general direction of the door. She wouldn't kick her best friend out no matter how early she was getting up in the morning. She did need to get her away from the dishes, however.

"You shouldn't have to cook *and* clean up." Merry put her arm around Grace's waist. They were the sister they'd each always wished for.

"You did the hard part," Grace promised.

"Going out with Alec tomorrow?" Merry guessed.

"Yep." Grace showed her the plant Alec had given her. "It's trying to sprout."

"Any idea what it will be?" Merry inspected it hopefully.

"A flower, I guess?"

Merry punched her playfully on the arm. "Yeah, let's hope for that."

They giggled the rest of the way to the door, where Merry wrapped her in a hug.

"Oh, I almost forgot." Grace stepped back while Merry slid into her coat. "How's your big project coming along?"

Merry lit up. "It's almost done!" She shrugged. "I got a rush job this week that's taken priority, but I've replaced the…"

Grace couldn't really follow the elaborate woodworking description that followed, but she payed close attention anyway. One of her best friend's fondest dreams was to do specialty orders only and restoring the antique writing desk would be a huge step toward achieving that.

"So I'll send him a message tomorrow." Merry finished with a sigh. "I mean, I could probably find another buyer if I had to, but I don't want to run the risk of him finding one between now and when I finish."

"That makes sense."

"On the other hand." Merry tugged at her coat front to straighten it, wishing she could finally lose that ever-elusive five pounds. "As soon as I tell him, he's going to want pictures. He'll start calling me once a week for 'updates.'" She wrinkled her nose unhappily.

"One of those, huh?" Grace understood perfectly. Some clients needed that extra interaction to feel like things were going well—which was really hard for an introvert like Merry.

"Unfortunately." Merry's lips twitched. "It's the price we pay for fame, I guess."

Grace snickered, but noticed that Merry had

actually gone pale. "Are you okay?"

"Fine." Merry claimed another hug, then opened the door. "Brrrrr. Stay warm!"

"You, too!" Grace watched long enough to be sure Merry got off safely before going inside again. Rubbing her arms, she wondered about that last hug. Merry loved hugs but rarely got them because there were so few people she was that comfortable with. And this one? It felt sort of desperate.

Blowing out a breath, Grace started loading her dishwasher. She couldn't fix Merry's anxiety any more than she could fix her own. However, she could and would include Merry in her prayers tonight. It was the least she could do.

After tidying up and changing for bed, Grace was still wide awake at 9:30 PM, prompting her to turn on some hymns. Needing something to do with her hands, she dumped her shoulder bag out on the couch and began sorting through it. A combination day bag and emergency kit, it held some of everything.

"Good grief, I've been looking for those!" was followed almost immediately by, "Ew, how old is that?"

Eventually, a much more organized bag sat on the table next to a pile of rejected items and a list of things she wanted to replace.

Kneeling by her bed, Grace bowed her head in softly spoken prayer, sharing her concerns for Merry as well as her own apprehensions about tomorrow's date. Of course, there was also forgiveness to be asked for. And she couldn't forget the struggling families in the area. Or the prophet. Or the missionaries. Or…the…

She must've fallen asleep praying, because she woke on her knees, stiff and cold. Dragging herself into bed, she huddled under the blanket until she drifted off again.

Chapter 13

The balloon, slightly deflated but un-popped, seemed to wobble mockingly every time she turned the page in her scriptures during study the next morning. The very *early* Saturday morning.

"Ohhhhkay," she muttered, trying to tie her boot while she hopped over to her phone. "Hold your horses, I'm coming." She got to it right before it vibrated off the counter and onto the floor. "Ten minutes, check. Plenty of…whoa!" She almost threw it when it buzzed unexpectedly with a text from Alec.

[Be there in five.]

"Showoff." Grumbling, she stuffed the rest of her peanut butter toast in her mouth and chewed furiously while she double-checked her messenger bag. "Sure would be nice to know what we're doing." Her shoe came undone and she stopped with a groan to retie it.

Leaving the pile of discarded items on the table, she dropped the bag's strap over her head and snagged her coat. Changed her mind and reached for her windbreaker. A coat and a sweater over a tee would probably be a little much for such a warm morning.

Hearing the rustle of tires on grass she hurried to the door, where she stopped, one hand on the doorknob. Dropping to her knees, she whispered another prayer for the success of the outing, then sprang to her feet and slipped outside.

Where she nearly ran into Alec on the porch.

"Hey." He steadied her. "You're ready!"

"Seriously?" Laughing, she pushed him out of her way and headed for his truck. "I'm a vet, not a drama queen. Of course I'm ready."

Hustling around her, he managed to open her door before she did. Barely. Climbing into the driver's seat a moment later, he put the key in the ignition, then paused.

"What is it?" Maybe it was the adrenaline from seeing him again. Or maybe she was loopy because it was so doggone early. However it happened, the words were out before she consciously registered his hesitation.

"Would you mind," he asked haltingly, "if I offered a prayer? It's a long drive, and even though the weather's been pretty good lately there could still be…" His words came out faster and faster until she interrupted.

"Alec." She took hold of his near hand. "I would love it if you would say a prayer." Before she bowed her head, she saw a tear slip down his cheek.

"Father in Heaven." Alec reverently thanked Him for the good weather and asked for a blessing of safety on their date.

Grace felt a shiver of self-consciousness when he said he was grateful for her faith, and murmured a shy, 'amen' at the end.

"Did you bring the gift bag?" He finished buckling himself in.

"Yes." She'd been surprised to get a text from him yesterday, asking her to bring it. That was almost all she remembered about the bizarrely hectic day. "I haven't had a chance to open it."

"No?" He brushed his thumb lazily across the back of her hand. "Honey, you work too hard."

"Maybe." Tugging her hand free so she could think, she dug the gift bag out. "It's a CD, isn't it?"

Laughing, he tore the paper off and showed it to her. "I mixed it especially for this trip."

"Great."

"Umm…or not?" Hearing a down note in her voice, he stopped, the case partially open. "Too early?"

"Kind of." She wrinkled her nose apologetically. "I thought I might sleep on the way to wherever it is that we're going. If you don't mind? I mean, I do want to hear the music, I just…"

Leaning close, he brushed his lips against her cheek. "You had me worried, Doc." He winked as he straightened, setting the CD on the seat between them. "Ready on schedule, already had peanut butter toast for breakfast, and so beautiful I can hardly look at you. A woman that perfect can make a man feel downright self-conscious."

"How do you know it was toast?" Grace reclined her seat while he turned the truck around, but it was useless. Even that tiny near-kiss was enough to snap her fully awake.

He reached up to brush at his mouth. "Crumbs."

"Are you saying that was a crumby kiss?" she teased.

"Well now, that depends." He arched his eyebrows. "Are you offering to replace it?" That sounded like a great idea to him—even better, it gave him hope that he hadn't completely forgotten how to flirt.

She blushed. "Maybe later."

A profound silence descended after that as they each privately pondered the idea. This was their second date, after all.

Which date became even more mysterious to Grace when they 'arrived' and transferred to the back of a van.

As the van turned down yet another dark road she asked, "Isn't it about time you told me what we're doing?" She didn't feel the least bit threatened or afraid. She was just…getting antsy from wondering.

"Five more minutes," Alec promised, squeezing her hand. "Whoa!" He threw up his free arm to catch himself as the van bounced, lurched, and came to a stop.

The driver jumped out and threw the side door open, revealing what looked a flame thrower aimed at two men holding something up.

"Alec?"

"Amazing, isn't it?" Alec knew he was grinning so big that his teeth were showing, but he couldn't help it. "I've wanted to do this for years!"

"And what, exactly," she let him help her down, "is *this?*" She didn't really want to know, did she? Well, given that it had to be what they were about to do, yes, she did.

"It's a hot air balloon."

Her gaze suddenly shot to the far right of where they stood. Yes, there it was. Yards and yards of brightly colored cloth, tinted mostly orange by the 'flame thrower.'

"Alec, I...I don't know. I don't mind heights, exactly. I do silks, for goodness sakes." She gulped as the flame thrower kicked it up a notch. "This, however—this is something else entirely."

Alec slipped an arm protectively around her. "I'll be right with you the entire trip."

She choked out a laugh. "Meaning you're not planning to take a parachute? Hop out mid-ride?"

Concerned at the rising emotion in her voice, Alec frowned at the balloon. Looked down at Grace, whose face had lost its normal, healthy color.

"I'm sorry, Grace." He sighed and turned her away from where the crew continued to work. "I should've asked you about this. I guess I got so excited for myself that I didn't think about it bothering you."

"Hang on." She dug her heels in instead of letting him lead her to the van. Blew out a breath. "You really want to do this. You should go."

"What?" Startled, he peered down at her in the weirdly dancing light. "Go without you?" He snorted. "What kind of a date do you think I am?"

"One that's nuts," she retorted. "You're that close!" She held up her fingers in the traditional inch-apart style, then changed her mind and pointed at the half-inflated balloon. "This close! C'mon! You have to go!"

"I'll go another day."

"You are so stubborn." She ground her teeth. Couldn't he understand how guilty she'd feel if he didn't go?

"Yeah, but you knew that already." Alec shrugged and rubbed her arms in an effort to soothe her. "Don't worry about it, okay? I'm not."

"If you were going to do this by yourself, you'd have done it already." Scrubbing her hand over her face, she glared at the balloon.

By now the crew members were exchanging looks, like they knew something was wrong.

With a gigantic groan, she punched his arm. "You promise you'll stay right beside me?" She watched his head move up and down. "The entire trip?" she demanded.

He nodded again, then stopped suddenly. "Hang on. You don't want to go and I'm not going to make you go, so there's no point talking about it." He held out both hands, palms forward. "I had a bad idea. I…I dragged you out of a nice warm house in the dark for no good reason and you deserve to have your revenge."

She muttered something he couldn't hear over the preparations, then marched past him to where a crew member was buckling on what looked like a safety harness.

"Do you have another one of those?" she asked boldly.

The man shoved his baseball cap, which read 'Ozark Air' in bright colors to match the balloon, back on his head.

"Yeah," he said at last. "Want me to get it for you?" He looked over her shoulder at Alec. "We only got the one spare, buddy."

Alec rested his hands lightly on Grace's waist. "That's fine, thank you." While the man went to hunt it up, Alec brought his mouth close to Grace's ear and asked quietly, "Are you absolutely sure?" She nodded and he hugged her gently. "Whatever you have in mind for revenge—I'll come quietly."

She did her best to laugh around the fear climbing the walls of her abdominal cavity. "You'd better."

"I'll take it." Alec took the harness from the man, who was most likely their pilot. "Between the two of us, we ought to be able to figure this out," he told Grace. He was relieved when she smiled, faint as it was. "After a lifetime of sorting out tack, this will be a piece of…"

"You've got it upside down." Grace sort of hated to bring it up, but the balloon was starting to lift itself off the ground. "Here." Flipping it over, she untwisted it and stepped in.

"There, see?" Alec grinned and offered her his arm. "I knew it'd be easy."

Laughing, Grace took his arm.

"Here we go, folks." The man with the baseball cap called them over to where the basket waited. "It's time to clamber aboard."

Grace eyed the stepstool they'd set up. "Here goes nothing." She did fine until she started to ascend the stepstool. Somewhere between steps, her knees turned to water.

"Grace?" Alec's hands settled on her waist again. "I've got you." She didn't respond,

Scooping her into his arms, he carried her up the last step, then swung them safely down into the basket.

"We can get right out again," he assured her.

She twiddled one of his shirt buttons while she considered the situation. "It's…all right. I mean, you may have to pry me loose afterwards, but for now I…" She looked up into his gorgeous gray eyes. They were so close. Swallowing, she asked, "How do you feel?"

"Fine would be an understatement."

The pilot, who'd scrambled nimbly aboard while they weren't looking, cleared his throat. "You can hook your harness up over here."

"Thank you." Grace didn't try to hide her smile as Alec set her down.

"Here we go." The pilot made eye contact, gave her rig a couple of quick, professional tugs to make sure she was wearing it correctly, nodded, and snapped a safety line to the D ring on the back of the harness. "Are we ready?"

"Nope." Grace smiled tightly at him. "Let's do this."

Uncertainly, the man looked from her to Alec, then at her again.

Alec took her by the hand. "We're ready."

At Grace's nod, the man spoke into his walkie-talkie.

She gasped at the first wobble of the basket, but Alec squeezed her hand tighter. "I've got you."

It was perfectly ridiculous to think that holding his hand would somehow save her from the consequences of a balloon crash. And yet—his touch settled her. Her heart slowed to its normal Alec-is-near pace. Her mind set her half-finished obituary down and snuggled into his arms.

Clearing his throat, Alec forced himself to look away from her and out over the edge of the basket. The light from the burner's flame, which seemed so bright when he was facing it, now seemed more like a puny matchstick compared with the endless, inky black sky. It was weirdly disorienting to not have any landmarks. To think of himself as just hanging between the earth and the sky, somewhere in southwest Missouri.

"Won't be long till sunup," he announced unnecessarily.

"I didn't realize we'd be able to see the stars."

His ears pricked at the hint of interest in her tone. "Do you see any that you recognize?"

"Mhmm." She slowly relaxed as she pointed out the constellations she recognized.

"Very good," he congratulated her. "You remember all of those from our date?"

She gasped. "Look!"

"What?"

"A shooting star!" She let go of his hands to point. "Another one!"

"Well of all the…" Astounded, Alec watched with her as a short flurry of lights streaked across the sky.

"Is…is it over?"

"I don't know." Bewildered, he shook his head. "That was probably part of the Taurids shower. Maybe? I mean, it runs clear from September to December, but I had no idea we might see some of it."

"Wow, that was kind of scary. And thrilling." As her hand settled on the basket's rim, she suddenly realized how far she'd traveled from its 'safe' center. "Yeah, um, and scary."

"Easy," he soothed, squeezing her arms gently. "I'm right here."

"Okay." She leaned back into his embrace. "Keep talking about the shower." She focused on the sound of his voice, the feel of it rumbling through his chest, and the occasional sighting of a meteor arcing across the horizon.

"You're shivering." Opening his jacket, Alec enveloped her in it, and kept holding her as the night began to give way to a new dawn.

"It's so beautiful." Grace nestled in his arms, completely unafraid. Before her was the miracle of the light pushing back the darkness, a true metaphor for life. Behind her, flooding her senses with each breath, was the man she loved and wanted for life.

A light wind edged them toward the east, making the sunrise seem to occur almost twice as fast as usual. Grays, pinks, and the searing white of the sun followed one after another. Hilltops became visible, then tree tops, and finally the one or two buildings that dotted the sparsely populated land below.

"They look like dollhouses." Grace shrank a little. "Exactly how high up are we?"

"I have no idea." He hunted for something to distract her with. "Can't believe how clear this air is. Do you think if we try hard enough, we'll be able to see tomorrow?"

That made her laugh. "Oh, I can see tomorrow

fine. I'm giving a talk tomorrow." In a congregation of some three hundred people, she wasn't often asked to speak in sacrament meeting, but she knew the bishopric had a backup speaker in mind in case she got called out on an emergency.

"You are? What's your topic?"

"Thanksgiving."

"Ah, how appropriate."

"And yet, I'm stumped." She was warm enough now that being wrapped in his jacket was getting uncomfortable. Easing out of it, she admitted, "I can't even decide where to begin."

"That's the hard part," he agreed. He wasn't cold exactly, but he'd enjoyed holding her and missed it immediately. "Is there any one thing you're grateful for this year?"

She looked up. "You."

"Grace, when you say it like that…" He searched her wide eyes, surprised by the depth of emotion in her voice.

"I love you." The words spilled out through the cracks in her safety wall. "I have ever since I knew there *was* a 'you'."

Alec shook his head to clear it, but thought better of asking her to repeat herself. After several seconds, all he could think to say was, "Now who's being impatient?"

"I can understand how it would sound that way to you, Alec." She searched his face for some clue of how he was reacting. "And I don't expect you to…to get down on one knee and propose because I said it." If her face got any hotter, the pilot was going to have to turn off the burner. "I just couldn't hold it in any longer."

"Alright, folks." The pilot dialed the burner down. "We're getting close to the end of our ride, so if you want me to take some pictures of you, now's your chance."

"Oh, we'll never forget this," Alec promised as he fished his phone out of his pocket, vaguely surprised that he hadn't taken a single picture the whole time.

"No, never." Grace handed over her phone as well.

"Say cumulous!" he joked as he prepared to take their picture. He'd sure been wrong about this couple. From the way things had started, he'd expected her to insist on ending the flight early. Instead, it was the fella who looked kinda queasy.

Chapter 14

"My parents are never going to believe this," Grace laughed as she climbed into his truck. "In fact, I better have them sit down when I tell them."

Alec chuckled with her, then asked, "How's your stomach?"

She blinked. "My what?"

"Your stomach," he repeated. He wasn't quite ready to discuss her heart. "I promised you a big breakfast, but I wanted to make sure you were up to it after that ride."

"Oh. Well." She shrugged. "That peanut butter toast *was* quite a while ago."

"Wonderful." He started the engine. "Why don't you pop that CD in?"

Reaching for it, she noticed something else on the seat. "What's this?" she held up the thermos. "Hot chocolate?" she guessed.

"That's right. With maybe half a pinch of cayenne pepper."

"Cayenne," she sputtered. "*That's* your secret ingredient?"

"Well, it *was*." He made a show of looking around the cab as if worried that they'd been overheard. "I brought it in case it was a cold drive in."

"Mmm, I could use some now." She shivered slightly.

"Cold?" he asked, his gaze dropping to her perfect mouth.

Deliberately, she put the CD in and relaxed in her seat. While she might not know when or if they would ever discuss what she'd said in the balloon, she needed both feet on the ground for their first kiss.

Amused, Alec headed for their next destination. Thankfully, the CD started, filling the silence—until it wound up prompting them both to sing. He could tell which songs she really knew because she would slip into a sweet low-soprano harmony.

"Oh shucks," she complained when he pulled into a parking lot. "Are we here already?"

Chuckling, he parked and switched off the engine. "Grace, I think we have the same taste in music."

"Eclectic?" she teased, opening her door out of habit.

"Exactly!" He met her at the front of the truck and paused to look down at her, wondering if he could get used to a woman who opened her own doors.

"I don't think they're open yet." Frowning, Grace pointed at the sign by the door.

"Now, now." Catching her by the wrist, he lifted her arm over her head and guided her through a slow spin, almost into his arms. "Don't you know it's impolite to point?"

She tried desperately to come up with something to say in response, something coy or at least flirtatious. All she could think of was that he had to be able to feel her pulse pounding under his fingertips.

Shifting his hold from her wrist to her elbow, Alec found himself face to face with temptation. He wouldn't even need to bend. Just tip his head forward.

Grace stifled a sigh and stepped to one side to wait for him to answer his phone. *Of all the rotten timing.*

Disappointed, Alec let his hands fall to his sides. Frowned. Some people claimed to hear music while kissing, but he hadn't… Suddenly it dawned on him that his phone was ringing!

"I—" He began slapping his pockets to try to find it. "Um, excuse me." Yanking his phone out, he debated rejecting the call. Unfortunately, he owed the caller a huge favor, so he couldn't. "Hey, Vince."

"Aaaalec. You did not tell me she was hot!"

Cringing, Alec took a long step away from Grace in the hopes that she wouldn't be able to hear his brother.

"Yeah, that's probably an eight on the inappropriate scale." The answering guffaws rang painfully in his ear.

"Same old Alec. Still haven't loosened up, huh?"

"That's right." Alec put his hand on his side and took a deep breath. Having a fabulously talented brother was great for when he needed a favor. If only Vince didn't have a knack for embarrassing him. "Still the same uptight stick in the mud."

Feeling a hand on his arm, he was startled to find Grace beside him. "One sec," he mouthed.

To his brother he said, "How about it, Vince? Are you going to feed us or what?"

"Don't I always? Get in here you doofus."

Pocketing his phone, Alec smiled down at Grace. He had an arm around her shoulders and she was resting naturally against him. How did that happen? Not that he minded, he simply liked to be aware of what he was doing.

"Everything alright?"

"Sure." Relaxing, he kissed her forehead lightly. "C'mon, let's go. My brother's a lot of things, but lucky for him that includes being an excellent cook."

"Your brother?" Grace bit her lip as she racked her brain for the name. "You mean Uncle Vince?"

Alec jerked as if she'd slapped him. "Yeah." Straightening, he dropped his arm from her shoulders and took her hand instead. "Let's go in."

As she accompanied him, more or less at arm's length, Grace had the most bizarre feeling that she was a child being taken for a walk by an adult. The feeling persisted through the meal. Waffles, bacon, and eggs had never tasted so much like sawdust in her life.

"So you're Grace? Danny's best friend, right?" A chair squeaked as Vince pulled it away from the table. "Serves me right for not coming out for Christmas all those times he invited me. I'd loved to find a package like you under my tree." He nudged Alec's elbow and grinned at an inside joke only he knew.

Inwardly Grace rolled her eyes. Fending off overly 'friendly' men bored her. The worst part was that some of them never matured past that stage. Vince, for example. He couldn't be more than a few years younger than Alec. However, where Alec was warm and considerate, Vince came off as brash and insolent.

"Under the tree?" She gave him as blank a stare as she could manage and still be polite. "Don't you mean on top?" She didn't actually think she was an angel, but hoped he'd get the hint.

Vince cracked up to the point of slapping his hand on the table to express his enthusiasm. "Awesome! This one's on the ball!" He moved on to smacking Alec's arm. "Thought you were nuts coming all this way for breakfast, but y'know, I think you're onto something."

Rising, he pointed at them with both hands. "Don't be strangers!" And walked away, whistling something loud.

Pulling her braid around so that it dangled over her shoulder, Grace flicked a glance at Alec through her lashes. He hadn't done or said a thing to discourage Vince. He'd been a bit off since the phone call in the parking lot, though, so maybe Vince put him out of sorts in general? Danny had never been keen on Vince, either, as she recalled.

Alec shifted in his chair. Stirred his eggs. Thought about how casually Grace had handled Vince. Like a bored matador sidestepping a clumsy bull. It took a lot of practice to get that good at something.

"…ketchup?"

Hearing her voice, he looked up. Watched her face soften and her hair fall forward as she leaned toward him.

"I said, do your eggs need ketchup?"

He swallowed. Shook his head. "Not as hungry as I thought." Setting his fork aside, he picked up a piece of bacon.

Unconvinced, Grace studied him. Setting her own fork down, she demanded, "Alright. Let's have it."

"Come again?" He raised both eyebrows innocently.

"You can't fool me, Alec Fitzsimmons. I know you too well." Folding her arms in front of her, she rested them on the table. "Something's bothering you."

"You're right." Reaching over, he picked up the bottle. "These do need ketchup."

"Alec." She put her hand lightly on his wrist. Held his gaze.

He'd seen her use this tactic on others. Now, as his resistance crumbled, he felt a deep empathy for them.

"Grace," he sighed. Putting the bottle back, he scrubbed at his face with his free hand.

"Run out of napkins, bro?" Vince recoiled from the twin death glares. "Sheesh, I was only kidding!" Neither of them blinked. "Um, okay. I came over to give you guys these," he gingerly set takeout boxes on the table, "and to say drive safe!" Hastily, he retreated.

Alec frowned at the boxes. What a morning. The hot air balloon ride nearly blew up in his face. Somehow he'd forgotten Vince's…personality. And Grace Myers thought she loved him.

"Let's go." He shoved his plate toward the center of the table and got to his feet. Picking up the boxes with one hand, he caught hold of Grace's hand and led her out the door.

"Alec?" She tugged at her hand. "Alec, talk to me."

"Not here," he muttered. This was one conversation he didn't care to have Vince intruding on.

"Then where?" She rotated the wrist he'd finally released and eyed the door he'd opened for her. "Why not here? And now?"

"Grace, please get in the truck."

"In a minute." Fuming, she folded her arms across her chest and walked rapidly toward the tailgate. *Ugh!* If he would just talk to her! Then they could figure out how to fix whatever was wrong and… She stopped and leaned against the back of his truck, her stomach churning.

"Grace?" Alec put the boxes behind his seat and slowly closed the door. "Grace, I'm sorry." Shoving his hands into his pockets, he cautiously followed her. "We've got a long drive ahead of us. The sooner we get started…"

"The sooner we'll be done." She turned to face him. "I know how it works, I'm not a child." Clenching her hands into fists, she asked, "Tell me one thing first. How did dating me get to be a chore?"

There it was again. That flare of temper that burned his notions of her as a child right down to the grown. Except…

"That's not what I meant." Frustrated and uncertain, he raked his fingers through his hair. "Why do women always complicate things?"

"Complicate things?" she sputtered. "You…you…" A dangerous light flashed in her eyes. "You want simple? Fine!" Grabbing him by his shirt front, she pulled him close and pressed her lips to his.

Off-balance, Alec grabbed for the truck to support himself. He'd bumbled into an electric fence once—it wasn't the kind of mistake a man repeated—and this reminded him of that. Electricity coursed through his veins, almost short-circuiting his brain. Still, a rusty reflex brought his arms around her, drawing her tightly against him while her arms crept up around his neck, her fingers curling in his hair.

As her heels settled back onto the pavement, Grace snuggled against his chest. "Simple enough for you?" She smiled as his answering chuckle rumbled through him.

"Do me a favor, will you?" He kissed her hair. "Never call Vince 'uncle' again."

Her eyes popped open and she pulled away. "Alec! You don't mean…" His kiss cut her off mid-sentence, but she didn't mind a bit.

"Mmm. So, new rule." She playfully touched the tip of her nose to his. "I won't use any of Danny's familial terms."

"I'd appreciate that." He tried capturing her lips again only to have her hide her face against his chest.

"We better go." She didn't want to. She needed to. Sure, she knew some women who claimed they could kiss for the fun of it. If she'd ever wondered, she could now state with absolute certainty that she was not one of them.

His arms tightened around her briefly, then relaxed. "Your chariot awaits."

They didn't talk much on the ride to her home, which now didn't seem long enough as they each tried to sort through the events of the morning.

She waited for him to open the door for her when they arrived, and they walked to her door together.

"It's been quite a day." He stood back a pace and watched her go through the simple act of pulling out her keys and unlocking her door. Drank in the graceful movement of her reaching up to tuck a strand of hair behind her ear.

He hadn't thought of a woman as…a woman in so long he could've sworn he'd forgotten how. Then Grace lost her temper and crashed through his perimeter fence, releasing a torrent of emotions he'd never expected to use again. And the way she'd held onto him—like she was never going to let go.

"It has," she agreed. Facing him, she couldn't help the blush that began stealing up past her collar. She thought she knew how the date would end, but nothing about this day had gone as she'd imagined. "I had…" 'Fun' didn't seem right. "Well, it was…" *I told him I loved him!* "Quite a day."

He smiled, relieved to see he wasn't the only one feeling off-balance.

"Listen." He took her hands in his. "I'm about as out of practice at this as a man can get and not be dead. No, wait." He lifted his eyebrows when she opened her mouth to interrupt. "I'm not going to keep trying to ignore our age difference. Doing that only makes me more uncomfortable."

"Alright, Alec." She searched his eyes as she added, "But you must know I don't care about that."

"I got that impression," he chuckled. "And I could kiss you all day, Grace Myers." If he touched her scarlet cheeks, would they singe his fingertips? "I'll admit that I have a few years of dust and cobwebs to shake loose from before I'll be able to think straight when it comes to you, but if you'll be patient with me, I know now that I…" He paused to clear the tears from his throat. Got a grip on his courage. "That being alone was what I had gotten used to. A habit. I've realized that, given a choice, I don't want to live the rest of my life alone."

He stopped there, unsure if he'd said enough—or perhaps too much?

Grace considered their joined hands. Her lungs had locked up when he hesitated, fearing he was about to propose. That sounded absolutely crazy given her earlier declaration of love for him, which he hadn't mentioned. Was that good or bad? Oh, she'd decide about that later. Right now, he was waiting for a response.

Squeezing his fingers, she said quietly, "All I can say is thank you. Thank you for taking a chance on dating. And for being honest with me."

Chapter 15

The next morning found Grace uncomfortably seated on the stand a few chairs away from the bishopric. Behind her, the organ was playing a lovely hymn in preparation for the meeting. Beside her, the youth speaker was in danger of fainting.

"Good morning," Grace murmured, smiling at the girl, who couldn't have been more than thirteen. According to the program, her name was Meg.

"Morning." Meg smiled wanly. "Are you giving a talk today, too?"

Not trusting herself not to chuckle at the artless question, Grace just nodded. Aside from offering the opening prayer, why else would she be up on the stand today?

Meg swallowed visibly. "Nervous?"

"You bet!" Grace made a show of squaring her shoulders. "But we'll be alright."

"Yeah." She didn't sound convinced.

Grace leaned over and touched her arm lightly. "I like to look at my parents while I talk. And sometimes I look way in the back, over the tops of peoples' heads."

"Over their heads?" Meg's nose wrinkled and she almost smiled. "That's pretty smart."

"Thanks." Hearing the music stop, Grace was mildly embarrassed to see the bishop rising to start the meeting. "Here we go."

She shared a hymnal with Meg to maintain a sense of camaraderie and prayed silently for the girl throughout her sweet talk.

"So to me," Meg finished in a quavering voice, "Thanksgiving is a time to officially stop and be thankful for all the things we forget to remember most days." She gave Grace a grateful smile on her way to her chair.

Grace returned Meg's grateful smile, then took a deep breath and got to her feet. At the pulpit, the first person she made eye contact with was Alec. Her pulse spiked and she dropped her eyes.

"One of the best things about preparing this talk was that it reminded me to be grateful as I went through each day. It also gave me the opportunity to revisit general conference talks that I haven't read or listened to in a while. Such as Elder Wirthlin's 'Come What May, and Love It' talk from October 2008, which I'll be using quite a bit." Deliberately, Grace looked out over the tops heads to the far wall, then to her right and to her left as she recounted an abbreviated version of the story from which the talk's title came. "He goes on to tell us four things that we can do to help us during those times when we may not think there's anything to be thankful for."

As she shared Elder Wirthlin's wisdom, she used her own experiences to illustrate each of his four points: "look for humor, seek for the eternal perspective, understand the principle of compensation, and draw near to our Heavenly Father."

"I remember being convinced that I had failed somehow, on a personal level. Failed to be worthy of the blessing I was praying for. Failed to present myself well at the interview. Failed, basically as a human being." She gripped the edges of the podium and willed herself not to cry. "I was so focused on getting what I thought I wanted, that I overlooked the possibility that the Lord had something far better for me. I couldn't even consider that until," she gave her parents a watery smile, "until I counseled with my parents."

It didn't take long to share the story of how she'd been invited to work with her dad at his veterinary practice and gone on to take it over when he retired. She touched lightly on the blessings she'd received after making that decision, such as being able to see her parents more often, and having the opportunity to support the people in her hometown. She choked up a little at the end, but managed to finish, then retook her seat by Meg.

The third and final speaker built his talk around a single verse of scripture, and ended with a warm, sincere testimony of the joy he'd found in Christ.

Grace shared her stash of tissues with Meg and they both dabbed at the tears brought on by his heartfelt talk.

After the closing prayer, she wove her way through the quietly milling congregation, smiling and accepting compliments on her talk as graciously as she could. She really wanted to get to Relief Society, though—and to get out of the chapel so the brethren could have their priesthood meeting.

Until her phone began vibrating in her hand. Recognizing the number, she looked sharply at Alec.

"What's wrong, Bart?" He already had his phone at his ear.

Grace answered her phone with a simple, "Doctor Myers." She listened intently as a sobbing Mrs. Brooke begged her to come to the Rockin' R immediately.

"They're sick! They're all… My babies, I…"

"I'm on my way." Grace cut the hysterical woman off. "Do exactly what Bart tells you to until I get there." She only waited long enough for Mrs. Brooke to agree, then stuffed her phone in her pocket and reached for Alec's. "If you'll drive my truck, I'll walk him through what I can."

"Let's go." He relinquished his phone with one hand and accepted her keys with the other.

"Grace?" Her dad frowned at her.

"Have to dash." She pressed a quick peck to his cheek, then her mother's. "I'll be home as soon as I can."

Ignoring those who'd stopped talking to listen in, Alec caught Grace by the elbow and towed her out of the building.

"Hang on, Bart." Grace hopped into the passenger side of the truck and, putting the phone on speaker, set it on the dash while she buckled herself in. Bart wasn't hysterical, which was a plus, but his answers were all over the place. "You're not making sense! Okay, let's try something simply. How many of the horses have been affected?"

"Affected?" Bart snorted. "Half of them are sick as dogs, if that's what you mean. We've got convulsions, colic, a mare that plain can't stand up…"

"Bart, take a breath!" Grace's mind and heart were racing. "Alec." She looked at his white face and swallowed. "Have you made any big changes lately, like changing your feed supplier?"

"No."

The one-word answer didn't rule out contaminated feed, but it did drop it from her top ten suspects. "So, how about poisons? Pest control, that sort of thing. Any chance, however remote, that the horses somehow got into it?"

"No way, Doc," Bart blurted. "We are super careful about that. Besides, we've got sick horses from different sides of the barn. Unless someone deliberately put poison in their stalls, they couldn't all have gotten into it."

"It still sounds like some kind of poison. The symptoms…" Frowning, she pulled her phone out and dialed Neil. While she waited for him to pick up, she asked, "Bart, do you still have…"

Alec swerved to miss a car that casually pulled out in front of him, doing about twenty in a forty-five. Muttering under his breath, he shot past it and accelerated toward the Rockin' R while keeping one ear on the conversation as Grace juggled two phone calls.

At some point, Mrs. Brooke got ahold of Bart's phone and demanded to know why they weren't there yet.

Grace countered with a calm but firm request for her to put Bart back on.

"'Scuze me, Mrs. Brooke. Grace?" Bart's voice came through over the sound of an indignant Mrs. Brooke. "Only enough doses left for the four worst cases, but we got it started. Sure hope it works!"

"Good job. Neil will be along as soon as he can, but he'll need help bringing things from his truck into the barn," she inserted crisply.

"We'll be ready. Anything else?"

"We're turning into the driveway. See you in a minute."

"Grace?" Alec touched her arm. "Just do your best."

She gave him a tight-lipped nod and was out of the truck almost before it stopped moving. It took too long to change, but coveralls over a dress were the worst and even sensible pumps were no match for a good pair of barn boots.

"Alec!" Bart hurried over to meet them at

the door.

Alec's gut clenched at Bart's grim expression. "We lost one."

"Which one?" Grace spoke crisply even as her heart picked up speed. The Rockin' R had close to a hundred head of horses, but the ones in the big barn were all personal acquaintances of hers.

Bart wouldn't look at her. "Celtic Viv."

Celtic Viv was a big, beautiful mare with a coppery-red coat and flaxen mane and tail. A three time cross-country champion, she had a mischievous streak as wide as the Grand Canyon, but one of the best brood mares Grace had ever known.

Her vision swam before her and she felt Alec's warm hand grip hers. "Show me."

"Doc, that ain't necessary. I give you my word." Bart gulped, then finished, "She's gone."

"I need to examine her," Grace insisted dully. She'd rather speak at general conference in front of several million people, but it had to be done. "I can't do anything for the other horses until Neil gets here with the supplies, Bart. I won't be long and I might find a clue."

Reluctantly, Bart wiped his nose, adjusted his hat, and stepped aside.

Grace fought for control as she walked to Viv's stall. Icy indifference had never been her strong suit. Stopped at the stall door.

"Do you want me to…?"

She shook her head as Alec offered to go in her place. "I need to see it myself."

Whispering a prayer, Grace felt a surge of peace wash over her as she entered. Yes, Viv's body lay before her, stiff and unmoving. But this was only the end of her mortal existence. And Grace knew without a shadow of a doubt that death was not the end.

Stroking a hand down the coppery-red neck, Grace murmured, "See you later."

Alec, who'd stayed outside to give her a moment of privacy, lurched through the door when he heard her call his name.

"What? Did you find something already?"

"Here." Grace showed him the drying spittle on Viv's muzzle. "And here." Opening the mare's mouth, she revealed a green stem.

"That's fresh." Which made no sense to him. All the horses in the barn got the same feed—hay and grain. "I don't think she's been out on pasture today."

"So where'd it come from?" Getting up, Grace began a visual examination of the stall. In the process of kicking aside some straw to see if by some bizarre chance a weed had sprung up, her boot heel connected with the wall behind her. Froze when the horse in the next stall squealed indignantly.

"That's just Windy," Alec told her when she raised a questioning eyebrow.

"Windy doesn't sound sick to me." She

stripped off her gloves as she left Viv's stall. Approached Windy's carefully. "Hey, handsome."

The spectacular animal pranced in place, as fit as the day they'd met.

"Doc?" Bart's shout echoed through the barn. "He's here!"

Alec started to turn toward the entrance, then stopped. Grace was still standing in front of Windy's stall, her brow knit in puzzlement.

"Hey." He touched her arm. "Neil's here."

"Yeah." Folding her arms, she leaned them on the door to Windy's stall. "Why isn't he sick?"

Alec frowned thoughtfully. "I have no idea."

"Me, neither." Whipping out her phone, she shot Neil a text instructing him to check the other horses for signs of fresh greens, then entered the stall. "Sometimes the aberration holds the key to the puzzle."

Windy nickered and investigated her pockets.

"You remember me, huh?" She laughed softly. "Sorry, no carrots this time. Here, let me see." She checked his mouth. "Is he still eating a special diet?"

"Not since last week."

"Mhmm." She ran her hand down his neck, over his withers and walked slowly to his rump. Began walking the stall.

"What're you looking for?" Alec wanted to help, but he didn't know how.

"For…whatever Viv got into." But she didn't

see anything. Straw, smooth walls, feed and water buckets. Nothing out of the ordinary. Flipping her braid over her shoulders, Grace tugged it hard enough to bring her chin up. Her gaze went up also, up the walls to… *Hang on.*

Tipping her head back, she checked the ceiling. "Alec!"

"What is it?" Alec stepped close and peered up at the ceiling.

"Mistletoe." She called Neil and related what she'd found. "If it's in one stall, I'm sure it was in the others. Yes, exactly, all the symptoms caused by the same thing."

Meanwhile, Alec called Bart on his phone and barked instructions for him to get ladders and check every stall in the barn. Stuffed it in his pocket and patted Windy's mane.

"Smart fella."

"Yeah." Grace smiled. "Lucky for him he didn't taste test it like the others."

"How'd it even get in here?" Alec didn't think he had any horse killers on his payroll.

She shook her head. "We'll figure that out later. Right now we need to get it down."

"Good point. I'll have Bart bring us a ladder."

"We don't need one." Walking across the aisle, she pulled a lunge line from an equipment cupboard. "Can you get this up over that rafter?"

"Sure." Alec was no cowboy, but he did know how to handle a rope. An expert flick of his wrist sent the soft, knotted end of the rope sailing up and over the rafter as requested.

"Perfect." Grace caught the loose end. "Can you hold me?"

"I'd love to." Alec was delighted to see her cheeks pink in response. Cleared his throat. "Yeah, go ahead." He watched in awe as she climbed the rope as easily as he climbed stairs.

Once at the top, Grace used her fingernails to free the packing tape that held the mistletoe in place. Twirled the sprig once, noting the cluster of red, shiny, deadly berries. Needing her hands, she stowed the mistletoe in her hair and slid down to Alec, who promptly caught her and kissed her.

"Sorry." His grin belied his words. "I'm a sucker for mistletoe."

"I'll remember that." *Hoo, would she ever!* Hearing Bart's voice, she slipped out of Alec's arms and handed him the lunge line.

"Grace?" Bart's voice boomed ahead of him as he hurried down the aisle. "I've got three ladders going, but it's in every stall I've checked. Who in tarnation would do this?!" He paused and she jumped in with a question of her own.

"Where's Neil?"

"Left him up front." Bart jerked his chin in that direction. "Had us bring up every horse that could walk."

"And those that couldn't?" She held her breath.

Bart blinked rapidly and shook his head. "He had to put 'em both down."

Grace forcibly swallowed the bile that clawed its way up her throat. Knowing that it could all have been avoided made it worse. "There is no cure for mistletoe. All we can do is treat the symptoms and hope." Lifting her eyebrows at Alec in silent farewell, she headed off to join Neil. She'd have to leave the rest of the mystery up to them.

"Hey, Doc." Neil greeted her.

"Hey, Doc." It was a terrible joke, but she laughed anyway. "Where do you want me?"

He briefed her while she put on a fresh pair of gloves and was about to walk away when she touched his arm.

"Neil. The horses that had to be put down. I'm sorry I wasn't there to do it."

He smiled tightly. "Better me than you, Doc. At least I didn't know 'em." With a short, sharp nod, he spun on his heel and walked to the end of the line of their patients.

Blinking away tears, Grace went to the other end. "Hey, Dart." The trim black filly whinnied pitifully and leaned against her. "Not quite your spunky self, huh?" She adjusted the horse blanket and spoke soothingly to the distressed horse.

Time slipped through her fingers as she worked her way through the horses Neil had assigned. Back and forth she walked, checking vitals and generally trying to make them more comfortable while Neil did the same for his horses. They bumped into each other on her third go-round. Or was it the fourth? She'd lost track.

"Think we've got 'em stabilized." Neil stroked a sweating neck. Glanced at her half of the horses and nodded wearily. "Yeah, they'll pull through." Giving Grace a short once-over, he suggested, "You've been doing most of the legwork. Why not let me take the next watch?"

She stifled a snicker and narrowly avoided putting words in his mouth. After all, if he'd been gracious enough not to say she looked like a wreck, she could do the same.

"That's a great idea." Alec, who'd just arrived from the main house, wished he'd thought of it. "Chef Toni sent some soup and sandwiches for you." He hefted the two small coolers he'd been tasked with.

"Oh, I *love* her cooking!" Grace took off her gloves and eagerly accepted one of the coolers. "Neil, you are not going to believe how wonderful soup and sandwiches can taste."

"I'd eat an old sock at this point," he retorted.

Alec forced a smile, but they only had eyes for the food. Shoving his fists into the pockets of his jacket, he slowly walked down the line of horses. Pausing at one of his personal favorites, a gorgeous dun with the unfortunate moniker of Crème de la Crème, he scratched under her chin right where she liked it.

"You're going to be okay," he murmured.

Chapter 16

"Here you go." Grace removed the halter and patted the horse's neck. "You made it, Wingding."

The mare whickered wearily and sank to her knees in the soft stall bedding. Grace was sorely tempted to join her, but it would be dawn soon. She'd be lucky to get home, get showered, and have breakfast before she needed to head to the clinic and handle whatever appointments Amy couldn't reschedule.

Latching the stall door behind her, Grace stomped her foot. Wriggled her toes. She'd barely taken so much as a bathroom break since supper and her whole body ached. She was about to stomp again when she heard something that made her stiffen.

Whoever it was sniffled again and Grace turned toward the tack room. Easing the door open, she stepped and found…

"Eddie? Sweetheart," she dropped to her knees beside the weeping young woman, "what's wrong?" Instinctively, she wrapped her arms around the shaking shoulders and hugged her tight. Eddie returned the hug, but only sobbed harder. "Shhh, shhh."

"F-f-fault."

Grace's ears pricked. It didn't seem possible for Eddie to talk given how hard she was crying, but…

"My fault!"

A chill swept over Grace. No. She couldn't believe Eddie was responsible for what had happened. Eddie was a handful by anybody's standards, but she had a soft spot for animals as big as the Grand Canyon.

"Just," Eddie gasped, "wanted pic…pic…"

"Pictures?" Grace supplied, her heart sinking. Of all the heartbreaking reasons for an animal to die.

Eddie nodded, tears still slipping out past her tightly closed eyes.

Shifting into a more comfortable position, Grace drew Eddie closer. "Let the tears come, sweetheart," she murmured softly. "Cry it out."

She cried, too. There hadn't been time before. There wasn't now—but she couldn't leave Eddie alone with her grief and guilt.

Eventually, Eddie lay still in her arms, swollen eyes closed and breathing shallowly.

Grace's heart constricted painfully as she tried to imagine telling Mr. Brooke. By now he knew about the mistletoe. He'd turn the barn upside down and shake it like a snow globe until he found out how this had happened.

"Poor little thing," she sighed. "You've got a tough row to hoe, no mistake." She sat there for she didn't know how long before someone spoke.

"Grace?" Alec stood in the doorway. He'd half expected to find her curled up in the corner of Wingding's stall. "What's going on?"

She shook her head, not sure how to tell him. Or even if she should. Eddie would sleep a while now, and it might be better to let her do her own explaining. Except…

Looking up at where Alec was still expectantly waiting, she mimed holding mistletoe in the air and kissing someone. She could tell the instant he got the gist.

The blood drained from his face and he pointed down at Eddie, eyebrows raised pleadingly.

Slowly, she nodded.

Scrubbing his hand across his face, he came over to sit beside them. *How am I going to tell Mr. Brooke?* Feeling Grace's hand slide down his forearm, he laced his fingers through hers. Bit by bit, her warmth seeped into him, melting some of the block of ice that had settled in his gut.

Grace twitched suddenly. Gave him an apologetic smile and withdrew her hand so she could get her cell phone out of her pocket.

Belatedly realizing that she was struggling with Eddie's weight, Alec rolled onto his knees and lifted the girl free.

"Thanks." Accessing her texts, Grace groaned and massaged her temple. "I…" Her gaze shifted to Eddie. "I can't walk off and leave her."

Alec opened his mouth to say he'd take care of her, then closed it. "Now that you mention it." He cleared his throat. "What am I going to do with her?"

Grace covered her mouth to stifle a giggle. "Sorry. I'm." She waved her hand. "Tired."

"Same." He nodded.

Eddie stirred and he nearly dropped her.

"Here." Grace quickly reseated herself and patted the floor beside her. "Set her down. Then wait outside."

Baffled, Alec did as he was told, but only retreated as far as outside the partially open door.

"Eddie? Wake up, honey." Grace felt like an ogre waking her up so soon after she'd cried herself to sleep.

"Hmm?" Eddie's face twisted into a pained wince. "My head hurts."

"I know, honey, and I'm sorry." She wished she'd thought to send Alec for some ibuprofen or something. The big goof was probably leaning over the door of Windy's stall, practicing how he was going to tell Mr. Brooke.

"Don't worry about it." Eddie sagged against the wall. "It won't hurt long. My dad'll kill me when he finds out how this happened."

"Eddie, that's not true." Grace squeezed her arm. "I'll go with you right now and we'll tell him together."

Eddie cracked one eye open and gave her a long look. "How come you don't hate me?"

Startled, Grace didn't answer right away. "Hate you? Eddie, how…" She grimaced. Maybe some shock therapy would bring her out of it? "How many did you plan to kill?"

"What?!" Eddie lunged to her feet. Gripped her head. "Are you nuts?"

Grace got up as well. "Pretty sloppy of you to put it up so high. Made it harder for them to get it."

"I didn't…" Eddie swayed slightly. Lowered her voice. "I just wanted some cute pictures."

Grace touched her arm. "And that's why I don't hate you."

Eddie's lip trembled and she walked into Grace's arms.

Grace's cell went off and Alec stepped into the tack room at almost the same instant.

"Thought you might need these." That was all the explanation he gave as he held out a bottle of pain killers and a bottle of water to Eddie.

She eyed them without taking them. "You know?"

"Yeah." He pressed the items into her hands. "And, I know you. Speaking as a dad, I think everything will work out all right."

Tears trickled down Eddie's cheeks as she mouthed, 'Thank you.'

Grace smiled and slipped her phone into her pocket. "I have to go. Unless?" She raised a questioning eyebrow at Eddie, who shrugged.

"I'll be fine."

Alec studied Eddie for a moment, then suggested, "It's not good to take those on an empty stomach. Let me see if I can find a sandwich or something for in the leftovers from earlier."

Eddie took a huge swig of water, then motioned for Alec to stay put. "I'm starving. If there's a sandwich in this barn, I'll find it myself." Winking broadly at Grace, she added, "You two take your time."

"Well that little monkey!" Alec eyed the adorably pink Grace. "There is something I wanted to say, though."

"Oh?" Grace fanned herself openly with her hand. If they ever figured out a scientific way to prevent blushing, she was going to volunteer to try it.

"Yeah." He closed the distance between them in a single stride. Cupped her face in his hands and tilted her chin up. "I've come to the conclusion that I love you, too."

If not for his hand's support, her jaw would've hit the floor.

"Alec, of all the times to tell me!" Pulling free, she looked down at her dirty coveralls. Lifted a foot to confirm that she was very definitely wearing rubber barn boots. "I'm a mess!"

"It must be true love, then." He smiled as she shot him a startled look. Brushing aside a loose strand of her hair, he wrapped his arm around her shoulders. His thumb brushed her cheek as his other hand slid into her hair, and he kissed her softly. "Love is not love which alters when it alteration finds," he quoted from Shakespeare's 116th sonnet.

"Or bends with the remover to remove," she whispered.

They quoted the rest of it together, finishing with, "If this be error and upon me proved, I never writ, nor no man ever loved."

Nestling close, Grace kissed his jaw. Allowed herself a moment of enjoyment, then drew back.

"I have to go." Her lips twisted in an apologetic smile.

He stole a final, knee-weakening kiss, then tucked her into a half-embrace at his side and walked her to her truck.

"You'll take care of her?"

"I'll even hold her hand while she tells her dad if she'll let me," he promised. Observing her slightly raised eyebrow, he chuckled. "Too much?"

"Not for me to say. Just read her cues." Grace lifted a shoulder and stole a kiss of her own.

"Right."

He was still standing there, watching her, when she looked in her rearview mirror. It made her giggle in a way that was completely unlike herself.

"You're awfully chipper for someone who's spent a long night tending sick horses." Mrs. Ivey twinkled at her as she handed her a towel.

"It's a beautiful day." Grace beat her own personal record for shortest shower, changed into spare clothes from her overnight bag, and, thanks to Neil's timely arrival, and had barely enough time to wolf down a container of Mrs. Ivey's generously donated yogurt.

Tag-teaming the appointments with Neil, they made it through the morning.

"Amy's got the afternoon whittled down to two simple appointments." Mrs. Ivey announced as the door closed behind the last customer.

"And at least I got a couple hours of sleep." Neil finished scrubbing his hands. "I promise, if anything gets tricky, I'll call you."

Laughing, Grace allowed them to herd her into the backroom for a nap. "Okay, okay. But wake me up in an hour. Any more than that and I'll have a headache as big as Alaska." Which would only be a few square miles worse than the one she already had.

"So like your dad." Mrs. Ivey handed her a container of pineapple-coconut water. "This will help head it off."

Chuckling, Grace took it gratefully. "One hour!" she reminded them as she closed the door behind her. Then, to be safe, she set an alarm on her phone.

"Hey, sleepyhead." Neil winked at her when she shuffled out an hour later. "Good news! Amy has rescheduled the rest of our appointments for tomorrow."

"Wow." The word turned into a yawn that stretched tight muscles clear down the sides of her neck, making her wince. There was definitely a heating pad in her future.

"We took a vote." Amy popped in from the front office. "Mrs. Ivey and I will prep things for tomorrow while you two take the rest of the day off."

"Hang on." Neil frowned. "Nobody asked me about this."

"Or me." Grace sectioned her hair with her fingers and began braiding it. "Besides, we got a shipment today that…"

"Never you mind." Mrs. Ivey breezed in from the breakroom. "Amy and I plan to lock the front door and order a large chicken and ranch pizza."

Grace's nose had wrinkled before she realized it and she quickly blanked her face. Nobody had complained about the options the Thursday when she'd made pizza for them, but she and Neil both agreed to preferring traditional red sauce.

"Well, when you put it like that." Neil grinned. "You at least have to let me stay long enough to move the heavy boxes, though." He flexed like a bodybuilder, cracking them all up.

"I can't leave you guys with all of this!" Grace declared.

"All of what?" Amy shrugged. "With no appointments to take care of, we'll be out of here in a couple of hours."

"While I do what, exactly?" Grace immediately wished she hadn't asked. Mrs. Ivey's expression shouted that she could think of a thing or two a single young woman could do.

"I don't know about you, boss, but I think I'll go for a run and then crash." Neil slung his coat over his shoulder. "If I'm up early tomorrow, I can always come in and do some paperwork."

"Right." Deciding that surrender was her best option, Grace slid into her own coat. Started for the door, then paused. "Amy?"

"Yeah, boss?" The girl grinned impishly as she mimicked Neil's tone.

"Charge the pizza to the clinic." She got in a wink of her own before stepping out into the crisp fall air. Inhaling deeply, she savored the smoky scent that foretold snow.

"Boss?" Neil took her elbow and walked with her to where their trucks were parked. "Do we know any more about how the mistletoe got into the stalls?"

Grace puffed up her cheeks and blew out a breath. "I know exactly how it got there." Pausing at her truck, she chewed on her lip while she studied Neil. "I trust you to keep this confidential. However, I don't know how it's going to affect you personally."

"Affect me?" Neil's face was a picture of confusion.

"She didn't mean any harm." Grace tried to ease the bandage off. "She just wanted some cute pictures with the horses."

Neil sagged against her truck. "Eddie."

"Yeah." Grace shoved her hands into her

pockets and flexed chilled fingers. "She's probably told her dad by now."

Neil's head jerked up. "Mr. Brooke! He'll..."

"He'll be fine." Grace cut him off and stared him down. "I don't know what Eddie's told you about him, but after knowing the man for over twenty years, I think I can safely say he'll do the right thing."

Neil raked his fingers through his short hair. "She says he doesn't care about her. That he treats her like an annoying puppy he has to take care of."

Grace looked away. "What do you think of her?" That was marginally more discreet than asking if Eddie had ever done anything to give her dad a different impression.

"Me?" His shoulders slumped. "I don't know."

"That's not a bad thing." Putting her hand on his arm, she squeezed it gently. "You met her what, two weeks ago?"

"Yeah, about." He kept his eyes on the toes of his shoes.

"So keep an open mind." Releasing him, she unlocked her truck. "She said she didn't mean to hurt them. And I believe her."

He took a deep breath. Gave her a tight smile and walked away. Passed his vehicle and kept right on walking.

Shaking her head, Grace got in her truck, where she turned on general conference to listen to on her drive home.

As sometimes happens after an emergency, the rest of the week was peaceful to the point of being dull. Until she drove out to the Rockin' R after work on Thursday.

"Eddie!" Lowering her window as she parked, Grace called out to the girl. Sliding out of her truck, she slammed the door shut and jogged over. "Wow, can I help you with that?"

"I got it." Eddie doggedly continued pushing the full wheelbarrow. She shot Grace a look when she fell in step beside her. "You come to check on the horses?"

"And you. Whoa!" Grace caught and steadied the girl when the overflowing wheelbarrow started to tip over.

"Ugh!!" Eddie dropped the handles and threw her arms out in frustration. "Why does it keep doing that!?!"

Grace spotted Alec leaning against the barn and waited a beat to see if he would come over, but he didn't bat an eyelash.

"The wheelbarrow is too full," she pointed out at last. The bits of scattered straw a few feet further along Eddie's path suddenly made sense.

"Full, of course it's full." Eddie stomped her foot. "And I'm still never going to finish!"

"Yes, you will." Grace caught and held her gaze.

"No I won't. I…" Eddie sniffled. "It falls over every time!"

"Eddie." Grace took her gently by the arm. "It's *too* full. If you only fill it to the top of the rim, the weight stays lower, is centered better, and easier to control."

"Really?" Eddie swiped at her nose with the back of a gloved hand and inhaled shakily. "That explains a lot."

Grace smiled. "Sure I can't help?"

Eddie seemed to hesitate. Then she shook her head. "I got this," she repeated.

Grace let her hand fall to her side as the stubborn young woman picked up the wheelbarrow handles and resumed her course. Shaking her head, she headed over to talk to Alec.

"Hey. What's up with…?" She stopped with a gasp when he pulled her in for a kiss.

"Hey yourself." Alec trailed a finger softly down her cheek. "How've you been, stranger?"

"Hmm." Flipping her hair over her shoulder, she teased, "That's the most unique way to greet a stranger I think I've ever seen."

His answer was to kiss her again, a leisurely kiss that left her breathless. "I got your text." He kissed her eyes, which didn't seem to want to open anyway. "And I have to work tomorrow."

With an effort, Grace dragged her focus to what he was saying. "I'm sorry to hear that."

"Can we go out tonight?" He suggested.

"Can't." Remembering that they were standing in the open where anyone could wander past and see them, she moved out of his arms. "I have a late appointment at the clinic."

"Oh." Disappointed, Alec ran his fingers through his hair. "That sounds like fun."

She managed a small smile even though she'd had her heart set on this date. Tipping her head toward the barn door she asked, "How're they doing?"

Hands in his pockets, he followed her at a professional distance. "Basically? Back to normal. We're still being careful of them…"

"Babying them, y'mean." Bart paused to shove a hand at her, which she happily shook. "Special training schedule, special food." He waved his free hand eloquently to cover the rest of it.

"Not a bad idea." Grace peered into a stall as she passed. Checked another. "They were in good health before, but being poisoned is a tough recovery." Which reminded her what she'd started to ask Alec.

Bart dropped his gaze. Cleared his throat. "Yeah."

Stepping into his space a little, Grace asked quietly, "How's Eddie?" That brought his eyes up and she searched them keenly. "I've been praying for her."

"Keep it up." Bart blinked suspiciously moist-looking eyes. "She's coping right now. That's about it."

"And the wheelbarrow?" She tried to look at them both at the same time while she waited for an answer.

"Hey, boss?" A voice rang through the barn. "Feed truck's here!"

"I've got it." Bart went to take care of the delivery.

After checking for listening ears, Alec quietly explained, "Eddie told her parents. They decided, as a family, that she needed to learn more about horses."

"From the ground up?" Grace covered her mouth with her hand. "That came out wrong."

Alec choked on a laugh. Hugged her.

"No, really, I didn't…"

"You're in serious danger of being kissed," he warned her.

"Ohhhkay." Moving out of range, she rubbed a hand over the back of her neck as she resumed checking stalls. "You should wear comfortable shoes. For our next date."

Intrigued, Alec prodded for more information. "Comfortable? As in hiking boots?"

She snickered. "Nice try."

He waited clear around the rest of the circuit. He answered her questions about the horses she checked and even carried her bag, though that was pretty much standard procedure for them. When it looked like she was about to head out, he asked, "Wait, that's it?"

"No." She quirked an eyebrow at him. "What're you doing on the 30th?"

"I…" He squinted at an invisible calendar.

"Two weeks from tomorrow?" Taking her bag from her, he set it in the bed of her truck and leaned in for a kiss, which she drew away from, eyebrows raised. "Danny's invited me out for Thanksgiving, but I can be back by that Saturday."

"Well." Grace tapped her fingers on his chest and chewed on her bottom lip. "I guess that'll have to do."

Chapter 17

At Noella's the next night, Grace chuckled to Merry as she listened to Harmony and Noella discussing ingredients. "Sounds like our Noella put her own spin on things."

"As always." Merry swallowed a bite of gingerbread, shot a glance at the others, then remarked in a lowered voice, "I'm worried about this year's Christmas play."

"What?" Grace's forehead furrowed. "Why?"

"Because the theater committee is sabotaging her at every turn."

Grace listened as she explained about having to replace the flyers for the Christmas charity play after someone claimed they had to be removed due to typos.

"So the flyers I've seen around town, those are the ones you put up?" Grace's frown deepened at Merry's nod. "Taking the first set down was a dirty trick."

"It gets worse." Checking again to make sure Noella was suitably distracted, Merry continued, "I practically had to twist arms to get the loan of one couch and one desk. And forget about a stage crew. Everyone's 'too busy.'"

Grace's lips quirked up. "I think I know where to find a stage crew." Casting her own glance in Noella's direction, she explained, "One of the…guests at the Rockin' R is majoring in theater. I don't know how much experience she's had with being boss, but I do know that she's got the entire male population of the ranch wound around her finger." Grace couldn't help the blush that sprang up at Merry's inquisitively raised eyebrow. Alec had a strict non-fraternizing rule and led by example. "Almost the entire population," she corrected herself, giving Merry a friendly shoulder shove.

"But if she's only going to be there over Thanksgiving break, she won't be here for the play. Poof, no more stage crew." Merry savored a bite of the gingerbread.

"Noooo." Grace hesitated. In her job as a country vet, Grace heard a variety of tales of woe and made it a solemn policy not to share them. From everything she'd seen lately, Eddie wasn't going anywhere anytime soon. "That's not it." Uneasily, she remembered that Eddie was home because she'd been expelled from yet another Ivy League college. What was she getting them all into?

"Okay." Merry hesitated, not liking the way Grace was rubbing her left palm on her jeans, an old nervous habit. "I guess it's worth a try—if she'll be around for the play."

"Let me ask her," Grace suggested abruptly. "I'll ask her the next time I see her."

"Ask who what?" Harmony asked, handing them each a plate of re-heated gingerbread men.

"I was telling Grace about our stage crew problem." Merry responded. "She knows someone she can ask to help out."

Grace appreciated Merry's diffident shrug. Hopefully they wouldn't get Noella's hopes up too high. Good grief, Eddie might say no!

"Magnificent!" Noella tried to clap her hands for joy and nearly spilled milk everywhere. "We have the theater. Most of the cast." She angled a sidelong glance at Harmony, who had eyes only for the serving tray of gingerbread cookies. "And maybe the stage crew. Yes. Very good!"

"Sounds like things are going great." Merry heaved a sigh of relief.

"Oui, but for one thing." Noella paused for a dramatic moment. "We have no draw." She'd found that word through an online translation system and now anxiously watched her friends' faces to see if she'd used it correctly.

"Draw? Like, a big name to draw in the crowds?" Grace half-guessed. Her experience with French didn't exactly extend to marketing, but in context that seemed the most likely interpretation.

"Exactly." Noella handed over the glasses of milk and plopped into her seat. "I hear the talk. Because Mrs. Arnold's children did not make the cast, the people will not come."

Grace put her foot lightly on top of Merry's, who looked close to violence.

"Of all the two-faced, double-dealing monsters,"

Merry growled. She smiled tightly at Grace and Harmony, who'd turned wide eyes toward her. "Mrs. Arnold is the committee chairwoman who sandbagged Noella at that meeting. Now she's upset that her 'little starlets,'" as the woman had often been heard to call her offspring, "didn't get three out of the five roles in the whole show?"

Grace rolled her eyes. "Sounds like her." She had her own experiences with the woman.

"I'll say," Harmony huffed. "Cadmia's queen bee strikes again." Mrs. Arnold had a long history of playing the town like a fiddle. Thanks to her vendetta against this play, not a single adult had auditioned. Which was why Noella wanted her and Grant to play the mom and dad, complete with a 'kiss and make-up' scene at the end. *Not* happening.

"It was one thing for her to turn the town against the idea of rezoning Fleischer's pasture for a mall," Grace remarked quietly. Privately, she was grateful for that bit of interference. "But the proceeds from the charity play go to paying for food, fuel, clothes, even Christmas presents for some of the families around here." Not to mention some of the pets in town.

"Maybe we need to remind people of that," Merry grumbled.

"How?" Noella stuck out her bottom lip. "The merchants, they have agreed to set up tables to sell tickets, but nobody buys them. I stopped at the newspaper office to beg them to write a story and they say it is old news. The churches, well, they buy a few tickets." She hesitated, her fingers fluttering. "That is where I hear about Mrs. Arnold."

"The play's only a couple of weeks away." Harmony bit her lip.

"But what draw is there that would counteract Mrs. Arnold?" Merry asked. "It's not like there's room in the play for," she waved vaguely.

"Helen Montgomery." Grace wondered why nobody else had thought of it. Although, from the way Merry was gaping at her, she might as well have suggested octopus wrestling.

"What?" Merry gulped.

"Helen Montgomery," Grace repeated uncertainly. "From what I can tell, she's all the rage right now."

"Yeah, she's popular." Harmony frowned. "But do you really think an indie singer is, well, spectacular enough to overcome the bee?"

"If we can get her to come, the teenagers will spend their own money to buy these tickets." At least, Grace knew of a few of them who would.

"This may be true." Noella's fingers fluttered descriptively as she added, "Everywhere I go, I hear the voice of this singer."

"The grocery store, the beauty salon, even the family-run restaurants are all playing her," Harmony agreed thoughtfully. "If you could get her, and that's a pretty big 'if,' she might put the play over."

"Wonder how much she'd charge?" Grace mused.

Merry frowned. "Who says she'll charge anything?"

Startled at the irritation in Merry's voice, Grace felt her antennae rising. Was it her imagination or was Merry anti-Helen Montgomery? And why?

"Oh, I dunno?" Grace shrugged. "She's a performer. I just assumed she would want some kind of compensation."

"We can always ask," Harmony pointed out. "Tell her it's a charity play, sort of a last minute emergency, and see what she says."

"Last minute is right." Merry shifted in her seat. "She probably has big plans with family by now." Her eyes fastened on Harmony, who was typing on her phone. "What're you doing?"

"Asking Helen Montgomery to sing in our play." Harmony didn't sound optimistic, but she did hit send.

Grace's attention came sharply to Merry, whose phone dinged right then.

"What?" Merry asked them all.

Grace's eyes narrowed, but she held her peace. Besides, what would she have said? *Are you Helen Montgomery?*

"Nothing…" Harmony frowned. "That was some weird timing, though." Her left eyebrow went up as if to ask, *Wasn't it?*

Oblivious, Noella clapped her hands. "This is wonderful! Helen will say yes. The play, it will be a success. And everyone will have a merry Christmas."

Grace opened her mouth to warn her that nothing was that easy, but Noella had already started the movie. And, though Grace did her best to pay attention, she couldn't help being nervous about asking for Eddie's help. The play wasn't until after Thanksgiving. How long could, um, *should* she wait to ask?

It was only the community center, so they'd wouldn't need much of a stage crew; four, maybe five, people. Someone to handle the sound, someone to manage the lights…props…and… Well, the others might have to take tickets or ride herd on a case of water bottles, but they'd feel involved, right?

Loud applause came from the TV, drawing her into the movie just in time for a dramatic auction scene. Amused at the way things turned out, Grace leaned over to whisper to Merry, but changed her mind when she saw the white line around her friend's mouth.

Wait, what was going on with her tonight? Had something gone wrong with Tyrel? No, that didn't seem to fit. She'd seemed intent on Noella's situation until…

"Okay." Harmony mock-swooned as the end credits rolled. "*That* was a kiss."

They all burst out laughing, even Merry. But

this wasn't her carefree, 'I've only got movies on my mind' laugh. Before Grace could figure out how to ask if something was wrong, Merry had gotten up and started collecting dishes.

Casually, Grace snagged the last empty glass and followed her into the kitchen. "That's a lovely shade of pink you're wearing," she whispered as she came up beside a lightly blushing Merry.

Merry flicked a glance at where Noella and Harmony were talking animatedly about the auction scene from the movie.

"Wow. Tyrel must be doing something right." Grace tested her earlier deduction by opening the door marked 'boyfriend.'

Merry's eyes narrowed. "How're things with Alec?" Score! Grace's fair skin betrayed her instantly. "This is good, right?"

"It's something." Grace blew out a breath. "Complicated. Yeah, that's it." What else could it be after seventeen years of being first invisible, then a colleague? Except she hadn't come over to talk about herself. If Merry wasn't upset about Tyrel, then maybe… "Enough about me. You better answer Harmony's email."

Concerned, she put her hand on Merry's arm when the other woman stopped breathing. Good grief, had she guessed right?!

"Hey, what do you two think?" Harmony's voice called to them.

"What do we think about what?" Grace squeezed Merry's arm and gently dragged her over to where the others still sat.

"We were talking about working Helen into the story," Harmony explained. "There's no room for another character, so I think she should play the mom." That sounded plausible, right? She'd already tried and failed to convince Noella to do it. Opposite Danny, of course.

"Ridiculous." Noella flapped a hand at her. "You wish only to avoid the role for yourself."

"Which means you have a different plan." Grace interpreted, mostly to cover for the fact that Merry was sitting silently beside her. And to banish the weird image of Merry—still assuming she was Helen—acting out a kiss-and-makeup scene.

"Helen will sing the Christmas music." Noella beamed at them, terribly pleased with herself. "The mother listens to music while she works. They all listen to music at the end. Voila. It is perfect."

"I don't know," Merry objected. "It's a two hour-long play. You want her to, what, stand stock still on stage for that long?"

Grace did her best not to wince at Merry's too-loud protest. That clinched it, though. Her best friend, Merry McKinney, was none other than the popular indie singer Helen Montgomery. But how? When? And so many other questions!

Noella's brows knit together. "No, that would not do. We will have to give her a chair. She can stand whenever she is to sing. With a spotlight."

"Then fade into the background again when the spotlight switches to the others." Grace suggested, thinking that might make things easier on Merry. "That might work."

"Yeah," Merry agreed halfheartedly.

"Alright." Grace wrapped Noella in a hug. "Enough plotting for one night." Straightening, she smiled at her hostess. "Thanks for having us over."

"Yes." Merry followed suit, hugging first Noella, then Harmony, who'd risen to hug Grace. "And the delicious gingerbread."

"I better go, too." Harmony collected a hug from Noella. "My place for a musical next time!" They skipped movie nights on weeks with major holidays, so that meant she was free until December sixth. Hmm. Maybe she should plan another getaway?

"Can't wait," Grace assured her. Catching Merry's eye as they all sorted out scarves and coats, she gave her the slightest of nods.

"Night!" Merry headed outside.

Grace followed suit, high-tailing it out to her truck and over to Blinky's.

Cadmia's one-and-lonely diner, Blinky's prided itself on its 'vintage' decor. A counter ran in an L-shape around the center of the room, allowing a peek into the food prep area and offering a row of uncomfortable vinyl stools for the customers who wanted a soda, a sandwich, or even gossip a la carte.

Whether they intended the atmosphere to extend to 'vintage odors' was unknown, but a wave of greasy, stale air pushed its way out the door as Grace let herself in. It was like trying to breathe through a mask made of old onion rings.

"Gracie!" Susan, the manager and owner's daughter, waved at her from behind the counter.

"Hey, Susan." Out of habit, Grace stepped only on the black diamonds as she made her way over. "Looks like you're keeping busy."

"Are you kidding?" Susan traded two order slips for a takeout box and stepped up to the register without missing a beat. "If we were any busier, I'd need two of me!"

Grace politely joined in the laughter while scoping out the booths in the back. This being a Friday, there wasn't much more than a square inch between teenagers, so she wasn't surprised to find all the booths occupied.

"Waiting on Merry?" Susan guessed, collecting correct change from the drawer.

"Yeah." Grace made a show of checking the time on the diner's one, massive clock. Deciding to play it dumb, she asked, "How'd you know?"

"She just pulled in." Susan grinned from ear to ear. "We've got some nice trout on special today. Interested?"

Grace shook her head more vigorously than she'd intended. "I think we'll probably stick with hot chocolate tonight." Trout was easily her least favorite, most fishiest fish.

"You got it." Susan patted her hand, waved to someone behind her, and meandered toward the counter. Nobody came to Blinky's strictly for the hot chocolate. What these two were really after was a private conversation.

Turning to face Merry, Grace gestured for her to take the lead. The tension in Merry's shoulders, not to mention the light sheen of perspiration on her forehead, told Grace a lot. As did the fact that she slid into a booth that hadn't been properly wiped down since the last customer's left, presumably because it was the furthest away from the noisy groups.

Watching Merry's eyes close, Grace took the bench opposite and offered her own silent prayer to know how to help her friend. They still hadn't gotten around to speaking to each other before Susan arrived.

"Here's your hot chocolate." Susan plunked the mugs onto the table. Waved a can of whipped cream at them. "Any takers?"

Still trying to act like this was an ordinary girls' night out, Grace cheerfully held up her mug for a heaping helping. Then, as soon as Susan was out of earshot, Grace set her mug down and took Merry's cold hands in hers.

"You know I won't tell anyone." That was their deal. Merry trusted her with secrets because Grace never told. She felt Merry's fingers flex under her own. Watched her eyes slowly lift so they were looking at each other directly.

"I know."

Grace sagged with relief at Merry's statement. It had taken a lot longer than usual for her to say that!

"I…I don't like…"

Sensing that she was struggling, Grace gently observed, "You always liked your secrets. I'm sorry I teased you at Noella's." She was rewarded with a small smile.

"Thanks."

"Of course."

"How did you know?"

"I'm not sure." Grace shook her head. She'd recalled other things on her drive over that made the connection seem blindingly obvious now. "The way you react whenever she comes on or gets brought up. All the years we spent singing while we pulled weeds and hauled wood. I guess I just know you."

Merry groaned. "If it's that's all it takes, I'm in serious trouble."

Grace laughed softly. "No, I don't think so." Faced with Merry's confused scowl, she shrugged. "I was also in the right place at the right time tonight."

"What you're saying is," Merry's shoulders slumped, "I could've played dumb and gotten away with it."

"Pretty much." Giving her hands a light squeeze, Grace released them and reached for her mug again. "Susan preps this to coffee temps," she warned.

Merry managed half a chuckle. "I always forget that." Wrapping her fingers around the mug, she stared at it for several long seconds. "I can't do what they want me to."

"Not even with help?" Grace offered. Merry's eyes met hers for an instant, then returned to the mug as if it was absolutely fascinating. That was hardly a flat refusal. So… Leaning on her elbows, Grace asked, "What would you need to pull this off?"

Merry shook her head, then shrugged so Grace wouldn't misinterpret that as a 'no.'

"Does anyone know what, um…?" Grace glanced around casually, but no one was paying attention to them. "What she looks like?"

"There's a picture on her website." Merry blew on the hot chocolate and tried a cautious sip. Set the mug back on the table with a disappointed sigh.

"Okay, let's see." Grace tugged out her phone and ran a search. Locating the photo, she tapped on it to enlarge it. "Whoa." A woman with hair brighter and redder than her own stared out from behind severely rectangular glasses that made her square jaw seem heavier than it was. She squinted at the image, looked at Merry, then at the picture again. "If I didn't know this was you…" Grace pursed her lips. "This could work."

Merry straightened slightly. "What're you

thinking?"

"First, let's see the email." Grace put her phone away and Merry got hers out.

Together, they skimmed the email and Merry shook her head. "There's hardly any information in this."

"Yeah, I don't think Harmony expects *her* to say yes," Grace agreed.

After Merry typed up a short response, Grace gave it a quick once-over to make sure it didn't give anything away, and then they spent an hour quietly scheming how to bring Helen to life for the charity play performances.

Susan's curiosity must've gotten the better of her, because she brought over a second round of hot chocolate—on the house—but Grace glibly switched the conversation to a story of a heifer currently staying at her practice and Susan went away as mystified as before.

Merry's phone buzzed in the middle of the tale and she slid it over so Grace could read it, too.

"Yes, that's better." Grace nodded as she read. "Dates, times, and how 'bout that, an address for the community center." Clasping her hands together, she proposed, "I wouldn't accept right away. I mean, you were right. She most likely has holiday plans and will need to check her schedule."

"So I should say no?"

"Do you really want to?" Grace couldn't ignore the hope that sprang up in Merry's eyes at the idea of finding a way off the hook. Getting up on a stage would be cruel torture for her.

Merry traced a figure eight in the crumbs, then shrugged. "They made it sound like having her come was pretty important."

Grace sternly warned herself against saying anything. She'd support Merry either way—once she made her own decision.

"Let's keep things open." Merry scrubbed her hand over her face. "In case they're right."

"You got it." Smiling, Grace helped her write a reply that was optimistic but made no promises.

"And maybe we should sleep on it?" Merry teased as Grace's face nearly split with a yawn.

"Sound idea." Grace nodded, winking. "Let's do it."

Chapter 18

"We're almost there." Grace chuckled as Alec reached for a non-existent steering wheel. Again. It was as if he'd been driving himself for so long he'd forgotten how to be just a passenger.

Shifting slightly, Alec willed his hands to stay in his lap. "You still haven't told me where we're going." Not that he really cared. It had been a long two weeks of phone calls and stolen moments when their paths crossed. Their date could've been a walk down the Rockin' R's driveway and he'd have been thrilled to be with her. Especially after what he'd learned about Danny and Noella over Thanksgiving.

"You'll see." Slowing, she signaled for a turn. "Right about…now." Pulling into a driveway, she slowed in case the dogs were running loose as usual. Three of the friendliest mutts in the county lived here and she didn't want to accidentally run over one of them.

"What's this?" Leaning forward, Alec craned his neck to see better. A snug farm house, white with a brilliant green trim, waited at the end of the driveway. A medium-sized barn and a few outbuildings supported the house, but gave him no inkling as to what they were doing there.

"Let's go inside and find out," she suggested, shifting into park and turning off the engine. Thank goodness the dogs were put away. And sleeping, apparently, because she hadn't heard any barking.

She waited for him at the front of the truck, then slipped her arm around his waist as they mounted the steps to the front door. His arm came naturally around her shoulders and it felt like coming home.

Alec let her enter first, then followed, thoroughly perplexed. "Grace?"

"C'mon." Catching his hand, she tugged at it. "The kitchen's through here."

He could've found it simply by following his nose. A smallish, oval table dominated the left center of the room, and was set with what looked like 'the company dishes.' On the right side of the kitchen was a well-loved stove, an industrial-sized sink, and miles of countertop—part of which was laden with covered serving dishes.

"It smells amazing in here!"

"That's because Lila Talbot is the best hobby chef in the county." Grace put on an oven mitt. "We'll have to serve ourselves, though."

Sniffing one of the pots that had a small splash of marinara sauce on its rim, Alec belatedly remembered his resolution to watch his weight. After stuffing himself at Danny's on Thanksgiving, he'd suddenly developed an acute awareness of a…soft spot around his middle. A lot of men his age had a paunch, but somehow he didn't find that at all comforting. Especially not when he was dating a beautiful woman.

"We have a lovely garden salad. Penne rosa with baked chicken, fresh-baked garlic bread, and…" Catching Alec watching her instead of the food, she lowered her eyes in confusion.

Crossing the kitchen to her, Alec pulled her firmly to him. Threading his fingers through her hair, he felt as if the heat from her red curls was coursing through his veins. Tilting her head back, he claimed her for a kiss.

Grace lingered in his arms, palms flat against his cheeks, cherishing the moment.

"Sometimes," he said huskily, "you have to start with dessert." He could've gone on kissing her until the food faded into oblivion, but reminded himself that he needed to take things slow. So instead, he swept her off her feet and deposited her in a chair at the table. "My name is Alec." He brushed his lips across her forehead, then straightened and began unbuttoning his cuffs so he could roll up his sleeves. "And I'll be your waiter this evening."

It wasn't quite how she'd planned for things to go, but he kept her so busy laughing and talking that she forgot all about plans in favor of enjoying their time together.

"Mmm." He polished off his piece of chocolate silk pie with a contented sigh. "I don't know how you stay in business when you let people pay their vet bills with food, but this was one of the most amazing meals I've ever had."

"I'll be sure to tell Lila." Grace had opted for the lemon chiffon pie since it was Lila's specialty. The Talbot's struggle with money was real, so she'd been glad to come up with this alternative to writing off their debt, which would've hurt their pride. And, of course, there was the main event still to come.

"You know, there's something I still don't understand about this date." Rising, Alec took their plates and silverware over to the dishwasher, which he'd been unobtrusively loading as the meal progressed.

"What's that?" Grace drained her water glass and followed him with a few more dishes.

"I believe you stipulated that I should wear comfortable shoes."

"Oh." Grace retreated to the table before he could mistake her blush as an invitation for another kiss. "That's for after dinner."

Collecting the last of the dishes, Alec frowned. What in the world?

Grace started the dishwasher, then took him by the hand. With her free hand, she queued up a music app on her phone. Unlike the somewhat cramped kitchen, the spacious front room sacrificed only a small amount of floor space to a couch and a single rocking chair.

Setting her phone on the mantle above the fireplace, Grace started the playlist.

A slow smile spread across Alec's face as he recognized a waltz. "Grace Myers, you're a romantic." Bowing slightly, he offered her his hand. Her bare ring finger seemed to call to him, whispering that he needed to do something about it.

They whirled and twirled and moved to the music in delightful unison. From a waltz to a two-step, then a cha-cha, and finally, a foxtrot.

As she slowly spun into his arms again, Alec chose to ignore the next song in favor of holding her tightly.

"I had a long talk with Danny." Brushing a loose strand of hair out of her face, he struggled to know how to proceed. He'd prayed most of the way back from Danny's, but that was the easy part. "I think he and Noella are getting pretty serious." That was something of an understatement, but he'd promised to let Noella tell her friends herself.

"Hmm." Grace swayed to the music with him, wondering where this conversation was going. She hadn't expected to discuss someone else's dating. "He must be a fast mover. They've only known each other about a month."

"Unlike me. I was so set in my ways." Alec's mouth twisted wryly. "I'm still not sure what I'm doing here, with you in my arms." Kissing her forehead softly, he pressed his cheek against her temple. "I'm absolutely not sure I deserve a second chance at an eternal marriage and children."

"Is that why it was so hard for you to ask me out?" Grace gently wiped a tear from his cheek.

He managed a surprised laugh, then a nod. "That and I was scared to death." They laughed together at that.

"Me, too." Grace admitted, suddenly shy.

"Really?" He performed an exaggerated sway to his right, then dipped her to his left. Kept her there. "I never knew."

"You weren't supposed to." She dredged up enough courage to add, "But I've wanted you for a long time, Alec Fitzsimmons. You and everything you just mentioned."

Straightening, he twirled her away from him, then brought her in again. Holding her tightly, he guided her through a series of easy spins that took them around the edge of the entire room.

Reluctantly, she stopped in front of the fireplace. "The Talbot's will be home soon."

She wondered if the spell would break as they left the cozy home. And as they waited in the bitter cold for her engine to warm. If anything, the rest of their time together enhanced the glow of the evening.

"I was wondering," he threaded his fingers through hers, "if you'd like to go to the Christmas play with me." Her hand twitched and he looked over to find her staring very hard at nothing. "Grace?"

"I, um…" Oh, crud. She couldn't possibly betray Merry's secret. "Did you know Noella's in charge of it this year?"

"Yes, she mentioned it."

"Well, I volunteered to talk to Eddie," Grace said hurriedly, "and ask if she'd oversee the stage crew."

"Stage crew?" Alec rubbed his thumb across the back of her knuckles. "Uh-oh. I foresee my employees being volunteered." He wiggled teasingly suspicious eyebrows at her.

"So do I," she hooted. Squeezing his fingers, she apologetically explained, "I'll most likely be volunteered to help, too." She hadn't thought as far ahead as the actual play, but she could guarantee Merry would need her support. She'd be perfectly positioned for that as part of the stage crew.

"In that case, I volunteer, too."

"Oh, uh…" Probably should've seen that coming? She chewed on her lip while she shifted into gear. "That might work." She doubted it, though. Not only could Alec be highly distracting, she didn't want to lie to him. Which she would almost certainly have to do under the circumstances.

"You don't want me to help?" He was genuinely surprised. And possibly hurt.

"What? No. I…" *C'mon, think of something!*

"So. What aren't you telling me?"

She blew out a breath and muttered, "There goes any hope of my ever arranging a surprise party for you."

"I hate surprise parties." He drummed his fingers on his leg briefly. Made a decision. "You don't have to tell me."

"What?"

"You don't have to tell me," he repeated.

"Thank you." She was still trying to figure out what had happened when he spoke again.

"I'm as curious as a cat who can't see what they're hearing, but…" He shrugged. "I'll live." A slow smile spread across his face as she burst into laughter.

"You are terrible!"

"Thank you." He loved the sound of her laugh, and managed to keep her at it for the rest of the drive by throwing out ridiculous guesses. "So." Her truck had stopped in front of his trailer, prompting him to unfasten his seat belt. "It's not a live elephant." He slid closer. "Or a juggling robot."

"Or a one-man band." She leaned in to share a kiss—and saw movement by the barn. "Is that…Eddie?"

Alec reluctantly turned to look as well. "I don't see anything."

"Well, she must've gone inside. That was definitely her, though." Unbuckling, Grace reached for her door handle.

"Before you vanish…" Alec slid out a split second behind her, trapping her between his outstretched arms and the truck. "I just wanted to say thank you for a wonderful evening."

Grace covered her mouth with her hands as her face flamed. "Oh, Alec, I'm sorry!" Her hands left her mouth and reached for him, coming to rest on his chest. "I didn't… I mean, I saw her and I remembered that I needed to…" She ran out of things to say when he took her hands in his.

"I've always admired your hands, Doc." He pressed a kiss to her palm that weakened her knees. "So strong. So capable. So gentle." He ran his thumb and forefinger up and down her left ring finger. "I've noticed you never wear jewelry."

Realizing he was waiting for a response, Grace swallowed hard, forcing her heart down into her chest where it belonged. Managed a shaky smile.

"There are too many things jewelry can get caught on. It's something my dad taught me." Her breath caught when he pressed a kiss to her other palm. "He didn't wear his wedding ring until he retired."

"I remember." He nodded. "Speaking of wedding rings." He stopped when she looked up at him, her eyes probing his. "You strike me as the sort of woman who likes simplicity. Who might prefer a ring that's practical as well as beautiful."

"I've never really thought about it." Grace didn't know why not, but she hadn't. Her fear that that was the wrong answer faded when he smiled.

"I love you." He tucked her hand into the

crook of his arm and walked her as far as the barn door. "I had an amazing time tonight." Stealing a final kiss, he discreetly took himself off.

Her heart was so full that it ached as she watched him disappear into the shadows. She might've dreamed of winning Alec's love, but she never could've anticipated the joy that would come with each moment of it.

With an effort, she drug her eyes from where she'd seen him last and went off in search of Eddie.

The main barn housed only horses, so unless Eddie's chore list had her soaping saddles and polishing stirrups at nine o'clock at night… And there she was, scratching Acorn's glossy brown neck.

Oh, blast. Acorn tossed her mane and whickered as soon as she saw Grace.

"Hey." Grace lifted a hand to Eddie, who had started guiltily. "Mind if I join you?" She took Eddie's one-shouldered shrug as an invitation. "You're out here awfully late." Another shrug preceded an explanation.

"Had to get out of the house." Acorn was nibbling on her hair, so Eddie found a ponytail holder in her pocket and tied it back. "Mom's been watching or reading something, I dunno what exactly, but she's in an organizing frenzy."

"Oh, fun." Grace couldn't decide whether organizing would be easier or harder with maids.

Eddie made a face. "The worst part is that

when Mom's done with her stuff, she's probably going to come after mine."

"Oh." Grace made a face of her own. "Any chance you could head her off?"

"Head her off? How?" Eddie's eyebrows drew together.

Grace puffed her cheeks. "Maybe you could go through your own stuff? Pick out the clothes you're done with, that sort of thing. And make sure you add it to her things while she's watching."

"That might work." Eddie nodded slowly. "Of course, it's too early for clothes.

"Too early?"

"Mhmm." Eddie tickled under Acorn's chin. "I think she's going through her books right now. Won't start sorting clothes until sometime next week according to this schedule she's following."

"I see." Watching Eddie interact with Acorn made Grace smile. "How's she doing?" she asked, running a practiced eye over the mare even as she stroked the silken neck. Acorn, a Clydesdale cross, was as big as a small shed and mellow as a sun-ripened pear.

"Okay, I guess."

"You guess?" Grace smiled. "Want me to take a look?" Thank goodness she'd opted to wear slacks!

Eddie perked a little. "Would you?"

"Sure." Grace kept the exam short for everyone's sake, but at the end she smiled and reached up to pat Acorn's withers. "She's in great shape."

"Will she be ready for the stud on time?"

Surprised, Grace evaded the question as she let herself out of the stall. "I didn't know you were interested in your father's breeding program."

"I wasn't." Eddie's lip trembled. "Except—while we were talking, Dad told me we could be grateful I hadn't waited until closer to Christmas."

A knife twisted in Grace's gut at the thought of over a dozen expectant broodmares with mistletoe poisoning. "There's a lot to know about horses," Grace inserted gently.

"Yeah." Lowering her hands, Eddie stuck them awkwardly in her pockets. "I'm learning, though."

"That's great." Grace leaned against the stall door, wondering how to bring up Noella's problem. "Guess that's going to keep you pretty busy."

"Bart says I've finally mastered how to clean a stall." Eddie couldn't seem to help rolling her eyes at that. "So we're moving on to grooming and tack."

"There's always work to do." Grace responded to Acorn's nudge by petting her. "I have a request to make, actually."

Eddie drew her arms up until they were around her stomach, as if to shield herself. "Yeah?"

"Yeah." Grace tried to keep a brisk tone despite the pang she felt at Eddie's uncertainty. "A friend of mine is in charge of the Christmas charity play this year and she's got a major problem we think you can help with."

Eddie's shoulders straightened slightly. "Me?"

"You've done some theater, haven't you?" Grace waited only for her nod, then plowed ahead. "The play's about three weeks away and she doesn't have a stage crew."

"Seriously?" Eddie blurted the word. Dropping her eyes, she shuffled her feet. "I mean. The, uh, the stage crew's pretty important."

"And you have experience with that, right?" Grace ignored the outburst, though she was impressed at Eddie's efforts to moderate herself.

"Some." Eddie frowned. "I don't know if I could handle one of Mrs. Arnold's elaborate shows, though. I remember one year when she used every colored light the community center had. And another year…"

"Mrs. Arnold isn't running the show this year." Grace couldn't believe how good that sounded. She hadn't realized exactly how irritating she found the woman until just that moment.

"She's not?" Eddie leaned against the stall door, too. "I'd like to help. If I can."

"Fantastic." Grace gave Acorn a parting pat. "Is it alright if I give my friend your phone number? She'll call you, probably tomorrow, and you two can talk it over."

Eddie bit her lip. "She needs a whole stage crew? Doesn't have anybody lined up at all?"

"Not yet," Grace agreed. "But from what I've heard the sets are super straightforward. The biggest job will probably be working the sound system."

Eddie's nose wrinkled spontaneously. "Whoever put that in probably stood on a brontosaurus' head instead of a ladder," she joked.

Grace laughed out loud, startling Acorn. "Shhh, shhh." She held her hand out to the prancing mare. "Stop being such a drama queen."

Acorn nodded her head enthusiastically, then came over and nosed Grace's hand.

"She wants a carrot," Eddie deduced. "Can she have one?"

"Mmmm." Grace wanted to say yes. "How many has she had today?"

Eddie looked to one side, then up. "Ummm…"

"That many?" Grace winked. "We better not."

Eddie smiled shyly.

"Thanks for being willing to help." Grace offered her hand, something she couldn't remember having the opportunity to do before with Eddie.

"Thanks for asking." Eddie's shake was firm, her gaze steady.

Chapter 19

A week before the play, Grace turned off Christmas carols as she pulled up in front of Merry's house. The workshop door was unlocked, so she let herself in.

"Merry!" She shouted to be heard. "You're covered in wood dust!"

"I'm a carpenter," Merry retorted even as she lowered the sander guiltily. "That's an occupational hazard."

"Uh-huh." Grace cocked an eyebrow at her.

"Okay, okay." Merry began putting things away. "Everything's ready upstairs. I'll be there in a minute."

"You better hurry," Grace warned, pointing at the enormous clock on the far wall as she started up the steps. "Tyrel will be here soon."

"He's seen me like this before," Merry muttered.

Grace almost fell off the stairs. "He *has?*" Hustling over to Merry, she coughed and waved at the slowly settling sawdust. "Tell me the truth, Merry. Are you sabotaging yourself?" Merry's low self-esteem sometimes caused her to try to prevent good things from happening, no matter how badly she wanted them to. And in the past she'd expressed strong doubts that she deserved anything as wonderful as true love.

Merry took Grace by the arm and walked her

over to the stairs where she could breathe. "No, I'm not. I mean." She tugged nervously at the end of her braid. "Maybe I wanted to the first time, but it didn't work." Gesturing at her woodshop, she explained, "He loves that I do all of this."

"Yeah?" Grace gently shoulder-bumped her friend. If that was true, well, she might have to approve of Tyrel marrying her best friend.

"Yeah." Merry took her dust mask off, revealing a patch of bare skin in the sawdust dessert that was her face.

"I'm happy for you." Grace caught the sleeve of Merry's shirt and gave it a little shake. "Now hurry. A man like that deserves to see you all prettied up once in a while, too."

Merry's cheeks colored, but for once she didn't argue.

Hurrying upstairs, Grace hung up her things and stepped out of her shoes. As she started to turn toward the kitchen, she stopped and…stared.

"You have a Christmas tree," she announced inanely when Merry joined her. A tree with genuine crystal baubles, miniature soldiers, birds of all colors, huge Christmas lights, and a six-sided star on top that looked like it was made of fine glass. Actually, it was kind of hard to see the smallish tree behind all the decorations.

"I know." Merry rubbed her forearm. "Tyrel wanted one."

Grace nodded slowly. "Good for Tyrel." She liked him more by the minute. Merry usually shrugged off getting a tree, claimed it was 'silly to get one for just me.' Translation: silly to waste the time and effort on herself. Silly goose. "It's really pretty."

"Thanks." Merry hastily pressed a finger under her nose to stifle a sneeze. "I gotta get changed before I accidentally start dusting in reverse."

Laughing, Grace waved her off and turned her attention to the kitchen. A pressure cooker sat on one counter, the light indicating a 'stay warm' setting. A glance at the remaining items on the counter made her laugh—a can of chicken, a bottle of Alfredo sauce, and a bag of frozen peas.

"Exactly like when we were in college." Shaking her head, she began setting three places on the island in the kitchen's center.

Grace busied herself with the lettuce, only pausing long enough to buzz in Tyrel, Merry's boyfriend, when he arrived.

"Hey." Long and lank, Tyrel hung his things beside hers. He was the one exception to Merry's 'no shoes' policy because of his prosthetic and he took extra care when he wiped his shoes on the mat, trying to get all the melting snow off them before he stepped onto the hardwood floor.

"Hey yourself." Grace sliced into a tomato. "You ready?"

"Sort of." Tyrel ran his fingers through his dark hair. "Explain this to me once more?"

Grace left the tomato long enough to check the stairs to Merry's bedroom. "You may have noticed that Merry doesn't handle compliments very well."

One side of his mouth quirked up. "Now that you mention it."

"So how do you think she'll react to being up on stage during the play?"

He shook his head. "She'll forget to breathe." His voice roughened with concern. "She'll pass out in front of over a hundred people and everyone will find out that she's Helen Montgomery."

"After which she'll change her name legally and drop off the face of the earth," Grace predicted.

"Point taken." Tyrel pumped soap onto his hands.

"So the plan is to lay it on thick tonight in the hopes that it desensitizes her for the play." Grace wiped her hands and began peeling the hard boiled eggs. "Just like preparing a horse for a parade."

Tyrel snorted. "That's a thought."

Grace flinched. "I didn't mean it like that." Biting her lip, she handed him an egg to rinse under the already-running tap. "We've been best friends since we were kids. I don't want to see her get hurt and this is the only way I know to protect her."

"Because she has to do this play, right?" His tone underscored the implied obligation.

Grace cocked her head at him and paused in handing him yet another egg. "You don't want her to perform?"

He met her gaze directly. "She made up her own mind. Under the circumstances, it's my job to support her."

"The circumstances?" Grace was unabashedly intrigued.

Tyrel half-grinned, half-grimaced. He'd already spoken with Merry's parents and met her family—yet somehow he wasn't surprised that he'd have to pass muster with her best friend, too.

Much to Grace's disappointment, Merry chose that moment to come down from her room. However, the way she lit up at the sight of Tyrel told Grace more than he ever could've.

"Ty."

"There she is." Tyrel scanned Merry appreciatively and winked, whereupon she promptly ran into a chair.

Wincing in empathetic pain, Grace focused on adding the tomato chunks to the salad.

"Oh." Merry twisted her hands together as she eyed the nearly completed dinner preparations. "Who's hungry?"

"I'm starving," Tyrel announced.

"Food's ready!" Grace felt a twinge of jealousy as the two of them shared an amused look that spoke of an inside joke. That would take some getting used to. Wiping her hands on a towel, she smiled at Merry. "Which do you want first?"

Merry paled slightly, but answered, "Let's get this over with."

Nodding, Grace joined them in the living room. Spun all the way around and pressed both hands to her cheeks. "Helen Montgomery!"

Merry froze like the proverbial deer in the headlights while Grace played it up, even going so far as to ask for her autograph on an imaginary program. She insisted on playing it through, too, not dropping the act until Merry had stiffly asked if she had a pen and 'signed.'

Tyrel's approach was less dramatic. "Miss Montgomery!" He offered his hand and calmly proceeded to pump hers. "I sure do appreciate you coming out all this way to Cadmia, I sure do. Must be awful hard on you, being away from family like this, and I…"

Grace hid a grin behind her hand as he gave a credible imitation of Toliver Beaumont, Cadmia's solemn bank president.

Merry sent her a pleading look and she called, "Time!" They spent a few minutes brainstorming how Merry could politely retrieve her hand, then tried it again.

When she saw that Merry was starting to relax marginally, Grace stepped it up a notch.

"I love her lyrics," Grace gushed to Tyrel.

"She writes the most meaningful songs!"

"You're not wrong," Tyrel chimed in. "But for me, it's all about her voice. Soft, kind of husky." He expressed the rest of his thought via a wolf whistle.

"Enough." Merry got up and walked away from them. Circled the kitchen island twice, then returned to her living room. "I can't do this." They both opened their mouths and she threw up her hands. "Look at me! Tell me I'm not beet red."

Grace chuckled. "I wouldn't say *beet* red. More magenta." She slanted a look at Tyrel. "Although, when he whistled, I think I saw a hint of scarlet…"

Merry buried her face in her hands. "This isn't going to work."

Grace watched in mild shock as Tyrel rose and wrapped Merry in a hug.

"Why don't you go upstairs and put on your disguise?" he suggested. "I'll prep the chicken pasta and Grace can finish the salad while you're gone."

"Okay."

"Pretty smooth," Grace observed once Merry was out of ear shot.

"Like I said." He headed into the kitchen. "I'll support her."

"Things must be getting serious between you two."

His response was to open the cupboards and

retrieve a bowl for the pasta. The correct cupboard. On the first try. Grace knew a few teenagers who couldn't do that in their own homes!

She let him get away with ignoring the question until she'd finished with the eggs. "Are you planning on a spring wedding?"

He cocked an eyebrow at her from where he was stirring the pasta sauce into the cooked noodles. "I wonder if Merry needs your help."

She folded her arms across her chest and poked the bear. "Meaning you don't?"

"Meaning exactly that," he answered dryly. He'd propose when he thought they were both ready and not before.

"Have it your own way." She pretended to huff her way over to the stairs, but could tell from the way he was shaking his head that he didn't believe her. Well, how about that. Maybe he was the right man for Merry after all!

"Come in." Merry answered her light knock.

"Tyrel kicked me out of the kitchen," she announced glibly as she wandered into the bathroom where Merry was. "So I thought I'd see how you were doing."

She bit back an exclamation of surprise when she got her first glimpse. Thank goodness she'd seen the website picture, or she'd have keeled right over. Never in her life had she met someone with hair red enough to rival her own!

As calmly as she could, she examined Merry's makeup critically. "Hmm."

"What? Am I breaking out?"

"Pfft, no," Grace laughed. "I was thinking about the lighting. Your look is perfect for a casual date night, but I'm afraid you're going to disappear on stage." Thankfully, Eddie had agreed to boss the stage crew, including the lighting, prop management, and… "Oh, have a heart," she groaned, suddenly realizing how Merry had perked up at the idea of disappearing. "It's for charity, remember? The audience will expect to be able to see you."

"Fine." Merry sighed. "But I don't have to like it."

Grace dissolved into laughter, for which she received a dark glare. "Wow." Grace inhaled deeply and fanned her eyes. She hadn't laughed that hard for a long while. "Hmm. Let's head downstairs before he comes up after us."

Tugging Merry to her feet, Grace gently herded her downstairs, where the next big test waited. How would he react? On second thought, maybe he'd already seen Merry in her makeup? Hang on. There was something…wrong with Merry's clothes. She couldn't put her finger on it, though.

"Just in time, ladies." Pulling out two stools with a flourish, he looked up and stared. "Wow."

"Is that my phone?" It wasn't, but Grace needed an excuse to give them a moment of privacy. She spent a minute pretending to hunt for her phone in her coat and ignoring their lowered voices, then pulled her phone from her jeans' pocket.

Oh! She had a new text from Alec. She crossed her fingers as she pulled it up, hoping he wasn't going to cancel for their date on Saturday. There were only a few showings of *White Christmas* to pick from this year.

"Sorry guys, I'll be right there. I've gotta…" Grace's voice trailed off as she read the text.

[Four o'clock won't work for me tomorrow. Can we go at one?]

Heaving a sigh of relief, she shot him a quick answer. Hesitated, then added a sparkly heart emoji to the message before she sent it.

"Everything alright at work?" Merry asked, a trifle too casually.

"Everything's fine," Grace assured her. She could hardly be amused at Merry when her own heart was leaping at the thought of being with Alec. "*White Christmas* is playing on Saturday and Alec wants to go."

Merry nodded. "Isn't that your favorite Christmas movie?"

"It's pretty high on my list," Grace agreed. Folding her arms for prayer, she appreciated Tyrel's willingness to offer it and his sweet supplication on Merry's behalf.

"I cannot believe you're eating this stuff again." She added pasta to her plate. "I *know* you swore off it after college." They both had. It was great comfort food once in a while, but they'd been reduced to eating it almost exclusively one semester, which could ruin any dish.

"I love it," Tyrel interjected.

"Oh, ok." Grace winked at them both. "I get it." She didn't, and fully expected Merry to pipe up with an explanation. Which she might've done except for a conspiratorial wink from Tyrel that left Grace hastily smothering a flicker of annoyance. *Wow.* Being on the outside of Merry's inside jokes was really going to take getting used to.

Snagging a slice of warm garlic bread, Grace changed the subject. "Before I forget again, what're you planning to wear to the play?"

Merry shrugged and pushed her pasta from one side of the plate to the other. "Clothes?"

Grace choked on the garlic bread she was chewing. So much so that Tyrel favored her with a painful thump on the back. Merry wasn't kidding, he *was* strong! Grace held up a hand to prevent more well-intentioned first aid and coughed her way to a clear throat.

"Are you ok?" Merry frowned.

"Sure." Grace downed half a glass of strawberry soda and cleared her throat. "Fine. I, um, thought I heard you say the rest of your disguise," she motioned to include the wig and glasses, "was jeans and a tee."

"What's wrong with that?" Merry couldn't help the touch of indignation in her tone. She loved casual clothes.

That's it! The realization of what was wrong with Merry's clothes hit Grace like a skittish foal's hind hoof, knocking the wind out of her. *They're too big!* While Merry's wardrobe was generally geared toward comfort, particularly where it came to breathing room, her shirt was much looser than usual.

"That might make you easier to identify," Tyler pointed out.

"Exactly." Grace drummed her fingers on the counter, her food forgotten. Merry had hardly eaten a bite. She should've remembered what anxiety did to Merry's appetite. What kind of friend was she, anyway?

"What're you planning?" Merry eyed her with suspicion.

"I'm not sure yet." Grace returned her gaze steadily, hoping that acting normal would help Merry loosen up. "We don't have very long to get you an outfit that half the town won't recognize." Oh yeah. Big help she was.

"I can order something tonight. It'll only take a couple of days to get here."

"Yeah, you could." Grace chewed and swallowed. "But I've got a better idea."

"I'm listening."

"The other day Eddie told me that her mom is in an organizing frenzy right now. Cleaning out clutter with a vengeance." She gestured broadly.

"And?"

"And she just started on her closets." Grace

leaned forward. "Her 'this is so last season in Paris' closets! Chock full of stuff that nobody in town has ever seen."

"Except Eddie," Merry snorted. "And isn't she a size two or something?" Her cheeks pinked slightly as she smoothed her shirt. "Besides which, Paris fashion isn't exactly synonymous with modesty."

"Hear me out." Grace held up her hands. "Eddie hasn't spent any real time with her parents since she started kindergarten. Sad as that is, it takes care of the problem of Eddie recognizing your outfit. Objection number two." She held up two fingers. "She's a size eight when she isn't starving herself. Objection number three." She grinned. "Alterations." She held her breath while Merry thought it over.

"We can try."

"Great!" Grace squealed, refusing to be put off by Merry's obvious reluctance. "This is going to be so much fun!"

Tyrel jumped in with, "I'll rent the limo."

"What?" both women asked in unison.

"The limo. Helen should arrive in a vehicle at least as fancy as her outfit." He lifted his glass as if to toast Merry.

"Perfect!" Grace agreed.

"I've never ridden in a limo," Merry admitted.

"You'll have to pick it up outside of town," Grace cautioned. "Like, waaaay outside of town."

"No problem," Tyrel laughed. "I've been wanting to take Merry somewhere fancier than Blinky's."

"Good old grapevine," Merry muttered.

"Grapevines are old-fashioned," Grace snickered. "This town went wireless a decade ago."

Merry rolled her eyes. "We'll have to do the same for any alterations. If we go to Sew Cut," she grimaced as she mispronounced 'cut' to sound like 'cute,' which was how the owner insisted on doing it, "MaeBell will tell everyone she knows before I get a chance to try the dress on."

"Already have that figured out." And a plan to stop at Merry's favorite restaurant for lunch. She needed at least one square meal a day and it definitely didn't look like she was managing that on her own right now. Grace hopped up and added her things to the dishwasher. "Be ready to go at seven-thirty tomorrow, okay?"

"Isn't that a little early?" Merry protested.

"We'll need every minute." Grace hugged Merry, nodded at Tyrel, and let herself out. Before she'd even reached her truck, she'd dialed an old acquaintance.

"Hey, Tammy? It's Grace. Yeah, hi!" She indulged in the usual catching up, then asked, "How's Myrtle these days?"

"She's doing fantastic!" Tammy's enthusiasm bubbled right through the speaker like soda fizz over the top of a short glass. "But you know that because I would never take her to anyone but you. So," her tone was that of gleeful expectation, "does this mean you're finally going to cash in that favor I owe you?"

Grace snickered. "You caught me!"

"Oh, I'm so excited! When are you getting married?"

"What? No, no, no." Grace corrected her quickly. "It's not for me. I mean, I'll be there and…" She stopped to take a breath. "I've got a friend who needs your talents."

Eventually, she managed to arrange an appointment for the next morning. Next she made a much shorter call to Moira, the maid who'd been tasked with disposing of the clothes slated for donation.

"No, I don't mind. I drive all over the county, including past thrift shops, so it's no trouble." She nodded as she approached the Rockin' R. "How about now? I'm only a few minutes away. Sure!"

She checked Alec's trailer as she drove past, but his truck was missing, so she headed around behind the main house. Moira thanked her as they loaded the clothes into the back of her cab.

"You're saving me such a hassle," the woman sighed. "She's got a list as long as my arm of things for me to do."

"No," Grace grunted as she heaved in the last of the garment bags, "problem."

They laughed and wished each other well. That

That left Grace just enough time to race home for some sleep.

"Good thing Neil gave you the day off tomorrow," she told herself as she started general conference. "Goofy world, where the junior partner gives the senior partner the day off. But, whatever works!" And really, he should be fine. Mrs. Ivey had been careful to schedule routine stuff.

The miles streamed by as she considered what each speaker taught about Christ. As the closing hymn for the session started to play, she switched it off. The apostles and other general authorities taught the rules, she knew that. Only one person had ever successfully lived all the rules their entire life—the Savior. She knew that, too.

She wiped away tears as glimpses of her life scrolled through her mind. Times when she'd called on the Savior's atonement for strength against temptations. For forgiveness after failing. For comfort while in pain or distress.

She was so blessed.

Chapter 20

On Saturday morning, Grace allowed herself a long, hot bath. She'd earned it. It would've been easier to herd cats than coax Merry through the fitting. Danny Kaye's antics later at the movie night had eased any residual tension between the two friends and Grace was starting to think they were going to survive this whole Helen Montgomery crisis.

Her favorite French Christmas album played while she dressed, a souvenir from her one trip to Canada. A soft, fluffy snow falling softly outside added the perfect seasonal touch, making her smile even as she reviewed her appointments for the next week.

Good grief, was time going faster now that she was dating Alec? She hoped not. She wanted to savor each moment. *Hmmm.* She stared unseeingly out the window.

Funny how he'd mentioned wedding rings on their last date. Her head didn't want to read too much into it—but her heart couldn't leave it alone. Mr. Brooke had sent him on a surprise business trip last week, leaving her with plenty of lonely hours to overthink the matter. Oh, Alec had called her. She'd called him. And she could tell he missed her company as much as she missed his.

She smiled as she watered the plant he'd given

her. Inhaled the daffodil's sweet scent. She loved daffodils, but had no idea when she would've told him that. Who knew he'd been paying such close attention?

Coughing, she cleared her throat of the tears crowding in. What a goof she was. Alec started talking about marriage-type things and she started crying.

Well, for all she knew that was normal. This was her first go-round—because having a blind date propose in college did *not* count.

Chuckling, she finished tidying up after the movie night (popcorn was like grape juice; when spilled, it got everywhere) and headed out to the barn to tend her patient.

Pixy, the pony she'd been tending a few months ago, had gotten out again and injured herself while exploring her owner's hobby farm.

"Hey, sweetheart." Grace enthusiastically scratched under Pixy's mane, prompting the pony to nod her head happily. "You might be trouble on the hoof, but you definitely don't need another medical emergency. When I take you home, I better inspect your stall personally. Oh, you think that's funny, huh?" It certainly sounded like the pony was laughing. "You might be right. You could have a stall Houdini couldn't break out of and all it would take is for Jazzie to forget to latch it properly."

The sound of a truck coming up the drive set

her heart fluttering. "Ohhhkay, Pixy. Be honest." She held her arms out to display her lavender sweater and best blue jeans. "How do I look?" She grinned when the pony nodded emphatically. "I hope Alec agrees!" Pulling an apple from the stash, she handed it to Pixy. "See you later!"

She paused at the sink by the door long enough to wash and dry her hands before going out to meet him.

Alec, who had just gotten out of his truck, spotted her instantly. A slow smile spread across his face as he looked her over.

"How do you do it?"

Flustered, she shook her head and started walking toward him. "Do what?"

"Get more beautiful every time I see you."

She missed a step and he caught her. Her breaths came erratically as he held her in his arms. All at once, he swung her around, opened his door, and lifted her into the cab.

"Am I driving?" She did her best to laugh despite her disappointment.

Stepping up onto the running board, he kissed her softly. Her hands framed his face as she kissed him back, needing his nearness.

Eyes twinkling, he carefully slid her over onto the passenger side, then seated himself. They held hands all the way to the theater, where she exited the truck much the same way that she'd entered.

"Not many cars here." Taking off his jacket, he draped it over her shoulders against the cold, effectively surrounding her with his presence.

"Maybe we'll have the place to ourselves."

His step faltered and he looked down at her. "You think so?"

"Maybe." Her eyes flicked over his face. "Is something wrong?" She couldn't imagine what that might be. Her heart constricted. Unless…was he breaking up with her? No, that was ridiculous. Everything was going so well.

"Wrong?" He held the door for her. "Nope." Taking her elbow, he steered her to the concessions stand. Only one line was open, so they'd have a short wait. "Want some snacks?"

"No, thanks." She hardly noticed the theater's festive decorations as her brain kicked into overdrive.

Was that a diversionary tactic? Was he letting her down easy? He made the date, so he was keeping the date, but afterwards he'd tell her—tell her what? That she was beautiful, but…

"Sorry, I didn't hear you." She flushed at his amused expression. "I was thinking." *Overthinking.* She shoved the irrational doubts away and listened.

"Oh?" He drew her with him as the line moved forward. "About what?"

She bit her lip. "Nothing."

"Why so worried about nothing?" He touched her mouth, softly pulling her lip free.

"What can I get for you?" The teenager behind the counter didn't look up from the screen he was resetting. Stupid glitches. Why couldn't his boss get a tech upgrade so the machines didn't freeze up on every other order?

Alec gave Grace another moment of his undivided attention. When she smiled—a fake smile, he was sure of it—and shook her head, he addressed the employee's question. "Two tickets to *White Christmas*, please."

"Ohhhh. Sorry, folks, the one o'clock is sold out."

Grace felt Alec's arm flex under her hand. Well, this was perfect. They couldn't go to the showing at four because Alec was busy and now the one o'clock was...

The teen nearly jumped out of his skin when his manager spoke at his elbow. Alec, on the other hand, relaxed noticeably at her appearance.

At least, Grace noticed.

"Is something wrong with your monitor?" The manager flashed them a dazzling smile as she addressed the teenager.

"Yeah. I, uh, had to restart it."

The manager smiled at Alec and Grace. "I can help you over here." She led them to the next monitor, her ponytail brushing against her collar as she walked the short distance.

"But it's..."

She cut the teen off with a look. "While you're waiting on that system reset, and before the next wave of customers, would you take a look at the Frosty cutout? I think the kids have been trying to climb on him or something."

Grace watched the exchange with rising eyebrows. Why did the manager want to get rid of the boy so badly? And what, exactly, was the meaning of the smile she was giving Alec?

It *sounded* routine enough as the manager confirmed how many tickets they wanted to which show at what time.

"So it isn't sold out?" Grace interjected as Alec started to hand over his credit card.

"Plenty of empty seats," the manager assured her.

Grace spent the rest of the transaction analyzing everything that she thought had just happened while simultaneously telling herself not to be paranoid. Even if Alec did break up with her, it would hardly be to date a younger woman. Right?

Ugh! So this was what insecurity felt like. First she didn't have Alec. Now that she had him, she was so afraid of losing him she could hardly think straight.

"Shall we?" Alec made up his mind to find out what was bothering Grace before the movie started. Her smile couldn't hide the worry in her eyes, not from him. Whatever it was could potentially spoil their date; or worse, his plans for afterward. He patted his breast pocket to make sure the surprise was still safe.

"Let's." She did her best to smile.

Pre-movie ads lit the theater well enough for her to see that they were the first ones to arrive.

"Where do you want to sit?"

"I…" She felt his fingers thread through hers and suddenly couldn't speak around the lump in her throat. So she shrugged. Gestured vaguely at the seats.

"Grace." Stepping in close enough to crowd her space, he looked down at her. "Don't shut me out."

Her mouth worked, but no words came out. An obnoxiously loud ad came on and she reached up to rub her temple.

"Headache?" He feathered his fingers through her loose hair, easing it away from her face. "Why didn't you say so, sweetheart?" Brushing his lips across her forehead, he eased her into his arms.

She ached to close her eyes and put her head on his shoulder, but she couldn't.

Sensing her reluctance, Alec drew away uncertainly. Studied her face. "I'll take you home," he offered. "We can watch this later. Next year, even."

"Next year?"

The wistful note in her voice caught his attention. "Honey." He massaged her temple with his thumb. "We can watch it every year if you want to."

"Every year?" Her eyes, which had begun to

drift closed as his ministrations eased her tension headache, sprang open again.

Something nudged him and he took a deep breath. This wasn't how he'd planned it… He dropped to one knee as the lights dimmed for the opening credits.

"Grace, I know this may seem premature. After all, we have only been dating for a little over six weeks. But I believe that dating serves a different purpose when two people already know each other as well as we do." He withdrew a slim box from his shirt pocket and opened it one-handed to display a ring. "Once I opened my mind to the possibility, it didn't take me long to realize I love you. Will you marry me?"

Dazed, Grace stared down at him. "You're…not breaking up with me?"

He came to his feet with an incredulous, "What?!"

Grace covered her mouth, then changed her mind. "Yes!" Taking his face in her hands, she kissed him with seventeen years' worth of longing.

"Ooops." Sarah Myers tried to back out of the theater and ran into her husband, Eric.

Alec recovered from the surprise first. "Come in, come in." He held out his hand to Eric. "And congratulate us. She just said yes."

Eric chortled. "Never any doubt about that."

Grace was instantly enveloped in her mother's arms. "Congratulations, honey!"

"I thought you two were going over to the McKinney's tonight." Grace looked suspiciously from her dad to her mom, who had gone over to give Alec a fierce bear hug.

"We are." Eric draped an arm around her shoulders. "For supper. After the movie."

"Oh, honey." Sarah eagerly returned to Grace. "Let me see the ring!"

"Over here." Alec held up the box he'd almost dropped during Sarah's rib-crushing hug. "A perfect fit," he murmured as he slipped the diamond-encrusted ring onto her finger.

"It's so beautiful!" Grace tilted her hand from side to side, admiring it. The tiny diamonds that covered the top half of the band caught the weak light from the theater screen and scattered rainbows along the walls.

"It's called an eternity band," Alec explained. "It was my grandmother's."

"Hey, we're missing the movie!" Eric pointed at the screen. "Come on, let's take our seats."

Alec took advantage of the neatly timed diversion to kiss Grace again. "Shall we join them?"

Twice during the movie Grace had to reach up and turn Alec's head toward the screen. Finally, she put her head on his shoulder and watched the rest of it that way.

"You know I've seen this before, right?" he whispered.

"Shhh."

After that he did his best to let the movie distract him from the woman beside him, even applauding with them as the happy movie couples shared a romantic ending.

Grace's brow furrowed as the house lights came up. "Hey, look. We're still the only ones here!"

"Well of course it is," laughed Sarah. "Alec bought it out."

"You didn't have to do that!" Grace's jaw dropped.

"I know, but I…I wanted it to be special." He also had a deep-seated aversion to the idea of being stepped on by other patrons while proposing, before or after the show.

"Alright." Eric came over and dropped a kiss on the top of Grace's head. "We're off to the McKinney's. You two be safe now."

"Safe?"

"Mhmm." Sarah kissed her cheek. "Alec has the most romantic evening planned."

Eric cleared his throat and took Sarah by the arm. "Which we'll let you get to." With a cheery wave, he ushered his wife out.

"A romantic evening?" Grace arched her eyebrows. "I thought you were busy later."

"That's right." Rising, he caught Grace around the waist and lifted her over the back of her chair to the theater's top level, then stepped up to join her. "Picking out a Christmas tree."

"Oh my!" She gasped. "That's right! It's

nearly Christmas!"

"Yet neither of us has a tree." Slipping an arm around her, he started for the door again. "So I thought we could pick one out together and decorate it."

"Alec, that's wonderful. And, since it's your idea, it should go in your trailer."

"You have more room," he returned quickly. Pausing at the outer door, he helped her into his coat, ignoring her protests. "Besides, I didn't clear a space for it."

"Neither did I," she pointed out, matching her stride to his as they hurried through the cold to his truck. "And your trailer will soon be *our* trailer."

"Um…" He helped her in on his side, then quickly clambered in after her. "How soon?"

"I'd marry you tomorrow if I could." She watched his eyes light up. "But I suppose Danny would like to be there."

"And your brothers." He started the truck.

"What about your family?" The thought had just occurred to her. "We have to at least invite your parents."

By the time he turned down the lane that led to his cabin, they had a very rough guest list and agreed that they would have to give fair notice if they expected people to attend.

"Hey, I know where we should put the tree!" she announced, suddenly excited.

"Really? Where?" He parked and pocketed

the keys.

"There." She pointed smugly at the cabin.

Delighted, Alec grinned. "That's perfect!"

They chuckled as they tramped through the trees, thoroughly enjoying each other's company.

"What do you think of this one?" Alec asked, stopping beside a stocky specimen.

"It's gorgeous. But, those drop needles with a vengeance."

Chuckling, he had to agree. "Y'know, I haven't really had a tree since Danny left."

"Hmm, too busy?" she guessed.

"That." He nodded. "And they're everywhere else. There's one at the main house. They'll have one at the Ward Christmas party. Stock's in town has that artificial monstrosity." The stiff green paper—or whatever it was—that stuck out from the metal limbs had either faded or fallen off over the years, leaving bare spots that no amount of ornaments could hide.

"Oh." She grimaced. "Isn't it terrible? I know it was a good buy." Which was the polite way of saying 'cheap.' "But I've heard several people hinting about his getting a new one."

"Getting cold?" He didn't need to see her rub her hands together to know he was right. "I have a brilliant idea."

"What's that?" Busy trying to find her pockets with frozen fingers, she was startled when he unzipped his jacket and wrapped it around hers. "Alec, you'll freeze!" It was one thing to wear it during the short walk into the theater, and another to wear it when he really needed it.

"How about you get things set up in the cabin," he kissed the tip of her chilled nose, "while I cut down the tree we're parked next to?"

"I think I could do that." She gasped when he stooped and, putting one arm under the backs of her legs and the other around her waist, proceeded to carry her to the truck, still more or less ensconced in his jacket.

"There's a tree stand behind the driver's seat," he told her, trading her the keys to the cabin for his jacket. "I'll only be a few minutes."

As good as his word, he hauled the tree inside in short order.

"I'll bet you'd like some of your hot chocolate about now," she joked as she held the door while he brought in the tree.

"I have soup." He settled the tree in the stand she had waiting for him. "Let me bring in the boxes first."

"Boxes?"

"Yeah." He grinned a bit sheepishly. "I never thought of using the cabin, but I figured you might need extra decorations, so I brought some of mine along in case."

Alec was humming along with a Christmas carol while he strung lights around the tree when he noticed that Grace had gone very still.

"Honey?" A shock of fear rang through him

as she turned to him, revealing tears on her cheeks. Dropping the Christmas lights, he fell to his knees beside her. "Honey, what is it? What's wrong?" He wondered wildly if she'd found an ornament marked 'Our first Christmas nineteen-ninety-something' and was upset by it. "We don't have to keep it, we can…" He stopped when her hand came to rest lightly on his wrist while her brows drew together in puzzlement.

"Of course we'll keep it. I think it's the sweetest thing I've ever seen." As she spoke, she held up the salt dough ornament she'd been studying.

Shifting into a more comfortable position, Alec lifted it out of her hand. "Wow. I forgot all about this." Turning it so the handprint faced him, he held it up to his own palm. Had Danny ever been that small?

Grace ignored the date scratched in the back of the ornament; not because she cared, but because she knew their age difference sometimes bothered Alec.

"We should make those." Meeting his eyes, she laughed at his comical expression. "I mean, when we have children." His answering look melted her like frosting on a hot day.

"I love you," he murmured huskily and leaned in for a kiss.

As the play's second night wound down, Grace made her way nonchalantly to the community center's locker room, ostensibly to prepare the borrowed wardrobe items to be returned to their owners.

'Helen' ducked in a few minutes later and gasped, "They're right behind me!"

"Quick, hide behind the partition!"

The rustle of Merry's skirts had barely died away before three teenage girls poked their heads into the room.

"Heyyy!" Grace shook out a shirt. "I can use some extra hands. Who wants to help?"

The girls recoiled as a unit and the one in the center mumbled an excuse as they retreated.

"Good thinking." Merry peeked around the partition. "I've got to hurry!"

"Relax, there's plenty of time." Grace locked the door and pointed to one of the lockers. "You know Blinky's will be inundated tonight. It's tradition."

"Yeah, that's true." Merry kept talking as she changed. "I just don't want to keep Tyrel waiting."

"And I can't wait to see Alec."

"This is the best Christmas ever." Dressed in a sweater and jeans, Merry took Grace's left hand and admired her ring. "For both of us."

"I still can't believe it." Grace hugged her. "Shall we?"

"Here goes."

"Girls!" Noella pounced the second they emerged into the hallway. "A success! Oh, what a success!"

"You did it!" Grace said quickly, to distract her from Merry's abruptly ashen face.

"Me?" Noella shook her head. "No, never. It was the whole group. The sound, the cast." She took one of the bags from Grace. "Wardrobe."

Laughing, they all headed toward the back exit. The theater committee had found something for Mrs. Arnold to do after all—they'd put her in charge of cleanup—so the girls were free as birds.

"Where's Danny?" Grace craned her neck, looking for her soon-to-be son-in-law and tried not to think about how weird that all was.

"He wanted to wait, but I told him I would meet him at the diner." Noella got starry-eyed as she considered her own engagement ring.

"So you need a ride?" Grace half-offered.

"Oui, unless we find Harmony and she…oh!" Noella stopped abruptly, but they were too late.

Harmony looked perfect in Grant's arms, even if she was blushing furiously.

"Don't mind them." Harmony's younger sister, Lydia, kept her eyes glued to a game she was playing on her phone. She'd arrived recently from New England. "They'll grow out of it in a few eons."

The tension dissolved in laughter at her absurd remark and Grant gallantly held the door for them as they stepped out into the snow.

"We don't even need the street lights." Harmony indicated the Christmas lights that hung in every window and on every tree as far as they could see.

"Can you believe we're supposed to get another foot of snow tomorrow?" Merry asked a little unhappily. The snowplows might've cleared the streets, but they'd made a mess of the curbs, leaving three foot high artificial 'snowbanks' for pedestrians to navigate.

"I sure hope it holds until Christmas." Grace beckoned for Noella to join her and Merry. There was plenty of room in her truck. Likewise, she signaled for Merry to add her garment bag to the bed of the truck, where Noella was less likely to see something she shouldn't.

"That would be marvelous!" Noella agreed enthusiastically. "Only four more days!" She kept up a running commentary all the way to Blinky's, which made the drive seem shorter.

"Good grief." Merry twitched at her seatbelt. "Where are we going to park?"

"Over here, I guess." Grace pulled in and shut the engine off. "Let's go for a walk."

It wasn't really that far, but Grace was more than ready for the hot chocolate Alec handed her when they arrived.

"Cold?" The twinkle in his eyes told her that he wanted to kiss her.

"Mhmm." It was just a peck, so the whistles and clapping surprised her. Until she looked around and saw that the other three couples had joined them. Even Merry and Tyrel, who had gotten stuck under the mistletoe near the door.

Grace couldn't help being glad it hadn't happened to her and Alec. She wasn't on speaking terms with mistletoe.

They had a jolly time over burgers and sides, but she noticed that no one lingered tonight.

Tyrel and Merry started the ball rolling with a round of hugs and well wishes. Harmony, Grant, and Lydia decided that they were tired, too, from a long day of building snowmen with their neighbors.

She and Alec walked Danny and Noella to where they were parked, and parted with hugs and wishes for a Merry Christmas.

"Hey." She tugged at Alec's hand as he started walking the wrong way. "We're both parked over there."

"Mhmm." Pulling her close, he wrapped an arm around her waist. "If we go this way," he indicated the direction he'd started in, "we won't have to say goodnight for ten more minutes."

Genuinely tempted, Grace hesitated.

"On the other hand, I don't think you'd be very happy as a popsicle." Chuckling, he moved her knit cap enough to kiss her forehead and started toward their cars.

"Do you get Christmas off?" she asked, watching tiny snowflakes sparkle as they floated down from the sky.

"Not this year. I trade holidays with Bart, and since I took Thanksgiving off to spend it with Danny..." He shrugged philosophically. "You?"

"Officially, yes. Unofficially..."

"You're always on call?" They chuckled. "We're going to have a lot of plans spoiled by our jobs, I think."

"Yeah." She sighed. "What're you doing Christmas Eve?"

He didn't answer until they'd successfully climbed over the snowbank by her truck. "Christmas Eve? I'm all yours." Hands on her waist, he drew her close.

"Oh?" She ran her hands up his arms and linked them behind his neck. "Any special traditions I should know about?"

"Just one." He grinned mischievously. "You have to be a good sport when you open your presents."

Her eyebrows lifted. "I'm...not sure how I feel about that."

"About being a good sport?"

"About opening presents on Christmas Eve."

"We can open them Christmas morning next year," he promised, kissing her softly. "In fact, I look forward to it."

His next kiss kept her warm all the way home, where she finished wrapping his gift.

Between her anticipation of Christmas Eve and the general mayhem at the clinic, it hardly felt like three days before she found herself standing in front of her closet trying to pick the right outfit. Finally selecting a heather gray sweater and her second-best blue jeans (her best pair met with an untimely demise while on a call earlier that week) and waved goodbye to her parents.

"Oh, honey, wait!" Sarah reached for her camera and Grace laughed.

"Not now, Mom." She blew her a kiss. "Save it for the wedding!" Her mom was tickled pink when all four brides—Grace, Merry, Harmony, and Noella—voted unanimously to have her as their wedding photographer. They'd also all agreed on March weddings, which often seemed too long to wait to Grace.

She arrived to find the cabin's lights already on, including a small Santa and sleigh on the roof that was new.

"There you are!" Alec threw open the door and welcomed her with open arms.

After a particularly tender kiss, she looked up to find a bunch of carrots hanging right above the threshold and couldn't help the laughter that bubbled up.

"Do you like it?" One arm still around her, he closed the door. "It's what some people use in place of mistletoe at their stables, so I thought it might work for us."

She drew him to her for another soft kiss. "I love it."

Straightening, he tapped her lightly on the tip of her nose. "First things first."

They were halfway through the living room when she abruptly noticed the changes.

"Alec!" Staring around her, she took in the new end tables that flanked the couch. The recliner that was cozied up to a bookshelf. The rug under her feet. "You redecorated?"

"I brought a few things over from the trailer." He rubbed his hands together anxiously. "And oh, the end tables are new."

Her attention shifted and she started for the kitchen with Alec on her heels. "What is that delicious smell?"

"Ah, that is me calling in every favor Chef Toni ever owed me."

She couldn't believe her eyes. The card table looked surprisingly grand with its covered dishes and fancy folded napkins. From the corner of her eye she saw something else new.

"You got a stove?"

"It was time." His hands settled on her shoulders and he turned her to face him. "Grace, I told you I'd move to this cabin when I retired. And," he took her hands in his, "if it's okay with you, I think I'm ready." She didn't say anything, so he hurried to explain himself. "If I stay on at the Rockin' R, I'll never be home. Between old habits and new emergencies, I'll wind up living my job again and I don't want that. I want us."

"So you're retiring…now?" She couldn't believe her ears.

"No, not quite. I expect to work through February at least." Leading her over to the table, he seated her. "I want to give Mr. Brooke plenty of notice."

"Of course." She relaxed slightly as he poured a glass of cold milk for her. "What did Mr. Brooke say when you told him?"

"I haven't yet. I wanted to discuss it with you first." He watched the tension ease from her shoulders. "I guess I should've started with that." He shook his head ruefully.

Slowly unfolding her dove-shaped napkin, she spread it across her lap. "Darling, if you want to retire, that's fine with me. I'm only concerned that you'll get bored."

They paused the discussion for a prayer over the food, then Alec lifted the lids and set them in the sink.

Over delectable goose, mashed potatoes with gravy, carrots, green beans, and feather-light rolls, Alec told her he'd been thinking about retirement ever since they first talked about it.

"I don't have a long list of things to do," he admitted. "But it's a start."

"I think you'll really love volunteering at the fairground. They can always use an impartial judge at the 4H competitions." And though she certainly didn't think he needed to join a gym, she didn't try to dissuade him. If he thought he would enjoy it, she certainly thought he should give it a try.

"Wait." Finished eating, he wiped his mouth. Spread his hands. "I have to be impartial?"

Rolling her eyes, she got up and started loading the dishes into the dishwasher, which was also brand, sparkling new.

"What's this?" She pointed at the tray on the oven that was covered with wax paper.

"Dessert." Alec whipped the wax paper off to reveal a tray of cookies cut in the shapes of charming elves, trees, etc.

"Oh, not Toni's sugar cookies." Grace nearly licked her lips. "Those are not good for my waistline." Alec's slowly rising eyebrow and appreciative perusal did strange things to her heart, which she pretended not to notice.

"I'm willing to risk it if you are."

She eyed the tray as he turned the oven on and slipped it inside. "I don't stand a chance against the smell of cookies baking," she sighed.

"Let me finish this." He took a dish out of her hands, grinning boyishly. "You go sit on the couch. We're almost ready for presents."

"We agreed on one present each," she reminded him even as she complied.

"Spoilsport!" he called after her, making her laugh.

Sooner than she would've believed possible, he had started the dishwasher and joined her on the couch.

"Who gets to pick first?"

"I do!" She got up and went over to a long, rectangular box. It was as heavy as she remembered.

"Need some help with that?" He sort of hated to offer under the circumstances. There was a very particular present he wanted her to open and this wasn't it. Come to think of it, he didn't remember using that wrapping paper, either.

"Please," she huffed.

"Whoa." It took two hands, but he wrangled the box over to the couch. "Now what?"

"Now you open it, silly."

He tapped his fingers on the box, trying to figure out what had just happened. He'd expected her to pick out a gift for herself.

"Hold this." He put her hand on top of the box to keep it from falling over. Picked up the biggest package and brought it back to her. "Here." He set it in front of her. "We can open our gifts together."

Running a finger over the silver paper her gift was wrapped in, she looked sideways at him. "Ready?"

He nodded and they each tore the paper away.

"Grace!" He whistled in admiration as he carefully set the box down on its side to open it.

"What a beauty!"

She breathed a small sigh of relief as he examined the telescope and its accessories.

"The reviews claim it's easy to transport." She giggled. "I figured that would be useful, before I knew…" She gestured at the cabin in general.

"Hey." He put the gizmo he was holding down. "You didn't finish opening yours."

"It's a suitcase, right?"

"Not *a* suitcase, no." Unzipping the top he showed her what was inside. "Three nesting suitcases. They'll be perfect for our adventures." He hesitated. "Do you like them?"

"Yes." She nodded vigorously. "Yes. I love the pattern, especially. The gold and red leaves on brown make it look exactly like fall in the Ozarks." Squinting at him, she asked, "How many adventures are you planning on?"

"Mmm, one a year for as long as we can, I guess."

She fiddled with the suitcase's zipper.

"Grace?"

"Good thing you got me new suitcases, then." She coughed to clear her throat. "I don't think my old ones would survive a hundred or more trips." Wrapping her arms around him, she kissed his cheek. "Thank you."

"You're sure you like them?" He wasn't and he needed to know.

"Yes." She stroked his cheek. "I've just never

been given a lifetime of presents all at once before."

Reassured, he brushed his lips across hers. "This lifetime is only the beginning."

Thank you for reading <u>In Due Season</u>, I hope you enjoyed it!

To learn more about Merry, Noella, and Harmony, read the rest of the "Gifts of the Heart" series.

Visit me at
leacarterwrites.wixsite.com/flinch-free-fiction

More titles by Lea Carter:

<u>*Contemporary Romance*</u>
"Gifts of the Heart"
Four single Latter-day Saint women find love in the tiny, fictional town of Cadmia.
A Country Mile
In Due Season
Food For Thought
Home Free

<u>Fantasy</u>
"Silver Sagas"
The ongoing adventures of the royal fairy families.
Silver Princess
Silver Majesty
Silver Verity
Troubled Skies
Dress Blues
The Seeker's Storm
Heartwood
Wedgewood
Fission – coming soon
Fusion (2021)

"Coddiwomple"
Three high-flying adventures in the fictional world of Jattori.
Dragon Sparks
Dragon Fugue
Dragon Thunder